WINTER DREAMS

WINTER
DREAMS

a novel

DON J. SNYDER

Doubleday

New York London Toronto Sydney Auckland

PUBLISHED BY DOUBLEDAY

a division of Random House, Inc.

DOUBLEDAY and the portrayal of an anchor with a dolphin are

registered trademarks of Random House, Inc.

1745 Broadway, New York, NY 10019

Book design by Chris Welch

Library of Congress Cataloging-in-Publication Data

Snyder, Don J.

Winter dreams : a novel / by Don J. Snyder.—1st ed.

p.   cm.

1. Royal and Ancient Golf Club of St. Andrews—Fiction.   2. St. Andrews

(Scotland)—Fiction.   3. Americans—Scotland—Fiction.   4. Loss

(Psychology)—Fiction.   5. College teachers—Fiction.   6. Friendship—Fiction.

7. Golfers—Fiction.   I. Title.

PS3569.N86W55 2004

813'.54—dc22

2003061173

ISBN 0-385-50850-6

April 2004

First Edition

1 3 5 7 9 10 8 6 4 2

For Colleen, Erin, Nell, Jack, and Cara,
who put an end to loneliness

—WINTER 2003, SCARBOROUGH, MAINE

The thing was deep in him. He was too
strong and alive for it to die lightly.

—F. SCOTT FITZGERALD

"Winter Dreams"

WINTER DREAMS

PROLOGUE

THE SUMMER I turned twelve years old the Wilcox Tannery went out of business, putting fifty families in Westport, Illinois, out of work and laying abandoned the long brick outbuildings that stood beyond the east border of St. Luke's Orphanage. Brother Martin, a young Benedictine priest from a small town somewhere in Florida who taught us literature and composition, ran the kitchen and always had five or six of us working with him to prepare meals and wash pots. He had given up golf when he took his vows, but in his tiny office across from the ovens, an office with wire-mesh walls like a cage and shelves of canned food, he kept the trophies he'd won in amateur competition, along with two dozen golf balls in a Wheeling's Mill flour sack, and a three wood with a head made of polished hickory and inlaid strips of persimmon. Nothing in an orphanage is as inestimable as history. Because it was the one thing each of us lacked and desperately longed to know, there were no limits to the personal histories we invented. One boy claimed to have been abandoned by a mother who drowned herself after finishing as the sixth runner-up in a Miss America pageant in Atlantic City. Another swore his mother had been decapitated while on a safari in the Congo. Our fathers, we insisted, were still alive; they were bankers and engineers, railroad tycoons and ventriloquists, men who, by implication, were too busy to raise us themselves, but after they met new wives whose beauty and resourcefulness matched that of our lost mothers, they would come for us at St. Luke's some fine Sunday afternoon—in our imaginations.

ALL THESE LIES about love took their toll, and by the time we were teenagers we didn't believe anything. Especially stories that assigned manly, real-world qualities and experiences to the Brothers who cared for us and whom we, as we grew older, showered with ingratitude.

But the summer that the tannery was abandoned I was young enough to believe urgently that the trophies in Brother Martin's office had been presented to him for astonishing enterprises at a time in his life before he dressed in the shapeless black robe of the Benedictine Brothers, when his future was a brilliant shining promise and he still wore pants. I defended him to the unbelievers and suffered my first bloody nose from an older boy named Kravitz when I refused to repeat after him that Brother Martin was a queer.

AT NIGHT, OFTEN under moonlight, Brother Martin stood outside by the picnic table behind the kitchen and hit golf balls over the grassy meadow that divided the orphanage from the tannery, launching each ball into a glorious flight across the starlit sky. Before each shot he would play the part of a radio announcer, narrating a golf match. "Ladies and gentlemen, a very difficult shot here facing Gene Sarazen. His ball is nearly buried in the first cut of rough on a downhill lie. He's likely to hit a flier from here. It's a shot that appears certain to jeopardize his slim, two-stroke lead."

Brother Martin could narrate these stories with various accents; slow deep Southern and British snob were my favorites. And though we didn't know it at the time, these moments he recounted before each shot were taken from championships of the past, moments that introduced us to the great golfers of the ages. Gene Sarazen. Ben Hogan. Harry Vardon. And the matchless Bobby Jones. We loved these performances and waited with delight for that moment after every swing when Brother Martin would raise his hand in the air for silence just before the ball made a marvelous whacking sound as it ricocheted off the brick flank of the dark tannery building and disappeared into the night.

THAT BEGAN A long stretch of time in my life when I looked forward to nothing more than the chance to hit golf balls behind the kitchen with Brother Martin. He devised a game where he would hit all twenty-four balls and then send us out into the meadow like Labrador retrievers to find them. Whichever boy found the most would have the chance to hit next while Brother Martin made suggestions about the grip, the stance, the position of the hands at take back, and the tempo of the swing. He, himself, possessed a beautiful flowing swing that gathered ferocious power from a synchronized, effortless, and perfectly timed unwinding of his hips and shoulders, and a snapping of his wrists, and we all worked hard to catch its rhythm and to imitate it. In the years he shared with us before he was transferred to a prison somewhere in Texas, Brother Martin pressed upon each of us the idea that the majesty of God was revealed in the rhythms of the world, from the way a baby learns to crawl and then stand, to the changing seasons. He reached even the teenage hoods who smoked cigarettes on the back steps of the metal shop and glared at the world with bored, superior expressions; in time they too took part in hitting and chasing after golf balls and could be heard arguing over who the great Scottish golfer Sandy Herd had beaten for the British Open title at Hoylake in 1902.

I WAS ONE of the boys who never learned the proper swing. Plagued with a terrible flaw that sent all of my balls flying off miserably to the right, for all the times I tried, I never struck a single ball well enough to carry it on a straight line across the distance to the tannery wall. I hung my head after each swing, and then tried again with Brother Martin's encouragement. He never gave up on me, and though his instruction was wasted on me, I think I became a teacher because of him. Looking back, I see that his gift to us was the way he took us seriously, always encouraging us to dream about what we might become in the world and using the time we shared with him to tell us things about life that I've never forgotten and that still retain a certain resonance and fitness in my memory. I am fifty years old now as I write this, but I remember as if it were last night an evening under moonlight when he paused before a shot to tell us that we would all fall in love someday. "And then you will understand, boys," he said, as he cocked his thin wrists, "that every love story is a small boat set upon an open sea. And those things that imperil it, the winds of betrayal, the waves of fear and doubt, are also what earn its dignity in our memory."

A DENTED GREEN sedan took Brother Martin away from us, off to his next assignment and the rest of his life. It was a late-autumn morning. Leaves blew around the orphanage courtyard, and when he was gone I felt trapped inside a hollow space. This would have been just before I turned thirteen and joined the hoods on the steps of the metal shop where we pretended nothing mattered to us as we steeled ourselves against the next person who would vanish from our lives.

The night before, long after dinner was finished, after the last of the pots had been washed and we were supposed to be asleep on our cots, I found Brother Martin out beyond the kitchen swinging his golf club. He looked different in some way, and it wasn't until I was a man myself that I realized he had been crying. Before we went inside he told me that I was going to want to play golf someday. "At times when you're confused or lost, you'll want to play the game," he said. "Trust me, you will."

He stood behind me and ran his hand the length of my left arm. "For a righty," he said, "the most important thing is to keep the left arm completely straight on the take back. If you forget everything else anyone teaches you about the swing and just keep your left arm straight, you'll have a decent chance. Here, pretend you can't bend your arm at all. Pretend your elbow doesn't work."

I tried a few swings which failed to win his praise.

"Well," he said apologetically, "you'll catch on in time."

"I'll keep practicing," I promised.

He nodded, then paused and looked up at the sky. "Some scientists say we're made out of stardust. Did you know that?"

"No sir," I said. I stared at the stars while he went on.

"You need to become a reader," he said thoughtfully. "Books will help you navigate your way through the world. All the great authors have wrestled with the questions about life that will confront you. Who are you reading now?"

"Just my schoolbooks," I admitted.

"How old are you?"

"Thirteen."

"Perfect for Jack London," he concluded. "Eight more years and you'll be ready for Thomas Wolfe." He smiled at this thought. "Coming from this place, being on your own in the world, you're different from most people. What you accomplish will belong to you and to no one else. And you'll make mistakes. That's all right, mistakes are good. You'll fall in love easily. You'll depend upon friendship more than most people do. And you'll be disappointed. That's all part of life. Learn to rely on books to carry you through the lonely times. Books and golf. Both will bring you comfort."

WHEN WE WERE back inside the kitchen he sat at his desk and wrote names on a piece of paper for me, not the titles of the books he loved best, but the names of their authors. "Read everything they've written," he said, as he handed me the list, shook my hand, and wished me well. I had already turned to leave when he called to me. "One more thing," he said. "I want to give you something else."

It was a handsome bronze cup mounted on a piece of mahogany. One of his golf trophies. I was embarrassed of course, awkward as I held the trophy in my hands; but an orphan, like survivors of the Great Depression and other catastrophes, finds it impossible to turn down charity and to walk away from anything he might put to some use after the next disaster strikes.

"Take these too," he said to me, reaching for his golf club and the balls in the flour sack. I started to thank him, but he raised a hand to stop me. "No, no, I'm thanking *you* for taking them from me. I've had a lifelong battle against my addiction to golf. I'm going to make a clean start in Texas. No golf to get between me and the Lord's work." He handed the club and balls to me, telling me to keep them for good luck, as if he knew that I would need good luck. As if he knew that I would be lost for much of my life, led by the reckless longing of my heart down a narrow path of sorrow and despair. Cursed and blessed and haunted by the story I am telling you now. It is one of those love stories that Brother Martin spoke about. And the sea I set it upon with these words lies far beyond our diminished hopes, in the vast open silence that holds everything we have not yet learned.

BOOK

I

ONE

I BECAME THE man that Brother Martin might have expected me to become. That's what I thought each time I gazed out at my classroom, watching my students file in to take their seats. It was the autumn of 1969, three weeks into my first semester of teaching American literature at the University of Massachusetts as a newly minted Ph.D. The town of Amherst had been home to me since I arrived from St. Luke's for my freshman year. Through four years of college and six years of graduate work I had led a solitary life here. A life of books and golf. And though I wanted, sometimes desperately, to engage the world, to make friends, to fall in love, and to experience the variety of life's chances, I had remained alone, caught in the solitary rituals of an existence that most observers would regard as empty. There were my students in front me each day, so far ahead of me really, though at age twenty-eight, I was already old in their eyes. Truth be told, however, I was a child in comparison to the living they had done, a stranger to love and unacquainted with death, I had spent my entire life in two small towns; I had never seen the ocean or flown in an airplane; I didn't possess a driver's license or a passport; and because I had lived so little, I, like them, was waiting for my real life to begin, believing stubbornly, in the way only a young person can, that life is more about fate than accommodation.

I suspect this was why I had fallen in love with college teaching; I was as idealistic, and as uncertain of my destiny, as my students were. We were fellow travelers on a night journey of expectation and discovery.

And while I could not tell them what lay ahead, around the corner, because I had never been there myself, I could bless them with the gift of literature, which is, of course, the knowledge that we are not alone.

AS I WAITED for the room to fall to silence and for the last student to settle in his chair, I felt a calm pass through me as it always did at the start of class. This had surprised me after spending the whole summer scared to death about facing undergraduate students for the first time. I don't know if America had ever experienced a more eventful summer—Senator Ted Kennedy off the bridge, sending men to the moon, the concert at Woodstock. But I was so encased in fear and self-doubt about teaching that those events seemed to be taking place on another planet. Then the moment my first class began and I realized that nothing mattered more than bringing to life for my students the great writers who had lived before us, all my fears vanished.

I closed the door at the front of the room and nodded to a football player in the back row to close the door beside him. "Thank you, Mr. Schmidt," I said as he lumbered back to his seat. In the row of seats along the windows, the tiny red-haired girl from Pennsylvania took off her boots, then lit a cigarette, the first of eight that she would smoke in the next fifty minutes, lighting each new cigarette from the last. I watched the stoop-shouldered boy whose last name was Kapelke pour three packets of sugar into the coffee he had picked up at the spa on the way to class. The Sylvester girl, whose father had died that summer in a fire at the textile mill where he worked, sat with her head bowed as she had through every class.

This was my world. The place where I felt safe and useful. And privileged. "Melville," I said softly, and the room grew even quieter. "We've got two weeks to figure out together what it is in Herman Melville's work that we need to take with us for the rest of our lives." I paused. "First of all, can you imagine ever naming your son Herman?"

Laughter, even from Miss Sylvester with her bowed head. I was off and running.

I WAS STILL thinking of her laughter late that afternoon as I rode my bicycle off campus, with Brother Martin's golf club resting across my handlebars. Maybe the only way we can measure the depth of our affection for someone is by the emptiness left when that person departs for an hour, or a morning that lasts forever. I could still recall vividly how in the days after Brother Martin left the orphanage there was an emptiness that I found difficult to fill. Particularly in the late-afternoon hours that led to dusk, that time of day when an orphan always imagines fathers returning home from work and mothers from their errands around town and children from school. Families reconstituting themselves in the last light of day, before the long night settled upon them. Gradually I learned to fill those hours with Brother Martin's passions, going off on my own somewhere to hit balls and retrieve them in the same comforting rhythm of that time I had spent with him in my boyhood.

My first week in Amherst I discovered an open pasture beyond the football field where I could hit balls from the tree line down a wide, sloping field to some railroad tracks. I always brought a book along to read in the fading light of dusk; as a student it had always been a book by one of the authors on Brother Martin's list. Now it was whichever writer I was teaching. I loved this time so much that often I would stay too long, and, unable to find my golf balls in the gathering darkness, I would count out the number I was short and then make myself find every missing ball the next day before I began hitting again. Somewhere along the way, numbers had become the music of my solitude. Twenty-four balls. Twenty-four swings. Counting slowly under my breath in two beats, one-two, on my take back and three! on my downswing. Trying, always trying, to establish a smooth, even motion. Then counting my steps across the meadow to each ball. Taking delight in the higher numbers that marked my longest shots.

By now I was averaging just under two hundred yards on my better shots, and I was able to hit one or two balls relatively straight out of every two dozen. Once, as I was searching for balls with night coming on quickly, I turned and saw a passenger train crossing the pasture, the long rectangular windows of each car lit up like aquariums. This enchanted me and set me counting madly—the lamps on the tables of the dining car, the silhouettes of people at the windows—before the train passed out of sight. After that I learned the train schedule and, like this afternoon, timed my last round of balls so that I could be out in the field near the tracks when the passenger train rumbled by. Today a woman wearing a pink hat waved to me. I was still waving back to her after she disappeared down the tracks, and all the way to my apartment I constructed a silent narrative in which she got off the train at the next stop and made her way back to me.

TWO

OCTOBER 22. I have marked that as the day my life turned. There was a cold wind blowing across the pasture bending the oxeyed daisies low to the ground and reminding me that winter was not far off. I had finished grading some Melville papers while leaning against an oak tree and was taking my stance over my first ball when a freight train appeared on the tracks. I fixed my grip then began my take back with my shoulders turning slowly. One-two, back. Three down. This time my swing was effortless and the club struck the ball so sweetly that I barely felt anything as it took flight straight and true, a low shot that was still rising when it cracked against one of the boxcars as the train roared past. I had never hit a ball so straight and far, and it was such a gorgeous thing to see that I gave out a triumphant Tarzan screech, and in the next moment the train crashed off the rails in a horrible squeal of grinding metal and a riot of sparks. I watched in disbelief and shock as the cars tore loose and ripped apart the pasture, some of them cartwheeling end over end, others bursting into flames.

IN THE HOURS that followed while ambulances and fire trucks arrived, I watched from a distance until I was able to move without being noticed into the crowd of townspeople that had gathered. Gradually I moved closer as word spread that three engineers were trapped beneath the locomotive. They were men from surrounding towns, and as it began to rain, their families assembled under a makeshift tent while rescue workers attempted to cut through the twisted iron. Floodlights and flares made the pasture luminous, and I remained long after most people had dispersed.

Though I knew of course that I could not possibly have caused the accident, I was left sick to my stomach and trembling with fear. The sheer coincidence haunted me as I stared at the wives and children of the trapped men.

Sometime that night a reporter from the local newspaper moved from one family to the next with his notebook and pen as he questioned them about the men, their fathers and husbands.

I moved closer to try to hear what he was asking. I was standing just a few feet from a woman who held two babies wrapped in quilts when suddenly her legs buckled beneath her and she dropped to her knees. The reporter took hold of her shoulders and steadied her. And I moved closer. Close enough to be looking into the eyes of one of her babies when the woman spoke through her tears. "He is everything to me. Have you ever loved anyone that way?"

The reporter wrote this down, then thanked her, slipping his notebook into his coat pocket as he walked away. I watched the woman as she began to rock slowly, back and forth, rocking in her pain, with her face turned to the ground. Her words—*He is everything to me*—seemed to hang above her, a declaration trapped in the mist.

Maybe the other thing that literature teaches us is to see the common ground we all occupy, to be alert enough to catch an unexpected glimpse of ourselves in another person. I was so struck by the woman's grief that night that I was not conscious of walking toward her until I was kneeling beside her, holding her hand as she looked into my eyes.

In the years since then, during times when I have been receptive to the idea that God moves our lives, I have allowed myself to believe that the train wreck took place before my eyes so that I could bear witness to an emotion I had never seen growing up in an orphanage: in that mother's grief I caught my first glimpse of a woman's love for a man, something that struck me even then as holy and fine and worth desiring above everything else a person might ever want.

THREE

MY OFFICE IN Lawrence Hall looked down onto the quad where students came and went on their way to class and the student center. I was standing at the window watching a few boys throw a football when the department secretary, Donna Bridges, knocked on my opened door.

"Penny for your thoughts, Professor Lansdale," she said brightly.

I turned and smiled at her. She was always so cheerful and down to earth. Because professors make their living asking questions that they already know the answers to, they are often full of themselves, waterlogged by their own egos, expecting to be treated like royalty. Donna cut through that; she had a few hundred ways of reminding all of us that we were no more special than the person who delivers mail for a living.

"My thoughts, Donna?" I said. "I can't stop thinking about the train wreck."

"It was on the radio just a little while ago," she said, "you didn't hear? Everyone was rescued. All three men are safe."

I couldn't begin to describe my relief. "I'm so glad," I said to her.

"Someone was looking for you this morning," she said. "Elizabeth Taylor."

"Who?"

"No, she didn't leave her name. But she looked just like the actress."

"Probably one of my students."

"Probably," she said. "How are you getting on in the faculty apartments?"

"Fine."

"You're sure? You don't need anything?"

"No, I'm fine. All I have is my books."

She just looked at me for a moment, startled, I supposed, by the cheerful way I'd said that. I sensed that had I been her son, she would have cautioned me about growing comfortable in an empty apartment. The whole world knows that you are not grown up until you own things too heavy to move by yourself. Appliances, automobiles, beds, and couches, the kind of possessions that anchor us to the world.

"As long as you're content," Donna said, "I won't bother you." She smiled. "Well, I'm on my way to tell Professor Peters that the department will not be able to reimburse him for the case of whiskey he bought when he took the honors students to Ireland last semester. He'll be heartbroken."

As she walked away she called back to me, "It's going to snow early this year. You'll be doing your golfing indoors before you know it, Professor."

Donna was the only person I had told about the barn where I hit golf balls during the winter. Coming from St. Luke's as a scholarship student, I'd worked in the university dining halls while holding down as many part-time jobs off campus as I could find. One of them had been weekend chores at a chicken farm two miles outside of town. On the property there was also an enormous barn that had been empty since the farmer gave up raising cattle. Here is where I spent my best hours reading and hitting golf balls up into the haylofts. By the time I finished my junior year I had read all the novels of Thomas Wolfe and Theodore Dreiser there. I loved the clattering noise the golf balls made when they ricocheted off the walls and rafters. It was a satisfying sound that turned every shot into a triumph.

The barn was also where I discovered that if I read slowly I could memorize whole passages from books after just one pass. To quiz myself I brought along chalk from the school and often wrote out passages on the wooden planks of the barn walls. This was where I had first rehearsed the role of college professor, pretending to be standing in front of a classroom of students.

My ability to read with such recall had made my undergraduate and graduate studies quite easy. Preparation for exams meant simply reading slowly through the texts and lecture notes. And it was also in the barn where I had written most of my dissertation, wearing three layers of winter clothing, writing the first draft on a black iron Remington typewriter whose keys carried a reassuring echo into the vast space above me.

IT SNOWED ON the last day of October, just a few inches, but enough to send me indoors. I was hitting balls when I heard a car drive up. Swinging open the heavy barn door, I saw her standing beside an old tan Mercedes. I had not seen many movies in my life and I never watched television, but even I recognized her as a stunning re-creation of a young Elizabeth Taylor.

She stood at the front of the car, attaching a Christmas wreath to the engine hood. I was staring at her when she turned to look at me. As I think of her now, across the years that have carried me away from that moment, I still feel the weight of my love for her. The physical properties of my affection. Against my ribs, the pressure of desire. On my shoulders, the heaviness of my fear that I would lose her. The crushing weight of jealousy on my back. My jealousy . . . I am most ashamed of that. In my first glimpse of her I was already jealous of everyone who would see the perfect heart-shaped bow of her lips, the fine high line of her cheekbones. Her pale green eyes, and her hair that fell black and straight over her pinned-back shoulders. She possessed that kind of beauty you will always search for, no matter where you are in the world, in the fading light of day, before night descends. A beauty that inspires devotion to it. I am talking of that part of devotion that is an unbearable affliction. That part of love that opens its own meaning, breaks its own laws, and haunts us to the end.

FOUR

"YOU'RE PROFESSOR LANSDALE?" she asked.

"Yes," I replied.

"A nice woman told me I might find you here."

"That would be Mrs. Bridges, the department secretary."

"I'm Julia Peterson. I'm a photographer for the school newspaper at

Smith College. I've just discovered something in this wreath I bought. Come take a look."

Down on my knees beside her. Her breath on my cheek. "Right here," she said, as she parted some of the pine boughs.

I couldn't tell what it was. Something the shape and size of a marble, but with a sharp point fixed on it.

"I don't know what it is," I said. There were red patches on her bare legs from the cold.

She had the patience of a scientist for this thing she had discovered, whatever it was. She kept looking at it and turning it in her hands until she knew what she had found. "The skull of a bird," she exclaimed. "Look, the sockets of the eyes. And the beak. Hold out your hand, Professor."

She placed the tiny skull in my palm. Weightless.

"Well," she said, "you don't find one of those every day."

We stood up together. She looked at me with more than a glance this time, as if she had just noticed me there beside her. "Did you think I was one of your students?"

"You might have been."

"Tracking you down here to complain about a grade?"

"This is my first term," I said. "I haven't given any grades so far, except for some short papers."

She nodded and put out her hand for me to shake. She looked more prepossessed than my students, and just as I was wondering how close in age we were she said very directly, "I'm too old to be one of your students."

Twenty-two or twenty-three, I was thinking as she explained that she had dropped out of Smith for three years to help her dad get his new garage up and running. "I imagine that my former classmates are already hosting Junior League luncheons on their way to becoming exact replicas of their mothers," she said with an ironic smile. "Do you like being a professor?"

"So far I love it," I told her.

She raised her eyebrows as if this surprised her. "You don't find it a little stifling inside the ivy tower?"

Now I was the one who was surprised. Surprised and hurt by this remark. But I could not oppose her or think of what to say in response.

"Most of my professors act like they're addicted to the sound of their own voice," she said. "I think there ought to be a rule that all professors are forced to go out into the real world and earn their living every three years."

She said this without looking at me until she'd finished. When our eyes met I thought she was waiting for me to defend myself. But I couldn't. "Your father owns a garage?" I said.

"Classic used cars," she said proudly. Then she looked past me to the open barn door. "So, what do you do here?"

Suddenly I cared what she would think of me hitting golf balls. "I come here to think, that's all," I said. "To read and think."

"It looks like a great place for that. And no one will bother you here, that's for sure. Well, except me. My father would love a barn like this. He's never had enough room." She smiled to herself. "Engine parts all over the house. Pick up the couch cushions and instead of finding loose change you might find a radiator hose. That's home to me."

"Where *is* home for you?" I asked.

"Mount Carmel, Pennsylvania. It's a small town. Want to take a look at this great old car?"

It was a wonderful car. A dashboard made of redwood. Leather seats. "Look in back," she said. The rear seat was depressed, its springs flattened. "The man who sold it to my dad sold safes. He used this car to deliver them. Just the small ones, but it only took two years to ruin the backseat."

"I can't imagine who would buy a safe," I said. "It's actually something I've occasionally wondered about. Safes, and . . ." When I hesitated, trying to come up with something equally as unnecessary, she beat me to it.

"Mounted animal heads," she said.

I laughed out loud. "Right, those giant antlers."

"You'd be surprised with safes," she went on. "The guy who owned this car told my dad all about the business. What do you think people put in them?"

"In their safe?"

"Yes."

"Money, I suppose. Jewelry."

She shook her head and said, "Mostly photographs."

"What kind of photographs?"

"Family photographs. Pictures taken when everyone was happy," she said as if I should have known. "Doesn't that say a lot about the human race?"

The silver bracelets on her arm jingled when she reached inside the car and took an envelope from the glove compartment. "Aren't you freezing inside that barn?" she asked.

"It's not bad," I said. Then, curious as to how she would react, I told her that I had read a hundred books or more inside the barn. "I've done a lot of reading in there. I fall asleep in libraries. Always have."

"Me too," she said. "What do you read?"

"The same books over and over. By the great writers."

Our eyes met again. "And what do the great writers teach us?" she asked as she looked away, then back at me.

"Many things," I said. At that moment nothing specific came to mind.

"Name one," she insisted as she smiled at me slyly.

"All right . . ." I began.

"You're stalling, Professor," she said.

"You're right. Okay then."

"Okay then?"

"Here it is . . . The great writers teach us that a simple life is best. You know? Thoreau. Whitman." I watched her looking deeply into my eyes, measuring my answer, or me.

"Is there any such thing as a simple life, Professor?" she asked.

I stood before her, mute and helpless, envious of her boldness. She possessed precisely what I lacked: the self-confidence to be bluntly honest with the world and to demand the same in return. She was light-years ahead of me, I knew this. And I think I also knew that though I would try for all I was worth to possess her, to win her approval and her love, in the end she would find me inadequate.

She wanted to see the inside of the barn. I followed a step behind her, like a child, while she examined and explained to me the architectural qualities of the structure. It wasn't long before I confessed about the golf, then teed up balls for her until she hit one that satisfied her. "That's a terrific sound," she exclaimed. "You know, there's a golf course at Mount Holyoke College. Somebody told me there are only five girls who ever use it."

"I don't really *play* golf," I said.

"Good," she said. "It looks like a dumb game to me. Bunch of blond guys from California and Florida in bad pants. I don't think much of polo either. My first two roommates at Smith brought their own polo ponies to college with them. They're the ones who tormented me my freshman year, telling me that I was going to turn out to be just like them. You know, find a rich husband, let go of your own dreams. Not me. I'm here for my education, then I'm heading back home."

"That's sounds good," I told her. "You have brothers and sisters?"

"Three of each."

"Big family."

"It's great," she said. "I love my family."

I just nodded, lost in the joy I saw in her eyes.

"Anyway," she said, "I was taking pictures at the accident last week. The train."

The top of my head began to burn when she said this. I had the terrible and crazy feeling that she had tracked me down as a citizen's arrest for the golf ball that had caused the train to derail. "I was hitting golf balls in that field," I said so nervously that she just looked at me for long time.

Then she opened the envelope and took out a photograph. She handed it to me. It was a picture of me kneeling in front of the woman whose husband had now been rescued.

"I want to use it in the newspaper," she said, moving closer and looking down at the photograph with me. I heard her say that she needed my permission. "When I saw you take her hand," she said, "I knew it would make a great picture."

I couldn't say anything. I was lost in the woman's face, remembering what she had said to the reporter that day.

"You can certainly use it," I said.

She thanked me. "I was hoping you'd say yes," she said. "I've never seen that look in anyone's eyes."

"I saw it too," I said. "She was so determined."

There was a brief silence. When I looked up from the photograph, she was staring at me. "I was talking about the look in *your* eyes," she said.

FIVE

THAT'S HOW IT began for us. And isn't that the way a love story should begin? I was pushing thirty years old, a man by all outward appearance, and yet I was aware even then that I was marching toward something I had never known. A certain momentum was already building, pulling me forward, and I was leaning in, assenting to it.

In the orphanage each of us had one set of nice clothing that we wore only when prospective parents came to St. Luke's to choose a son. Dark blue slacks and a white shirt with a button-down collar. I never put on those clothes without believing that I would be chosen. There was no doubt in my mind that out of all the boys, they would take me home. And this hope of mine, this completely exquisite hope, was my great failing. When I built my life of solitude—filling the chairs in my apartment with books instead of people, playing golf in an empty barn rather than out on a course—it was to protect myself from my own unrealistic hope.

But I was lost after spending that first hour with Julia. How could I help being lost? How could I keep from giving myself away to a person who had noticed me?

I SAW THE photograph in the Smith newspaper a week later. This gave me an excuse to call her. I left word at her dorm and then immediately began to wait for her to return my call. I kept a vigil by the telephone: in case she called while I was in the shower, I left the bathroom door open so I'd hear the phone ringing. I did my reading by the telephone as well; no more trips to the barn, no more golf. After I held my classes, I hurried back to my apartment and waited for the phone to ring.

Finally she called me on a Sunday morning while I was reading my students' papers. As soon as I heard her voice I apologized for never asking her what she was studying at Smith. "Your major," I said. "I meant to ask."

"That sounds like a professor's question," she remarked.

I might have apologized but she didn't give me the chance. "I've had four majors so far," she said. "I'm afraid I wouldn't be chosen as a poster girl for Smith College. I can't seem to understand why it matters what someone majors in. Tell me, what major would be best for a garage mechanic?"

I wanted to give her a thoughtful answer but suddenly found that I didn't believe in majors either. She had won me over.

"I'm not planning to set the world on fire," she said. "I might just decide to work with my father at the garage."

"As long as you're happy," I said.

"Oh, I want to be more than happy," she said. "I want to live every day."

"That sounds wonderful, Julia," I said. As soon as I spoke her name I worried that this would make her uncomfortable. "I called to tell you that I saw the photograph. Thank you."

"You called me?"

"Yes, I left word at the dorm."

"Oh, nobody takes messages here. They pretend to but they don't. I'm calling you to see if you want to take a ride."

I stood up in my kitchen. "Sure," I said. And then, "I'd love to."

"Have you been outside, it's like spring. Bring along your golf clubs."

"YOU HAVE JUST one club, Professor?" she asked when I got in her car.

"I travel light," I said.

She looked at me and smiled. "If we're to be famous friends, maybe I should call you by your name rather than your title."

"Yes," I stammered.

She raised her eyebrows.

"Oh," I said when I realized she was waiting. "Ross. Yes, call me Ross."

"I will," she said as she shifted gears.

She drove us to the course at Mount Holyoke College. There were patches of snow on the fairways, but the grass was lush and green. All I wanted to do was take a walk beside her but she insisted that I play.

I swung too hard and shanked my first drive badly.

"I think it went over there to the right," she said.

"Strange," I said, "they usually go straight."

I hit a few more bad shots and then persuaded Julia to take over. "You're a natural," I said after she hit three balls in a row that went straight. Not far, but straight.

"Wait until I tell my pop that I'm a golfer now. He'll order me home immediately."

Behind the seventh or eighth green we came upon a marvelous hill, shielded from the sun by a row of tall cedar trees and still covered with crusty snow.

"*This* is a sledding hill," I proclaimed.

She looked out over it and smiled. "I agree," she exclaimed. "All my kingdom for a sled."

I told her that when I was a kid we used to go sledding on the metal lids from pretzel cans.

"Pretzel cans?"

"The minister at the Baptist church loved pretzels and used to supply the orphanage with gigantic tins of them. We'd sit on the lids and go flying down the hill."

"You grew up in an orphanage?"

"Yes. In Illinois. St. Luke's. It was a good place to grow up. I was very happy there. Fond memories and all."

"And your parents?" she asked without hesitating.

"Killed in a car accident," I said. My standard line that I'd told the two or three people I'd known well enough to have asked me.

"I'm sorry," Julia said.

And that night, back in my apartment, I kept picturing her face when she said that. Her eyes so full of sorrow. I couldn't fall asleep and was up trying to read a book of Robert Penn Warren's poems, but I kept reading the same verse over and over again while Julia's face lay across the page.

WE LIVE INSIDE our own truth, reassured by it, weighed down and hemmed in on all sides, tracing the boundaries of our illusions until we awake one morning to discover that nothing is the way we always thought it was.

THE TRUTH THAT I had constructed in order to be alone in the world was that I didn't need anyone. That I could even be a better professor this way. Free from personal commitments, I could devote myself to the literature my students and I were exploring together. I had it all figured out. It made perfect sense.

That was before I met Julia. In the days that followed, while I replayed our first minutes together, kneeling in front of her car, her breath on my cheek, my whole outlook began to change. One day after class I found myself walking the Sylvester girl (Amy was her first name) down the crowded corridor, encouraging her to talk with me about her father's death. "If you need time to go home and be with your mother, I can certainly work that out for you," I told her. She was grateful for my concern. "I want to go home," she said. "Every time I think of my father, I want to drop out of school and go home."

"I understand," I said to her. There were tears in her eyes and when one began to fall down her cheek, I cast aside the prohibition against touching a student, reached across the space between us, and dried her face with the cuff of my shirt.

It was so unlike me that I felt like I was observing myself from a distance with a certain curiosity. *Here is a man*, I thought, *who is trying his best to take down the walls that separate him from the world. I wonder what will become of him now.*

Some evenings I would be brushing my teeth before bed, standing in the bathroom in my slippers, or lying in bed in my pajamas trying to read, when I would put down my book and rally against my dull routine. I would get dressed and go take a walk across campus, saying, "Hello, beautiful night, isn't it?" to anyone I passed.

One night, I rode the bus to Northampton and found my way to Julia's dorm on the Smith College campus. I stood in the shadows, looking up at the windows for a long time, first just counting the lighted rooms and the dark rooms as if I were an indifferent observer, and then imagining myself in one of those rooms with Julia, talking with her through the night. I was at peace in this illusion until a girl began undressing within my view. I turned away in shame and knew that I could never stand there again.

IN THOSE DAYS after I met Julia I took a good look at my wardrobe for the first time in years and decided that I needed to buy some clothes. I owned four suits, which I alternated wearing to class, and two pair of khaki pants and a U Mass sweatshirt that I wore everywhere else. Up until now these had seemed perfectly adequate. But one day I looked carefully at the way my male students were dressed, and soon I was studying the attire of all the boys in all my classes. There was one boy, a sweet kid named Ed Mahoney, a sophomore sensation on the football team, who appeared exactly the way I wanted to appear the next time Julia saw me. I went to the Varsity Shop with him in mind, but there were too many sweaters to choose from and a selection of shirts that all looked the same to me. Eventually I asked for his help. "Sure, Professor," he said. "I'll go shopping with you any time."

"IT'S FOR MY nephew," I said to him when we were walking side by side down Main Street. "He's in college in Boston and he doesn't have much money. I thought I'd help him out."

"I hear you," he said.

My lie reminded me that I had lied to Julia about my parents. I wondered if the farther I ventured from my own little world, the more lies I would have to tell. Suddenly I felt terrible about this, and I promised myself that when I saw Julia again I would confess.

"All right," my student said to me as we stood in front of a selection of sweaters. "He'd love these."

He handed me a Shetland wool crewneck, dark blue.

"I should get him three, I think, Ed."

"Well, you want navy blue. Wheat. And dark green."

"Yes."

"I don't know how the kid dresses."

"Oh, well, he's never had any decent clothes. He grew up on a farm. And as long as we pick things you'd be comfortable in, that should be fine."

That's how it went. I admit that when Ed chose dark socks instead of the white ones I had always worn, my feelings were hurt. But I got through it, and it was quite an education for me.

"The main thing is this," he explained. "You see the advertisements in magazines and on TV and they're always pushing new styles. You know, they trick us by making us feel like we have to change. Tell your nephew to stick with the basic, classic look. No bright colors. No big floppy collars. You know, the stuff that only looks good on fruitcakes."

"Fruitcakes?"

"The Italian models, you know."

"Oh, right, I see."

"These things you're buying, they're cool."

"Cool, yes. Good. Thanks a lot for your help, Ed."

He shook my hand and said, "Right on, man."

SEVEN

ID I KNOW this was crazy? Yes. Well, no. Or, let me put it this way: I had lived in a great dark house all my life. Now someone had turned on a small lamp somewhere on the top floor, and I was walking toward it, stumbling along, banging into furniture on the way.

THE FIRST WEEK of November it snowed every day. I finally got up my nerve and called Julia. I had gone out to the grocery store earlier that morning before class and bought two large tins of potato chips. Hopefully. They only sold small bags of pretzels. Coming back to my apartment the cabdriver had looked at me in the rearview mirror. His name was Tom. He'd been giving me rides for years. "You having a party, Professor?"

"You know me better than that, Tom," I said.

"Well, there's a first time for everything, they say."

I had paid the fare and was standing outside the cab with one tin under each arm when I said, "May I ask you for some advice?"

"Fire away, Professor," he replied eagerly. "As long as it's not about women. I've been married three times and I still can't figure out why."

I laughed nervously. "Well, actually," I began, "I've met this girl. Not one of my students, of course."

"Right, I understand."

"She's just a girl I met. But I can't stop thinking about her."

"Oh, no," he said.

"I need to see her again and I don't know if I should call her."

He nodded slowly. "Well, the telephone is better than sending a message by pigeon. I'd recommend the phone. That's what they're for."

"Yes, but . . ." I couldn't finish.

"Here's my theory about life, Professor," he said. "Life is short. Call her."

WHEN I DID, all I could manage to talk about was the snow. "Don't you love it?" I said.

"I've been thinking of you sledding at the orphanage," she said.

I told her that I'd gone shopping for pretzels but couldn't find any that came in tins. "I got potato chips," I said.

"That's fine by me," she said. "When are we going?"

This took me by surprise. "We could meet at that hill on the golf course," I said.

"I have a better hill," she said. "I'll come get you."

I PUT THE cans of chips on the backseat then climbed in next to her. She was wearing something on her lips that made them glisten. And her hair was pulled back into four braids, two over each shoulder, something I had never seen before.

"I thought you were just going to bring the lids," she said.

Idiot, I thought; I'd been so damned nervous. "I wasn't thinking," I said.

"No, the chips will be perfect for where we're going," she said.

WHILE WE WERE driving I had the momentary dream that we were just starting out on a long journey across the country in her marvelous car. Looking out the windows at Niagara Falls and the Mississippi River. Giving rides to hippies who would tell us their stories of life on the road. We would sleep on the soft leather seats at night, listening to the radio until we couldn't stay awake any longer.

She drove with both hands on the wheel, impatient, I thought, with the slow pace of the traffic. "People drive like they've never seen snow before," she remarked as she punched the accelerator and we swung out into the passing lane. I grabbed the handle of the door when our back tires fishtailed across both lanes. "Don't worry," she said soothingly, "I'm a very good driver." And she proved this by calmly bringing the car back into her control. "I drive just like my father," she said.

Somewhere along Route 9, I decided that what I really wanted more than I'd ever wanted anything in my life was to never reach the sledding hill, to stay with her as long as I could. *Live with her*, I thought, *right in this car.*

WE DROVE MAYBE ten miles before we came to a large old brick building standing on a hilltop. "I called ahead and told them we were coming," she said.

I looked out the window as we turned onto a narrow lane. I think I already knew where we were just by the feeling in my chest, but when I saw the mailbox set on top of a short post, low enough to the ground for a child to reach inside, I turned to Julia.

She was smiling. "They call it a group home, not an orphanage. I don't know what the difference is really," she said. "I hope this was the right thing to do, Ross."

I felt my eyes fill with tears and I turned away. She took the mitten off her hand and touched my face. "I'm sorry," she said.

"No, you don't need to be sorry," I told her. "It's just that no one has ever done anything like this for me before."

I SAW MYSELF in all of the children. The ones who clung to our legs. The ones who wanted us to carry them up the hill and those who insisted on marching up the hill on their own to show how capable they were. Those who cried and those who hid their tears. "The chips are a big hit," Julia said to me while we stood watching the children devour them.

"I have to tell you something," I said to her. She turned to me. Her cheeks were red from the cold and she looked so strong and pretty. "I didn't tell you the truth about my parents. I don't know why I lied. It's a story I started telling when I was about the same age as these kids. It was easier that way. The truth is, I don't have any idea who my parents were. And I'm so glad you brought me here."

We looked into each other eyes. She was smiling at first, but then her expression changed. I thought she suddenly looked frightened.

BEFORE WE LEFT we had to promise we would be back again with more potato chips. One little boy lagged behind the others as we got into Julia's car. The man and woman who ran the place were calling to him, but he turned and ran up to my window and tapped on it with his hand. I rolled it down. "We're coming back again, don't worry," I said to him. He just looked at me and said nothing. Then he looked at Julia.

"Do you people have any boys of your own?" he asked.

We both shook our heads. "No," I said.

He looked at us again, chewing on the ice that clung to his red mitten. "You need one then," he said before he turned and ran away.

EIGHT

THAT NIGHT JULIA called my apartment.

"If you're asleep, just hang up," she said.

"I'm wide awake. Reading," I said. "Trying to read, but thinking about you." It was a dangerous thing to admit, but I said it. And in the silence that followed, I regretted what I'd said.

"I'm thinking about you too," she said at last. "Come downstairs."

What to wear, what to wear? I said the hell with it, and put on the clothes I'd worn sledding.

The stairs opened to a common room with couches and coffee tables. When I crossed the room, I heard her call my name. She was standing in the telephone booth with the glass door open. She waved me over and when I got within a few feet of her she held the telephone receiver in the air and said, "It's for you, Ross."

"For me?"

"Yes," she said with a serious expression. "It just happened to be ringing when I walked in. Step in the booth here."

She stepped out so I could get in. I put the receiver to my ear and reluctantly said hello.

"Hello," Julia said, looking right into my eyes. She stepped closer to me, and then closer so she could close the door behind us. "Hello, Ross," she said. "It's your mother calling."

I looked at her, trying to figure out what she was thinking. "I don't have a mother," I said. "Remember?"

"Everyone has a mother."

"I don't understand."

"You don't know her, but you still have a mother. And I just wanted to tell you something," she said, gazing into my eyes.

I felt like I was falling backward off my feet. "It's been a long time," I said into the telephone.

"I know, I'm sorry about that. I've been lost."

"Lost?"

"Yes. It can happen. It was just last week that someone told me my son had grown up to be a wonderful man. A college professor. A very kind man."

I thanked her for this.

She went on. "I've heard that you're all alone in the world. Is that true?"

All I could do was nod my head.

"Well, you shouldn't be alone," she said.

I looked into her eyes. She smiled faintly as she leaned toward me and softly kissed my lips. One kiss, that was all.

Just then a girl carrying books came in the front door and walked toward us. Julia slid open the door of the phone booth and the girl said, "I need to call my professor upstairs and tell him I'm here. Will you be on the phone long?"

I was about to hang up when Julia said, "I don't know. It's his mother. She hasn't spoken to him in a long time."

She turned to me and whispered in my ear. "How old are you, Ross?" I told her and she turned back to the girl. "She hasn't spoken a word to him in almost thirty years, so we may be a while."

"I'll just go on up then," the girl said as she turned toward the stairs.

Then Julia took my face in her hands and kissed me again. This time a long kiss. I kept my eyes open. Hers were closed. When she opened them, a worried look passed over her face.

"What's wrong?" I said.

"Nothing," she said.

"Are you sure?" I asked.

"No," she said. "Kiss me again."

NINE

I REMEMBER SPENDING hours in this little coffeehouse on Wesley Street in Northampton, just a few blocks from Julia's dormitory. She did her studying there and I corrected my papers. We always sat in one of the booths near the windows where a bunch of marijuana plants hung in macrame slings above a life-sized cardboard model of Bob Dylan standing beside a surfboard. Usually music by Judy Collins would be playing, or Joni Mitchell.

We went there one evening after taking a long walk in the snow. While we drank hot chocolate, Julia slid down in the booth so she could put her feet in my lap where I wrapped them in my coat to warm them. A small thing, I suppose, but I couldn't have been more moved if I'd just stepped inside the Sistine Chapel. Her breasts rested on the table across from me. I drifted away for a moment, staring at them until she lowered her head and looked up at me.

I was caught.

"I'm up here, Ross," she said sweetly.

I apologized.

She smiled. "I want to ask you something."

"Okay," I said.

She took a box from her leather bag. "I'm going to have a smoke," she said.

My eyes went from her face to this box maybe six inches long made of tin and painted pale blue with black lettering. Bishop's Biscuits. Inside she had a silver lighter with the Texaco logo on both sides, a red-and-black star. A can of lighter fluid. Papers. Tobacco in a leather pouch. I looked up at her. Her forehead was wrinkled and her eyes were narrowed in concentration. I watched the smoke brush her face as it drifted above her. "My mother hates the smell of cigarette smoke," she said. "My father and I do our smoking together in his garage. We always stand at this window that looks out into a field where you can see deer."

I told her that her father was lucky to have her love.

"Oh, I miss him all the time, ever since I've been at Smith. But now I have to ask you, in all the literature you've studied, have you ever come across a story anywhere about a girl who has pledged herself to a boy when she was very young, a girl in every sense of the word. Their wedding has been planned forever, it seems. It's the only boy she's ever touched. And she loves him, she always has."

"Is she sure?" I asked.

She looked into my eyes. "Yes," she said. "She loves him, but you see, because they were so young when they met, she never *fell* in love with him."

She looked away, out into the street.

"I'm sure it would be a story by Fitzgerald," I told her. She didn't look back at me.

"How does it end?" she asked.

"I'm not sure," I said.

Now she turned and faced me. "Have you ever fallen in love, Ross?"

"No. But not because I haven't wanted to."

"Tell me."

"There's nothing to tell. Two dates in boarding school." It was painful just recalling this. "They weren't interested in me. Disaster is the only word that comes to mind."

She reached across the table and took my hand.

"What is his name?" I asked her.

"Jack."

"Is he in college?"

"He's in the army. He's a soldier."

"Where is he?"

"He's in Germany. He's been there for two years."

"Not Vietnam," I said.

"Oh, God, I hope not. But he wants to go. He's volunteered. He's a soldier, Ross. That's all he's ever wanted to be. And I love him for that. But—" She stopped and pulled her hand free from mine.

"I'm not asking you for anything," I said. "I just like being near you."

She thanked me sweetly. "I have to tell you this, though," I said. "More stories than we can count have been written about people who try to measure their love for one person by falling in love with another. And they always end badly."

She listened to this and said, "Look at me, Ross. I could never do that to you."

"Would I have a chance?" I asked.

"A chance?"

"Against Jack," I said.

"A chance?" she said. "We never have more than a chance, do we, Ross?"

BEFORE WE PARTED that night I asked her if she had ever read much Walt Whitman.

"I celebrate myself," she said.

"Good."

"No, it's not good," she said. "Most of it went in one ear and out the other."

I told her that I was teaching a seminar on Whitman. "We meet Thursday night at seven. Would you be able to come this week?"

"I'll be there," she said. She kissed my cheek, then asked, "What are you thinking?"

"I'm just waiting to see you again," I told her.

TEN

WHEN I WAS in high school I had a crazy English teacher who came to class once dressed as Walt Whitman. He'd had the theater department put on makeup, the whole nine yards. He just stood in front of the class and recited Whitman's poems by heart. He was an eccentric guy and all the kids made fun of him. His name was Train, and we all called him Caboose. Standing there as Whitman, the kids began laughing at him. I didn't have the courage not to go along with them, even though what I wanted to do was stand up and applaud him.

I told this story to the graduate student who was on duty in the theater when I arrived just after dinner. And then I asked her if she would help me.

"I'm teaching Whitman in my seminar tonight, in the English department. Can you make me look like him?"

WHEN MY STUDENTS arrived I was slouched in a chair at the front of the room. Wild gray hair. A bushy gray beard. Dressed in a yellowed silk blouse and a moth-eaten tuxedo with the lining hanging out. Holes in the soles of my black felt slippers. A quart of whiskey on the table beside me.

I had been nervous walking from the theater department to my office. But that had passed. The makeup and costume were so perfect that the person who was nervous had disappeared and there was just Walt Whitman in his place.

I recited Whitman's poetry in a low, raspy voice, with my head bowed as if I were too weary to move. I was so completely lost in my performance, it wasn't until I'd finished the last poem that I realized Julia hadn't come.

There was still half an hour left, but I dismissed my students. I took Whitman's *Leaves of Grass* from my leather satchel and stood at the windows looking over the lights in the valley of the scattered farmhouses and the cottages in a ring around Porter's Pond. A carpet of lights at the small airport off in the distance. Suddenly I was drowning in disappointment. "It's your own fault," I said out loud. "You get your damned hopes up so high."

I was just beginning to gather my things when I heard Julia's voice.

"You were wonderful." She was standing inside the doorway. "I got here just as you were starting. I didn't want to interrupt so I stayed in the hall."

I thanked her and we stood at the windows together for a moment. "I love looking at the stars," she said.

I told her what Brother Martin had said about how some scientists speculated that we might be made from stardust. "That's a nice thought," she said, smiling.

"He's the man who introduced me to books," I said.

I took her into my office and watched her moving slowly down the length of the bookcases, running her hand over the covers.

"Here, come look at this," I said, as I took Brother Martin's list of writers from my desk drawer. We stood together while she read through the names.

"You've kept this since you were thirteen?"

"I've kept everything. When you don't have much to keep, you don't throw anything away."

"Exactly how many of these writers' books have you read so far?"

"Most of them," I said.

"Show me."

She held the sheet and I ran my finger down the list, naming by memory the titles of their books. "But since I met you, I've slowed down some," I confessed.

"I'm sorry."

"No, it's just that the time I used to spend reading, I spend with you now."

"Living instead of reading, you mean?"

"Yes, and dreaming. Dreaming of you."

"You've been dreaming of me?"

"Yes."

She looked into my eyes and sighed. I was embarrassed and I tried to make light of what I'd said. "I'm dreaming of you years from now, living a simple life."

She looked at me carefully. "There's that simple life again," she said. Then she asked me what I wanted.

"I don't know what you mean," I told her.

"I mean, what do you want most from life?"

"I'm not sure," I said.

"I am. I want to always feel like I'm alive. Like I feel right now."

She stopped talking and seemed lost in her own thoughts. And then out of the blue, she said, "I need to measure you."

She had brought a cloth tape measure. "I want to learn how to knit, and you're going to be my first experiment."

I took off the tuxedo jacket, which I'd forgotten I was still wearing. "Stand still now," she said as she stepped behind me. I closed my eyes while she drew the tape measure across my shoulders. I stopped breathing when her hands circled my waist. "Raise your arms, Ross," she said softly. I opened my eyes and she was staring at my face. "Measuring Walt Whitman," she said, smiling. "That's something you don't get to do every day."

I laughed with her as she took hold of my wrist. Then she stopped suddenly. "I want to go somewhere," she said.

"Where?"

"Anywhere that isn't your college or mine."

WE WALKED THROUGH town and stopped at a white clapboard church where yellow light from the windows fell across the sidewalk. A choir was rehearsing. We opened the door slowly to a dark vestibule. As soon as we stepped inside the door I kissed her mouth. A brief kiss, but when I started to pull away, she placed her hand on the back of my neck and pulled me closer until I had my arms around her. And I didn't believe any of it was real. Suddenly everything felt unfamiliar. As if the world had been only space that I walked through until now.

With her face lying against my chest, Julia told me that she wished she could go back and start college again. "From the time I first got here I closed myself off to everything that might tempt me. I was so determined not to change from the person I was at home. When I saw you kneeling beside that woman where the train had crashed, when I looked at you through the lens of my camera, I realized this for the first time. I never realized it before, Ross. Or maybe I did, but I didn't want to admit it."

I waited for her to go on, but she was quiet, still in my arms. "What happens now?" I asked her.

"I don't want to know," she said.

ELEVEN

IN THE END it wasn't Whitman but Shakespeare who brought us closer. *Romeo and Juliet* was playing at the movie theater in Northampton and Julia wanted to take me. The film was so powerful that both of us were barely breathing by the time the doomed and star-crossed couple spent their night together before they parted. They were lying naked in bed in the early-morning light when Julia took my hand. When I looked at her face I saw the reflection of my own desire. Like a quick spark of light.

After the movie ended we sat silently until everyone had left the theater, then walked slowly up the aisle. We were still holding hands outside, both of us startled by the world of passing cars and traffic lights. Across the street was the elegant Hotel Northampton. A four-story red brick building with white Georgian columns and balconies off the upper floors, which were strung with colored Christmas lights. Below, the broad, white-trimmed bay windows of a pleasantly lit café overhung the sidewalk and made the people inside seem part of a live theater to the people passing by. As I looked up to the third floor a man and woman stepped outside through French double doors whose lace curtains blew in the breeze. He held a bottle of champagne, and she the glasses. If I had someone else's life instead of my own, I thought, I might be the kind of man who would walk Julia across the narrow street, take a room in the hotel, and hold her all night long. Just hold her. That was all I wanted to do.

I paused, wondering what that would be like, before turning to her just as a gust of wind blew her scarf across her face. When I reached up and moved it back onto her shoulder, she looked at me. "I'm always going to be honest with you, Ross," she said softly.

I said nothing. I didn't know what to think.

We walked to her car, and rather than let go of my hand, she opened the passenger door and crawled across the seat, pulling me in next to her. She never let go of my hand and we didn't speak for the fifteen or twenty minutes it took to reach the planetarium.

"This is my church," she said when we started on the walkway that led to the door. She didn't ever go inside, she told me, the door was either locked or there were people inside. Instead she led me to a stone bench that we stood on, looking up at the sky. "Do you go to church?" she asked.

"No, not anymore," I said. "At St. Luke's we had to go every day."

"It's just a story," she said, almost as if she were talking to herself. "All of religion was made up to make dying easier, don't you think?"

Before I could answer she said, "If you can't drive a car in heaven, I don't want to go there. What about you, Ross?"

"Well, I don't drive so—"

She turned to me. "What?"

"I don't drive," I said. "I've never had a license."

She still didn't believe me. "It's true," I said. "None of us at St. Luke's got a driver's license. The Brothers had a hard enough time riding herd over a hundred boys."

"They were probably afraid you would just drive away. Go see the country. But what about when you got here for college?"

I was feeling a little embarrassed now. "I don't know," I said. "I just never thought about it. You've got the buses and taxis here. It's a small town."

"But still, you need to drive. Your poor, deprived soul needs it. Trust me, you'll love driving."

AND SO I had my first driving lesson there in the parking lot of the planetarium. At first the clutch was too confusing for me and the car just bucked forward and stalled. Julia kept telling me that I would get it. "Nobody gets it right away, don't worry," she said. Finally we were moving forward across the ice- and snow-covered asphalt.

"Yeah! Yeah! Now turn, turn. No! Not too sharply. Just get us going in a circle, Ross."

That turned out to be within my ability. And it was fun. I got us going a little faster, and then faster, and then suddenly the back half of the car flew out of control. I slammed on the brakes.

"No!" Julia yelled, laughing at the same time and pressing against me. She grabbed the wheel and threw the car into a tight 360-degree turn just in time to keep us from slamming into a snowbank.

"Next lesson I teach you how to pull out of a slide."

"Tomorrow," I said eagerly.

She looked at me and smiled. "Tomorrow I have to study."

"Oh."

"Final exams are coming. You should know," she said. "We'll have to celebrate the end of my exams and your first semester of teaching."

"That sounds great," I said.

She looked out the window, and then leaned across my lap and pointed to the sky. "When people are far apart, they pick a star to look at, to make them feel closer. Did you know that?"

"No," I said.

"So, if we become great friends, and we end up being far apart, which star do you want to look at and think of me?"

"All of them."

"No, that's not fair. Just one."

I finally chose one for her.

"I'll look at the same star and think of you," she said.

With Julia so close and with the feeling that my life was opening to me at last, I didn't want to think about Jack. About which star was his.

T W E L V E

SOMETIMES I STAND at my kitchen window, wrapped in my blanket, with the cold linoleum beneath my bare feet. My whole life has passed. It is strange. I am an old man standing at a window looking out upon a world that contains Julia as it does the people who are my mother and father, its vast spaces separating us. I wander back to bed and close my eyes. I close my eyes and I can see her face. Her hair. Her eyes. Her fingers. Her lips. Like someone packing carefully for a long journey, I am committing these things to memory with the sense that I will always be somewhere where I cannot find her.

JULIA HAD HER finals to prepare for, and I had plenty of work to fill the next ten days. Papers and exams to read. Final grades to record. Like all new professors, this work, rather than being a burden, energized and excited me. Here were these marvelous young people, sharing their ideas with me, someone they barely knew. Engaged in a dialogue about books and writers who meant everything to me. Some evenings I would count out a certain number of papers to read before I quit for the night. I'd finish, go to bed, and then get right back up and wade into more, too enthralled to sleep.

LATE ONE AFTERNOON I completed the final grade reports for all four of my classes, left them on Donna's desk to be passed on to the registrar, then went to the library, determined to find a poem by Sylvia Plath whose verses had been banging around in my brain since I'd felt myself falling in love with Julia.

I searched the stacks for hours until I was one of the last people in the library. I was turning pages like a madman when someone called to me. "Hey, Professor, have a nice Christmas." I looked up and saw Ed Mahoney with his arm around a beautiful girl. I thanked him and he raised one hand and pointed to me. "Nice threads, man," he exclaimed.

"Excuse me?" I said.

"The sweater," he said.

He'd caught me. "Yes, thank you, Mr. Mahoney. I kept this one for myself."

When I finally found the poem I called Julia in her dorm and asked her to meet me in the lobby.

"I'm in the middle of an art history study group," she said.

"You have an exam tomorrow?"

"My last one," she said. "And then we can celebrate."

"Please, five minutes," I said.

She agreed and I took a taxi there.

SHE HAD JUST walked across the lobby toward me when the dormitory mother cleared her throat loudly. She remains the only woman I have ever known who looked exactly like George Washington, and she ran the dormitory like a minimum-security prison.

I suddenly felt defiant and brave. "Madam," I called to her, "I want to read this young woman a poem by Sylvia Plath. I've spent hours looking for it and it's a matter of grave importance. I think the survival of this college may depend upon it."

I was just going to read the poem, but when I saw the dorm mother craning her neck to watch every move Julia and I were making, I jumped up onto the arm of a couch and recited the poem loudly.

"Get down off there!" the dorm mother snarled.

Julia was looking at me with a big smile on her face. She began walking away, holding one finger to her lips. "Tomorrow night. The coffee shop at six."

I nodded. Then spoke two slightly altered sentences from *Romeo and Juliet*. "In an hour there are many days. By this count, I shall be much in years before I again behold my Juliet."

"Go home before you get in trouble," she said, still smiling.

"Good night, fair maiden," I said to George Washington on my way out.

THIRTEEN

I DON'T KNOW how long Julia had been sitting across the table from me in the coffee shop, but when I awoke she was staring at me and her eyes were red from crying. She said she was sorry for being late, and when I asked if she was all right, she dried her eyes with her sleeve and tried to pretend that nothing was wrong.

"*Look Homeward Angel*," she said, looking down at the book I had been reading before I dropped off.

"You've been crying about something," I said.

"It doesn't matter," she said. "I'm fine." She lowered her eyes. Her heart wasn't in this denial.

"I want to know what's wrong," I told her.

Without looking up she asked why. Her face was blank and there was no light in her eyes. A moment passed. Then she sat up straight, took something from her coat pocket, and laid it on the table for me. It was a magazine of some kind that she had folded in half. On the front there were color photographs of brides in wedding dresses.

"They look like pieces of candy, don't they?" she said. "Go on and open it if you want."

Inside, square pieces of white cloth were glued to the pages. Four small pieces on each page. I had no idea what I was looking at. I turned back to Julia and shrugged.

She smiled faintly at my reaction. Then something swept over her face. She reached across the table and took my hands in hers while I looked into her eyes. "Do you have an opinion about whether I should choose taffeta or lace for my wedding gown?"

I couldn't speak anymore. I just shook my head slowly.

"Good," she said. "This came in the mail today from Jack's mother."

I looked away from her and she saw my disappointment. "Let's go, Ross," she said suddenly.

What she needed to do, she said, was see people. Not students, but real, live people living real lives. "What are *we* living?" I asked.

"Oh, you know what I mean," she said. "I get so tired of thinking about myself. Everyone here is so self-absorbed. I miss regular people. People who pump gas for a living or deliver the mail. I'm one of *those* people."

So we sat in her car, parked along Main Street in front of a bank. She

47

smoked her cigarettes and we talked for a long time. "I drive home to-morrow," she said.

A chill ran through me. "I hear there's a blizzard coming tomor-row. All the roads between here and Pennsylvania will be closed. You can't go."

"You're sure?" she asked.

"Positive."

She drove me to my apartment. From the street the building looked bleak.

"I want to go to your orphanage someday," she said.

"Why?"

"I want to find out what kind of little boy you were."

"We can go tomorrow instead of you driving home," I said.

"The blizzard," she said, turning to look into my eyes. "I'll be back in three weeks," she said. "You'll be here."

"No. I'll be gone."

"You'll be here."

"You haven't heard?"

"Heard what?"

"I've joined the French Foreign Legion."

"Silly."

"I'll perish here without you," I said, trying to make this sound light-hearted, though of course I meant every word of it.

She kissed my cheek. "Merry Christmas, Ross," she said. "I have to go now."

I tried to keep from asking her, but couldn't. "Will Jack be home for Christmas?"

"Yes," she said.

Now that the door was open, I marched through it. "When did you last see each other?" I asked.

"June," she said. She looked very sad, and I knew I was making things difficult for her. I opened the car door, and before I got out, I thanked her for the evening. I was walking up the steps to the front door when she called to me. I turned back.

"I'm going to be sad too," she said.

I CLUNG TO those words in my sleep that night. And when I awoke in the morning, though I knew she was on her way home, already hundreds of miles from me, I was okay. Three weeks and we would be together again.

I was standing at the kitchen sink, making coffee, when there was a knock on my door.

When I opened it, she was standing there. "You've got ten minutes to get ready," she said with a mischievous grin.

"Ready for what?" I asked.

"I'll be in the car," she said, turning and running down the stairs.

FOURTEEN

MY HOME-FOR-CHRISTMAS outfit," she said as we pulled away. She was wearing an ironed white blouse that held the faintest scent of bleach and reminded me of the laundry room at St. Luke's, a gray pleated skirt, and nylons, which I had never seen her wear before. I felt a tightening in my chest when I thought of her pulling the nylons up over her calves and thighs.

"You told me once that you've never seen the ocean," she said.

"I haven't."

"Well, that's where we're going."

"We are?"

"We are."

"What about Pennsylvania?"

"Tomorrow. I'll be home for Christmas, like the song says."

I nodded my head, smiling. "And I've never seen anyone as pretty as you."

"That's silly," she said as she floored the accelerator and sped through a yellow light. "Ten more years and my hair will be completely gray. Like my grammy's. Everyone has always told me that I look just like her."

"You'll be stunning with silver hair," I said.

"Maybe not," she said.

"I want to see you with silver hair," I said.

"Maybe you will then," she said.

IT HAD JUST begun snowing when we crossed the iron bridge onto Cape Cod and I got my first smell of the salt air. "Look below us," Julia said. I raised myself up and peered through the skeleton frame of the bridge. A slow parade of tankers and cargo ships made their way beneath us, ghostlike in the snow, their red-and-green lights blinking.

"Someone told me about a place just a few miles from here. It's supposed to be beautiful."

WE PARKED ALONG a narrow beach in a town called Cataumet and stood together looking out to the bay. The water was black beneath the gray, snowy sky. I had imagined the ocean blue, a deep, wondrous shade of blue. And not nearly as rough as it was today. There were shorebirds ticking along ahead of us on the wet sand like windup toys. And gulls crying while they circled the swells.

"It's amazing," I said. "But I've always read that the ocean makes you feel small. I don't feel small right now."

I saw her gazing out across the tops of the waves.

"Your Jack is over there," I said. "Somewhere across the sea."

She smiled. "Nope. He's in Pennsylvania by now."

"And you're here with me. I feel guilty."

"I'm here with you," she said, "because I want to be. Now stay right here, I've got to get something from the trunk."

I turned and watched her running back to the car.

"Your Christmas present!" she hollered.

SHE HAD BOUGHT me a set of golf clubs. She stood beside them, smiling happily. "They're not new," she said, "but they're very good clubs. The man told me they're the kind of clubs you can use your whole life. What do you think?"

"They're beautiful."

"Ben Hogan irons," she said, as if those three words held great meaning to her now.

"You shouldn't have done this," I said.

"Don't ever say that when someone gives you a present," she said.

I pulled the four iron from the bag, aware suddenly that golf had vanished from my life once Julia entered it. I had filled my empty hours with her or with thoughts of her. I took a few swings with the iron, working my shoulders and hips. It felt weightless and heavy at the same time.

Julia had knelt down and opened one of the side pockets on the bag. "You have to hit these balls while I take your picture," she said. "I have tees too."

I hammed it up for the camera, striking the baronial pose of a long-dead British Open champion, then affected the snobby accent that

Brother Martin did so well. "Here we are on the final hole at St. Andrews in Scotland with the championship hanging on this very shot." I sliced the ball so terribly that it flew a couple of hundred yards down the shore and landed on the beach without making it into the sea. "A rare mishit, ladies and gentlemen. Must have been that second glass of whiskey I had with my tea."

I set up another ball and kept talking, warmed by Julia's wonderful laughter.

WE ATE DINNER in a small Italian restaurant, sitting in the back where there were no windows, and when we finished and came outside, the light snow had turned to freezing rain and everything was coated with ice. "We can't drive back in this," Julia said. "We'll fill up with gas and sleep in the car until morning."

"Music to my ears," I said.

"Before my father would let me bring the car to school he stocked the trunk with everything you'd need to drive across Siberia. We'll be fine. But when's the last time you got drunk?"

"Me?"

"Yes, you."

"Never."

"Professor Lansdale, sometime you're going to have to explain to me just what you did for four boring years of college. Let's go."

WE PULLED INTO a parking lot with a bottle of wine and the contents of her trunk: a sleeping bag, two wool blankets, gloves, flashlight, and candles. "There were chocolate bars but I ate them long ago," Julia said.

We huddled in the front seat, talking. The windows were caked with ice and it wasn't until Julia lit a cigarette and opened the car door for some air that we discovered the parking lot we had pulled into was lined with boats that had been hauled there for the winter. All around us there were huge yachts on wooden cradles, like whales that had gone off course and washed up on the shore.

"Oh, Ross," she said excitedly. "Do you know how lucky we are? Follow me."

We found a ladder and climbed onto the decks of five boats before we found one whose cabin wasn't locked. Then we made our way down below where we followed the flashlight into mahogany-paneled staterooms with real beds. "We'll be sleeping in style tonight," Julia said. We chose a room with a round window just above the bed and watched the sleet change to snow.

"You can't be shy tonight," Julia said, just before we fell asleep. "You're going to have to hold me to keep us warm."

IN THE MORNING I saw the sun rise on her face. I had no words to tell her how privileged I felt to see her awaken, to watch the day enter her and return her from wherever it is we go when we sleep. I wondered if this was how you got to know another person, by watching them carried back to you in the first light of each new day. I looked out the round window and saw a full moon floating above an open field. When she opened her eyes she said, "I wonder if love stories are different from all other stories."

"How do you mean?" I asked.

"If you have the beginning, like this. And then the end. And then the long middle part." She rolled closer to me. "Maybe that's why we can love two people at the same time. You and I are at the beginning. Jack and I are in the middle. I have to figure this out while I drive home today."

FIFTEEN

I WATCHED HER drive away at noon. She had connected a strand of colored Christmas lights to the car battery and hung them inside the rear window of her car. After I saw her turn off Main Street I walked a little way with the Christmas shoppers. Inside the front window at Wight's Sporting Goods I watched a store clerk wearing a blue apron show a set of golf clubs to a father and his son. I waited until the clerk was free then asked him if he sold any used clubs.

"I have a few sets out back," he said. "Nothing much left though. I sold a beautiful set of Ben Hogan irons to a girl from Smith just a few days ago."

I bought a set of ten-year-old Wilsons and spent Christmas Eve sawing them off and putting on new grips in my kitchen. Then on Christmas morning I took a taxi to the group home that Julia had discovered, where I was the next best thing to Santa Claus when I showed up with the golf clubs. I lined the kids in a long row at the top of the sledding hill and watched them hit golf balls until we'd lost them all in the snow.

Before I left I shot a few games of pool and talked with the boy who had lingered with Julia and me when we had come here together. His name was Frankie. He was seven years old. He told me that he had lived in Erie, Pennsylvania; Boston, Massachusetts; Providence, Rhode Island; and someplace in Maine where he was born. "I don't know the town," he said. He had big brown eyes that darted wildly, never focusing on anything for longer than a second, and hair that hung over his eyebrows.

"You've done a lot of traveling," I said after he told me the list of places where he'd lived.

"This is the best place," he said, " 'cause they let us play outside a lot."

"Nice," I said. "I grew up in a place like this too."

"You did?"

"Yes. Far from here."

"Which state was it in?"

"Illinois."

He tried out the word, then asked, "How old were you before you got adopted by somebody?"

It was a loaded question, and if I'd answered truthfully, I knew it would take away what hope he had left. "How old are you?"

"Seven and a half," he said.

I remembered the boys at St. Luke's who had left and then returned after a probationary period with prospective parents who were trying them out to see if they might adopt them. They called themselves rejects and pretend sons and Pinocchios when they came back, and they told the rest of us that out in the real world there were times when certain places could suddenly feel like places they had been to long ago, in the time before they were first given up to the orphanage. Places imprinted in their memories.

"I was eight when I was adopted," I told him.

"Were they nice?"

"Yeah, real nice," I said.

He nodded his head knowingly. "I'm going to be a pro golfer when I grow up, did you know that?"

"You've got a great swing already," I told him.

"Yep. I know it."

Frankie walked me to the taxi after I said goodbye to everyone. When I put out my hand for him to shake, he jammed his hands into the pockets of his pants. "We have to shake hands," I said to him.

"I never did," he said.

"Nobody ever taught you how to shake hands?"

He shook his head.

"Well, it's time then," I said. "Give me your hand. Right hand."

He smiled. "I like it," he said, still gripping my hand.

"Always make it a strong handshake," I told him. "Wherever you go in this world and whomever you meet, give them the strongest handshake you can. But you don't want to pump it. Just firm and steady. And remember this, you shake someone's hand when you meet them, and again when you say goodbye. Even if you're disappointed with the person, you still shake their hand. Okay? Do you understand?"

"Yes."

"Want to try?"

He gave me everything he had. I dropped to my knees in the snow pretending to be in pain.

"Like that?" he asked proudly.

"You got it, Frankie," I said.

THAT NIGHT I couldn't stop thinking about St. Luke's. It had been five or six years since I'd last spoken with anyone there. It seemed that once I no longer needed transcripts of my high-school grades or copies of my birth certificate, I had lost touch. I felt bad about this now, and I called to ask for Brother Martin's telephone number in Texas. I was told that he had left there. "Do you know where I can reach him?" I asked.

"I'm not sure," he said.

"Is this Brother Thomas?" I asked.

"No, Brother Thomas is no longer here. I'm Brother Whitcomb. But if you leave your telephone number, I'll try and help you."

In the background there were the sounds that I remembered so well. Someone crying. Someone fighting. Someone racing up the stairs. I closed my eyes and pictured the place. The kitchen with the aluminum pots stacked on the shelves beneath the window. The black gas stoves. The blue glass pitcher we used for iced tea on hot summer days. And the office with the wire-mesh walls where Brother Martin hung each week's menu. The wood-paneled dining room with the long Formica-topped tables where five generations of boys had scratched their names in the hope that their lives would be remembered. I could see the staircase rising to the room where we'd slept in rows, a wooden box for our possessions at the foot of each bed, and on the top of one of those wooden boxes the painted black-and-red squares of a checkerboard. I had always believed that the past was just a time, but I knew now that it was also a place.

Sitting alone that Christmas night I felt like I had ventured far from St. Luke's in the time I had spent with Julia. Such a brief time still. No more than a sum of hours that barely equaled a full day. Lying beside her in the boat, her back pressed against me, my arm around her, holding her hand while she slept, I had watched the sun rise with a burst of gold light from the sea that I had never seen before. I had closed my eyes then and said a silent prayer that somehow the two of us could go on together to make a life. When she awoke I had told her that I would love her better than anyone else ever would.

"Will Brother Martin remember your name?"

"He may not," I said. "Tell him I'm the kid with the wicked slice."

SIXTEEN

EVERY COLLEGE IN America spends the weeks over Christmas break interviewing candidates for teaching positions that they anticipate for the following fall semester. And the responsibility for this task always falls on junior professors, who complain bitterly about having to sacrifice their personal time.

For me, it was exciting. And the perfect way to fill the days while Julia was at home. We had only two openings to fill. One in the classics program, and one to teach expository writing. Because I had no driver's license and couldn't chauffeur people around, I was assigned a one-hour private interview with candidates for both positions. These consisted of twelve men in their thirties from predictable backgrounds and nearly identical academic records, with the exception of the two finalists for the writing spot. The first was a young poet from Flint, Michigan, who had won the Yale Younger Poet's Prize and was being courted by at least five Ivy League colleges, which perhaps explained his attitude. He lit up a joint in the middle of the interview, seemed completely uninterested, declined a tour of the campus, and announced at the department dinner that night that teaching poets laid more undergraduate students than regular professors because they had perfected false modesty.

The second young author was Johnny Durocher, who had recently published his first novel to considerable reviews and notice. I liked him immediately when, five minutes after we met, while we were walking down the corridor of Lawrence Hall, he took out his wallet and showed me photographs of his two little children, a boy and a girl with white hair. ("A new one in the oven right now," he said proudly, "four months to go.") And a picture of his wife as well.

"I almost brought Linda," he said to me. "Boy, is she going to love this place."

"You're a lucky man," I told him.

"I am. I don't deserve them," he said with such sincerity that I knew the road he had traveled to get where he was had not been easy.

In my office at the end of the day he noticed Brother Martin's trophy on one of my shelves. "Junior Amateur Championships 1951," he read aloud. "Someone you know, Professor?"

"An old friend," I said, "yes."

"Do you play?" he asked, still staring at the trophy.

"You want to go hit some?" I asked him.

Now he looked up, his eyes wide with excitement.

———————

WE WALKED THROUGH the snow, stopping at my place to pick up a few clubs and balls. "Oh, baby," he said, when he saw the clubs Julia had given me. "Old Ben Hogan blades."

The rest of the way to the barn I told him how I had been introduced to the game.

"For me," he said, "it was my old man. The only time he ever talked to me was when we played golf."

Inside the barn he stepped away from me and gazed up at the rafters. "Man," he said, "I could spend the winter here."

I told him that I had hit maybe twenty thousand balls here. "It's been my refuge," I said to him.

He noticed the writing on the wall nearest us and walked up to it. "What's this?" he said. "Wait a minute. *Anna Karenina*."

"Junior thesis," I said. "I've written the first drafts of probably fifty term papers on these walls. Plus the beginning of my doctoral thesis."

"I'll say, man, this is amazing." We walked the perimeter together. I told him I used to steal the white chalk from my professors' classrooms. "Man, it's truly wild," he exclaimed. "Oh, you've got old Robert Burns here. 'A Man's a Man for A' That.' Tough old Scot. Wonder if he played any golf in his day."

I showed him the hayloft with the sliding door where I lay on warm days reading peacefully. "Whole days," I said.

"I hate reading," he said. "Don't tell anyone. I just need to be moving. I think most writers prefer watching television."

I laughed along with him. "Your novel," I said. "It's working its way around the hiring committee now. I'm eager to read it."

"Well, it's nothing really. First book, you know."

"What's the first line?" I asked him.

He turned and faced me. "First line?"

I picked up a piece of chalk and waited.

"I'm honored," he said. "Okay, first line. 'At a distance, men in uniform satisfy our vague longings for grace and order.' How's that?"

I wrote it along the wall. "Very nice," I said.

"Not quite up to Tolstoy and Hemingway, but at least I made the wall."

SLOWLY HE TOOK off his overcoat and suit jacket. Then he hit balls with such passion that I could do nothing but stand there and watch. He didn't have a beautiful swing with the classic line of Brother Martin's, but he made solid contact on each shot, and every ball flew in the same low, explosive trajectory. When he had just one ball left to hit, he rolled up his sleeves and turned to me. "Every ten years the most prestigious amateur tournament in the world is held at St. Andrews, in Scotland. Christmas Eve. One round on the Old Course, by invitation only. Guys like me wait their whole lives and never get in. My old man submitted my name to the invitation committee when I was twelve years old, so I'm on the list, just waiting for the call."

He turned back and set himself in his stance. "Someday," he said just before he began his take back. This time he hit the ball with such force that it blasted through the barn wall like a bullet.

I watched in disbelief. "I think I got all of that one," he said.

I SAID GOODBYE to him outside the student union where a driver waited to take him to the airport. We shook hands. "I really enjoyed this," he said. "How long do you think it will be before I know something?"

"I'm going to read your novel tonight," I told him. "I'll report to the hiring committee on Friday. Middle of next week, I would think."

Before he got into the car he thanked me. "That barn," he said, "I'd like Linda and the kids to see that."

I could have said *They will,* but I didn't.

"I stuck a little golf in the book," he said as he climbed into the car. "I hope you like it."

Johnny Durocher, I said to myself as the car drove away.

SEVENTEEN

THE LAST PERSON I expected to show up at my office in Lawrence Hall was Tom, the cabdriver. He was holding his hat in both hands and he looked very nervous.

"Never was any good in school," he said when I told him to come in.

"Sit down, Tom."

"That's okay, Professor, you know me, I've been sitting all day. I just thought I ought to tell you this. I hope I'm not out of line or nothing."

"Tell me what, Tom?"

"Well, it didn't make any sense to me, but two nights ago I dropped your—" He paused. "The girl you've been seeing? I dropped her off at the Hotel Northampton."

"Julia?"

"Yes."

My mind started racing. "Two nights ago?"

"That's right."

"It can't be, Tom. She doesn't come back for another week."

"She's back, Professor," he said grimly.

I thought, by the tone of his voice, that she must have been with another guy. Jack.

"Were they—" I started to ask.

"Just her, Professor. All alone. One bag. She didn't look good though. She tried to give me a hundred-dollar bill for a two-dollar fare."

"Where did you pick her up?"

"Just outside town at the A&P."

I didn't think about calling the hotel first. "Drive me there, Tom, can you?" I said.

W H E N   I   S T O O D outside the hotel I recalled the night Julia and I had gone to the movies across the street, how I'd looked up at the hotel just as a man and woman stepped out onto a balcony on the third floor with a bottle of champagne. I don't know why, but as I walked across the carpeted lobby for the first time, passing the broad fireplace and the handsome antique furniture, I thought of all the parents who had stayed in this hotel over the years. Dropping off their daughters at Smith, or visiting on parents' weekend. Maybe sharing a bottle of champagne to mark the end of a part of their life. I wondered how it felt to let go of a child that way.

I rode the wooden elevator to the third floor, which was lit by small brass lamps mounted along the hallway. I found the door to Julia's room open a few inches. The first thing I saw when I looked inside was her navy blue pea coat and leather boots, and something on the floor beside them that I couldn't identify until I knelt down and held it in my hand. Two darning needles connecting a small square of pale blue knitting.

I heard a sound, and looked across the four-poster bed to the windows where Julia was sitting in a stuffed chair, smoking. I called her name and she turned and looked at me with a strange smile on her face. "That's your sweater," she said when she saw that I was holding the knitting.

I walked over to her but she didn't look up or give me her hand or acknowledge me in any way. She was in another world, just blowing smoke from her cigarette out the open window. Finally she leaned forward slightly. "Not very happy people," she said, nodding to the street. I looked down into the square where people were coming and going. "I've been watching them, Ross," she said. And I was relieved to hear her speak my name, as if I'd thought she had forgotten who I was in the two weeks we had been apart. "Only one out of seven people is smiling."

Her voice was so flat and lifeless that I knelt down in front of her. I took hold of her hand and looked right into her eyes. "You caught me," she said.

"Caught you at what?"

"I've been drinking," she said.

Then I saw an empty bottle on the floor. I picked it up. "You didn't save any for me?" I said, teasing her.

"You don't drink. You're Professor Plum."

"Professor what?"

"You don't know who Professor Plum is?"

"No, I don't, Julia."

"You've never played CLUE?"

I shook my head.

"You've never been drunk or played CLUE. Or been engaged. Or been married. Or—"

I touched her face to stop her. She closed her eyes and asked, "Don't you like your sweater, Ross?

"It's a little small, don't you think?" I just wanted to make her smile or laugh.

"That's as far as I got before everything—" She closed her eyes, then finished the sentence, "—everything fell to pieces on the floor."

I looked around the floor to try and see.

"No," she said, turning her head slowly. "Not here."

"At home?"

"Put me to bed, please," she said.

"Are you sick, Julia?" I asked.

"No," she said.

She raised her arms to me with her eyes closed again. I lifted her from the chair and carried her to the bed like a rag doll. I took off her shoes, then covered her with the blankets.

"I'll just sit beside you," I said to her, though I wanted to be closer than that. I wanted to lie beneath the covers with her, but I felt uninvited.

"Do you know what it means to hot-wire a car?" she asked, just above a whisper. She pulled me close and kissed me. A long kiss. I opened my eyes and saw that hers were closed tightly and her forehead was wrinkled as if she were concentrating hard, putting everything into this kiss. She pulled away from me then, glanced at my face, and closed her eyes again. A faint smile was on her lips. She was just about asleep, I thought.

"I think so," I said.

"You're going to have to learn how to do that to me, Ross," she said, opening her eyes briefly, then closing them again.

"I don't understand," I said.

"We can't make love," she whispered. Then waited.

"No," I whispered, shaking my head slowly as she shook hers.

"We should though," she said sadly.

"We should?" I said.

"But we can't," she said again, as if deciding finally. "But there are other ways to start the motor."

She was asleep then, having left me with no idea of what she meant. You could have searched the world for a man my age who knew less about sex than I, and come up with no one.

I lay next to her for a long time. Richie Havens was singing in the theater that night, his great raspy voice crying out for freedom.

EIGHTEEN

I AWOKE BEFORE sunrise with Julia's hair across my face. She was sleeping peacefully. I watched her breasts rise and fall beneath the blanket and then I looked down at my right hand and saw that it was twitching. The thumb and forefinger rubbing together in a steady motion the way I had seen the youngest boys at St. Luke's rubbing their blankets to comfort themselves while they fell asleep.

I took a shower and walked up Main Street in the cold morning air where I bought coffee and some flowers at a small shop. I handed the clerk my money and when I reached out to take my change, my hand was twitching again. I stared at it with an odd fascination, then put that hand in my pocket self-consciously.

In the elevator, I looked at my face in the reflection of the copper ceiling. Different, I thought. You look different.

JULIA WAS IN the bathroom when I got back to the room. The water was running in the tub and I waited for it to stop before I called to her.

"I've got coffee here," I said.

"You're a saint," she said. She opened the door wide enough for me to pass the cup to her. She had a towel wrapped around her, and her hair pulled back.

"Are you feeling better?" I asked.

"Just a minute," she said. And then she told me to come in.

She was in the tub, all but her face and shoulders submerged in a bubble bath. The cup of coffee sat beside her on the toilet seat where she had a cigarette burning in an ashtray. She told me to sit down beside her, and when I did she touched my face with her hand, tracing her wet fingers along the line of my jaw.

"Never go home for Christmas," she said, trying to smile.

"This is my home," I said. "I have nowhere else to go."

"I know," she said. "I should have stayed here with you. I shouldn't have left you alone."

"You have to tell me what happened," I said.

She reached for her cigarette first. "My father left home," she said. "It seems he's fallen in love with a woman in the church choir. I've known this woman my whole life. I've never liked her very much. Not at all really. In fact, I've always hated her. Can you believe that?"

She turned and looked at me but I could tell she didn't know I was there. "So my mother is a wreck, as you can imagine. And the whole family has been turned upside down. At Christmas, for God's sake. My father wanted to bring the woman by when we opened our gifts on Christmas morning."

I told her I was sorry.

"And there's another thing, Ross. I know you're not going to want to hear it, but it's my life right now. Jack's gone to Vietnam. He didn't tell me he was going until the night before he left. That was the day after Christmas. So there I was, trying to help everyone. My brother, Sam, stayed drunk the whole time. Which probably wasn't a bad idea. My little sister, Peg, who's only ten, cried herself to sleep every night. Oh, Ross, I should be home there with her right now. Poor Peg."

I put my hand on her arm and told her again how sorry I was.

"You are a saint," she said.

"No, I'm not. But I love you," I said.

She looked at me through the smoke. "Take this," she said, handing me the cigarette. Then she sat up in the tub so that her breasts were visible above the soapy water. I looked away modestly. "Your hand is twitching," she said.

I made it stop. "Do you want to get out now?" I asked her. "Do you want to go somewhere?"

"I don't know," she said as she slid back beneath the water.

I told her that I had to go to a department meeting.

"Go," she said.

"But I don't want to leave you."

"It's all right. There's a paper bag in the other room. Will you get it while I get out?"

A moment later, wrapped in a towel, with the bathwater running down her face and legs, she took the paper bag from my hand and dumped its contents onto the floor. Hundred-dollar bills.

"What's this?" I asked.

"Fifteen hundred dollars," she said. "I sold the car."

"Why, Julia?" I said.

"I've spoken to the desk clerk. The room costs fourteen dollars a night. Here, wait, there's a piece of paper where I figured it out."

She found it on the floor and handed it to me. "Fifteen hundred dollars divided by fourteen dollars a night, including tax; that's one hundred and seven nights. And I checked the college calendar. That will take us up to Easter."

She got into bed and covered herself.

"I don't know what you mean," I said.

"We're in a boat together here, Ross," she replied. "Let's think of it that way. Outside the door there's only the ocean. You remember how it looked, so angry and churned up. We'll just stay in this room together until the money is gone."

I smiled at her, but she didn't smile back.

"I'm serious," she told me.

"You have school. I have school."

"No," she insisted. "This is what we have, right here. This room. Our boat. And the money."

"You'll need to go out for cigarettes," I reminded her.

"I'll stop smoking."

"Food?"

"Room service."

I walked to the windows silently.

"You can't be happy with just me?" she called.

I felt my hand twitching again. I cursed it under my breath and pressed it against my leg to make it stop. Then I turned and faced her. "I have to go to the department meeting in an hour," I said. "My job, Julia." When she didn't say anything, I walked over to the bed and sat down beside her.

"I've been a good girl all my life," she said.

"I know you have."

"Please come right back after you're done with the meeting," she said.

"I will. But what about you?"

"I'm not going anywhere."

"Classes start in a week."

"I'm not going back to school," she said.

"Yes, you are."

"Why?"

"Because, you have to. We both have to."

She turned her head away from me on the pillow. I said nothing until she turned back and looked up at me.

"You'll go to school, young lady," I said.

She nodded slowly. "I'm sorry about your father," I said as I kissed her cheek. "I'm sorry about Jack too," I said. And I kissed her again.

"Jack who?" she said. "Please don't go."

NINETEEN

THAT WAS THE first department meeting I ever missed. I felt so guilty about it that I made Julia strike a bargain with me: I would allow us both one week of what she called "R and R in our Ship of State," but when classes resumed we would rejoin the world.

"After one week, it's up and at 'em for you, okay?" I said.

She leaped onto the bed and jumped up and down in the pale blue flannel nightgown one of her sisters had given her for Christmas. "Yes, sir, Captain!" she said, saluting me.

"And I'm going to quiz you at night to find out if you've been working."

"You'd better!" she quipped, mocking me.

THAT PART OF the deal never worked out. Our evenings were too precious to squander on homework. Instead we spent them the way lovers should, lying in our four-poster bed under our quilts below the chandelier and the pink stamped-tin ceiling, while the snow mounted on the window ledges and the granite battlements of city hall. I read Shakespeare's sonnets to her by candlelight, while she knitted my sweater. In the mornings I brought her coffee from the café downstairs before I left for work, paying the desk clerk for our next night before I went back up to the room with the coffee. This was a time when wives stayed at home, waiting for their husbands to return from work. Leaving Julia to go to my job brought me the consolation of having finally become a man, joining that army of men blessed with the privilege of being waited for at the end of each day.

Once I came back and found Julia lying in bed in the same position she was in when I left in the morning, but she had pushed the bed across the room, up against the windows. When I came in, she raised her arms.

"Come here, Ross," she said, as she sat up.

She wanted to show me something. "Right down there is where the bus drops you. See? I watch you coming back to me. It's a busy place in the late afternoon."

"People out walking on the ocean," I said, taking her hand. "Would you like to take a walk?"

"Maybe later," she said. "But first I want to be close to you. Closer than we are. I love having you hold me and kiss me, but I want more, don't you?"

"I want everything," I said. "I want to have you all to myself."

"Lie down beside me while I tell you something," she said. "Make yourself at home."

I did and then she told me that Jack had given her something when they said goodbye at the airport. "You know the army has a manual for everything? How to take care of your feet and teeth. How to search for land mines and change the air filter on a jeep. And they also have this one for the wives and fiancées of soldiers who are far away for a long time. It tells them how to satisfy themselves sexually so that they remain true while their soldiers are gone. Lead us not into temptation, they call it. It's so the wives don't run around with other men and the fiancées are still virgins when their men come back. Do you know what I mean, Ross?"

"The army has a manual for that?" I said.

"Some of the wives and girlfriends put it together. They did these little drawings. If you want to look at them with me, I can show you."

I felt my hand begin to twitch again. "Are these things that you do with Jack?"

"Some of them."

I thought for a moment, trying to put Jack out of my mind. "Are there some things that you and Jack haven't done?"

"Yes," she said.

THUS BEGAN MY education, over a period of days and nights when Julia was all that I could think about. Kissing her with my eyes open. Slowly unbuttoning her nightgown, then watching her breasts fall into my hands, their surprising weight like an apple in each palm. My lips against the soft skin at the base of her neck. It was as though we were climbing a ladder together, without knowing what we would see at the top. In the moment when we parted I was already waiting to climb to the next rung when we were together again, dreaming of each rung that we would pass on the way with sweet familiarity. The anticipation of this could take my breath away. It could overcome me in my classroom and leave me silent, gazing out the window, a college professor suddenly transformed into a lovesick boy. Such was my hunger for Julia. A deep physical hunger. An ache.

I was insecure enough to never take Julia for granted. And this heightened my excitement and my appreciation of every small thing she gave me, every glance, every sigh. Each time Julia was in my arms, I expected it could be the last. That it was only a matter of time before I lost her. And this fear of losing her and of returning to the world alone as I had always been before made me realize that in a life when a person longs for your touch you are truly blessed. To have that, to see in another person's eyes her desire for *only your* touch, is enough to live for. Nothing else in life, none of the treasures we dream of possessing, compare to this, or to the emptiness when it is gone. There were many times when I was holding her, kissing her and praying at the same time, praying that God would never let her pass from my arms, or if she were to marry Jack, at least let me live in the same town so I could see Julia from time to time.

In those nights we had together I learned to listen for the sound of her desire for me. Her desire which was the exact measure of my own worthiness as she reached her hands into the air so I could pull her sweater over her head. And then her blouse while she insisted that she would always remember these times. Our love was so complete that we inhabited each other's dreams—dreams with vivid details of the small world that enclosed us. The porcelain handle of her hairbrush coming to rest on the glass top of the vanity just before she came to bed. The bright chorus of her silver bracelets brushing my chest as she took me in her arms. The first time I brought her to her pleasure, riding her nightgown up her thighs, then pressing my hand against her while the simple chords and harmonies of Simon and Garfunkel from Carnegie Hall played on the radio beside our bed with its flickering yellow, lighted dial.

—Kathy, I'm lost, I said, though I knew she was sleeping—

The audience yelling, "More! More! Please!"

I GAZED AROUND our room one night while Julia slept peacefully beside me, her hair lying across my left arm and chest. I felt a pleasant narrowing of my life. Everything that mattered to me was now directly in front of me, in my path. None of the troubles or complications of the world could reach us here in the square, silent space of our room. I thought of the plain room at the orphanage that I had shared with fifteen other boys my age. How I had fallen asleep in that room every night of my life from as far back as my memory reached, and never once had I imagined life as sweet as it was now.

TWENTY

S HE HAD FINISHED the front half of my sweater and held it up for me to see one morning as I was shaving. "I just have to do the back now," she said.

"What about the middle?" I asked her.

"There is no middle, silly. You're the middle."

"Are you sure?"

"Here," she said. "Let me do the rest for you."

She took the razor, then stepped behind me. In the mirror I saw her pull her nightgown over her head and let it fall to the bathroom floor. Naked, she pressed against my back and began shaving my face.

"You're going to class today," I said. "You promised last night. Remember?"

"I know. But what if we make love instead?"

"Why are you saying that?"

"For real this time, Ross."

"What about Jack?" I asked, watching her eyes in the mirror. I saw her lower her face. She dropped the razor in the sink and walked out of the bathroom.

"I'll get dressed now," she said.

ON THE WAY home that night I stopped at a jewelry store to buy her something. I looked at necklaces with a woman who worked there trying them on for me. Then I asked her if she would show me the rings. There was one, the most beautiful ring I had ever seen. A diamond set in a narrow band of white gold, with a small sapphire on both sides of it. As I held it in my hand I pictured the moment when I would put it on Julia's finger. "Marry me," I would say. And she would say, "I will."

"Can you hold this ring for me?" I asked the woman. It cost just over four hundred dollars.

"You'll have to give me some money down, and your telephone number," she said.

She couldn't take a check, so I walked to the hotel and went up to our room and borrowed a hundred dollars from Julia's money. She had gone to class and the room had been done by the chambermaid. The bed was made for the first time since we'd checked in eleven days earlier. I stared at it before I left and it made me feel sad. Almost as if we had never been there. Or maybe it was because this was how the room would look one day after we were gone. No trace of us left here. And no one in the world to acknowledge what we had shared together.

I put a down payment on the ring and when I walked back to the hotel I felt a warmth inside me, a certainty that Julia and I were meant to be together. I was so excited that I turned left instead of right after entering the hotel and crossed through the café. I'd gone only a few steps when I heard Julia's laughter. I was certain it was her and I followed it to the room behind the kitchen where the dishes were washed. The door was opened wide enough for me to see Julia sitting on a chrome table, smoking a joint with two guys in white aprons. One of them I had seen before, a marine back from the war, whom I sometimes passed in the mornings on my way to the bus stop. I watched them while my right hand began twitching in my pocket where I'd put the receipt for the ring.

Another man wouldn't have read anything ominous in this. He would have simply gone in and introduced himself. But I was crushed. I wanted to evaporate from the spot where I was standing.

———

UPSTAIRS IN OUR room I waited hours before she finally returned. I heard her giggling to herself as she opened the door. "Anybody home?" she called.

I didn't answer. But she knew I was there. She could see me across the dark room, standing at the lighted windows.

I heard her take something from her purse, then the sound of paper ripping. "Don't move," she said. "I'll be done in a minute."

She turned on the light by the bed before she came up to me. "Look here, Ross," she said. She unbuttoned her blouse and pulled it open. She had taken the wedding dress samples from the magazine and stuck them all over her. "Which do you prefer?" she asked, as she looked down over her breasts.

It gave me a sick feeling and I turned away.

"Jack's mother wants me to decide. Help me decide, Ross."

"I'm not choosing," I said. "Let Jack choose."

"Jack is a million miles away," she said.

"Didn't you go to classes today?" I asked her. She didn't answer. Instead she said that she wanted to talk with me about something.

"What is it?" I asked.

"What I told you before about love stories. Do you remember?"

"Yes. A beginning, a middle, and an end."

"Yes, but not in that order. The excitement of the beginning ends. And then you live out the middle. But I was so young when I met Jack that the beginning was never fulfilled. We've been in the comfortable middle for a long time. And I know that's where we'll stay after we're married. Do you understand, Ross?"

"Yes, I think so."

"It's the same thing with my little town, which I've always cherished. I was so comfortable there before I went home for Christmas. And now I wonder if I can ever go back again. Hold me, please," she said at last.

When I took her in my arms she said, "I don't think I love Jack. I used to think I did. But now I think I love you."

TWENTY-ONE

THE MARINE WHOM Julia had been smoking pot with in the hotel kitchen was Joe Hill. He was a daredevil, one of those guys who would try anything. Even in the snow and ice he rode his motorcycle, sometimes with Julia on the back, her arms wrapped tightly around him. She called this time she spent with him her great awakening. He told her what he said was the truth about the war in Vietnam. She began watching the news on television at night, sometimes cursing President Nixon when his face appeared. "Secret plan to end the war, my ass!" she exclaimed one night, sounding more and more like Joe. "People elect him because he has a secret plan to end the war? What kind of bullshit is that, Ross? He keeps it a *secret* until he's elected while more boys are dying every day? If he really had a way to end the war, wouldn't he just tell somebody so it could be over! Then he wins the election and all he does is drop more bombs on innocent people. And Joe says he's already secretly moved soldiers into Cambodia and Laos."

"I don't think he could do that without someone finding out," I said.

"Joe says he already has. He knows guys who were wounded in those countries."

"Well, if Joe says so, it must be true," I said sarcastically.

ONE DAY I came back from class and as I passed the dishwashing room, Joe Hill called out to me, "Hey, Professor Plum, come have some

one-hundred-year-old scotch, courtesy of the United States government."

"My name's not Plum," I said, stepping into the room.

He laughed and so did the other two guys, who wore kitchen aprons.
I should have just kept walking to our room, but I didn't. I took a drink
to try to prove something. Then another.

We drank steadily for an hour, then Joe challenged me to a test of
bravery that he and his buddies in the Marine Corps had devised. He
rolled up the sleeve of his right arm, lit a cigarette, and laid his arm on
the table. "You put your bare arm against mine, Professor," he said, his
speech now slurred by the booze. "I'll lay this cigarette where both arms
meet and we'll see who pulls away first."

I didn't hesitate. I moved one of the other guys out of the way and
laid my arm down on the chrome table next to Joe's. "I'll never move
my arm," I said. The other two guys mocked me with catcalls.

Joe took a deep drag on the cigarette to get its coal burning bright
red, then he laid the cigarette in the crease where our forearms met.

It took maybe ten minutes for the cigarette to burn down to the filter
and extinguish itself. I just stared into Joe's eyes the whole time while
the room filled with the rank smell of our burning flesh. When it was
over there was a neat hole in both of our arms. Through my melted
flesh I could see the dull gray surface of a bone.

I left the room and went outside. I laid my arm in the snow until the
cold had numbed it.

"Why are you crying?" Julia asked when I returned to the room.

I hadn't known I was and I was sick with shame. "I took a walk. It's
just the sleet stinging my eyes," I said.

I went into the bathroom, locked the door behind me, and wrapped
a towel around my arm.

Julia tried to open the door. "Tell me why you've been crying, Ross,"
she called to me.

"Because you're already taken," I said.

———————

THE FEEL OF her skin against mine took the fight out of me. How could I oppose her when she was touching me like no one ever had?

"I'm going out to get some iodine for your arm," she said, as she sat up in bed. "But first I want you to do something, for me. Find my clothes and dress me."

I found her socks in the bed and knelt down on the floor in front of her. What is more beautiful than the body of someone we love? And to be granted access to that beauty? To be trusted with the delicate bones of her feet in my hands. She stepped into her panties and I pulled them up over her knees, my fingers brushing the luminous skin of her thighs. I touched the tight cords of her neck as she stood there with her head drawn back, breathing peacefully. Her black hair spread over her white shoulders. I had done nothing in my life to earn any of this.

"You're not finished," she said.

I pulled her jeans on and buttoned them. She held her arms out for the bra. I kissed both nipples before I turned her around and brushed my lips against her spine. The impossible clasp, my opposition, so simple in its construction and yet as difficult for me to fasten as to unfasten. I closed my eyes and tried to commit it to memory.

I finished with her white Irish sweater then turned her around to meet my lips. I felt her trembling. I asked her what was wrong. "I want to incorporate you into myself," she said breathlessly.

WHILE SHE WAS gone I stood at the window watching a family walk across the town square. Father with a young child riding high on his shoulders. Mother with two more, one holding each of her hands. It seemed to me a fine portrait of love. In those little bundled children, a purpose to live for.

TWENTY-TWO

I AM YELLING at Julia for the first time. In the bathroom, she is in the tub and I am washing her hair, telling her that no matter what her father has done, no matter what might happen to Jack in the war, she has to pull her life together. "I won't be responsible for you failing out of school."

"Why would you be responsible for anything I do?" she snapped at me.

"*Why?* Because one of us has to behave like an adult, that's why. And I'm older than you."

"That's just dumb, and you know it, Ross."

"What's dumb is you staying in this room every day."

"I don't stay in this room every day, for your information. You're gone all day, how do you know where I go?"

"Okay, so you go down to the dish room and smoke dope with your marine."

"*My* marine?"

"Yes. For some reason that escapes me, you think he's the answer to your problems."

She stands up suddenly, grabbing a towel and storming past me, out of the bathroom, water running off her beautiful body. I go after her, throwing aside everything in my path, the stupid army manual, her boots, my half sweater that she seems to have lost interest in along with everything else except Joe Hill.

Everything falls to silence when I take hold of her arms and lay her across the bed. I can hear myself breathing. And then the two of us are breathing together, both of us moving toward the same still point until there is no place left to go. I can hear her say, "It's like I'm lying in silk. Can you feel it?"

And then I am crying like a little boy. I try to pull away from her, but she holds on to me. "We weren't going to make love," she whispers. "But we are."

I start to apologize but she puts her hand over my mouth. "Now that the damage is done, let's keep going," she says. And she is smiling at me as if everything will be all right.

BUT NOTHING WAS ever right after that. Even after she began going to class again. Even after her father called to say he had returned home and he was sorry for what he had done to the family.

I don't know why we fought so often. I was grateful, always grateful, for the fact that she had given herself to me instead of Jack, but I was also ashamed. There was that terrible contradiction of Julia making love to me with breathless passion and Julia sitting across the room from me with a distant, cold look in her eyes. I kept trying to reconcile the two Julias. I think I lashed out at a part of myself that I saw in her. And she did the same. Weeks would pass and the arguments would pile up and rather than trying to resolve them we would make love again, fighting in each other's arms like some doomed couple in a dance marathon, until we reached that ground of silence, too exhausted to speak or reason.

In March she went on assignment for the school newspaper to cover an antiwar rally in Cambridge where students from Harvard and Radcliffe were taking over an administration building. I watched the local news while she was there. Cops on horseback chasing down students who were racing through the streets, smashing windows.

"That's not the way to end the war," I said to her when she returned.

"Those were brave students," she argued.

"It takes courage to break windows?"

"You don't know, you weren't there."

Finally, thinking I might please her, I joined a group of professors in a protest march against the administration after it was revealed that the university was turning over to the draft boards the names of male students involved in antiwar marches. When some of the professors demanded a meeting with the president of the university, I backed down, afraid that I might lose my job.

We fought over this too. I watched her putting on her coat. "Where are you going?" I asked.

Her back was to me. I saw her hesitate before turning around. "I have to go to the hospital now to find out if I'm pregnant," she said angrily. "And because of you I don't even have a car anymore."

I WENT WITH her of course, following her down the corridor. She took the stairs instead of the elevator. Out in the street we hadn't walked far before she let me catch up to her. I took her hand and it felt different in mine. I looked at her face and let the word "wife" sit on my tongue for the first time. My wife. She would marry me now and I could finally stop worrying about losing her. We would be together until the end of our time. Soon we were walking hand in hand, stopping every few yards to throw our arms around each other and kiss. The nearer we got to the hospital the more frequently we stopped until we finally gave up walking altogether and kissed with such passion that neither of us could move. Suddenly Julia fell backward into a snowbank, pulling me on top of her. "I love to feel you wanting me like this," she said breathlessly.

Somehow we made it into a rest room inside the front doors of the hospital. She raised herself onto the front edge of the marble sink. "I want you to go inside me, and listen to me," she whispered.

"Yes," I said.

"Slower," she said.

"Slower."

"There. Now listen."

"Yes?"

"Whatever happens . . . If I am pregnant, you don't have to marry me."

"I will marry you, Julia. Nothing would make me happier."

She put her hands on my shoulders and gently pushed me away so she could look into my eyes. "I don't mean it that way, Ross," she said. "I mean you shouldn't think that just because a girl wants you to make love to her, it means you'll be together forever."

I was so filled with hope at that moment I didn't interpret this to mean she might not want to stay with me. "*We'll* be together forever," I told her. And then I watched her close her eyes. *I will remember this day,* I thought, as I held her. This small room with the toilet, wastebasket, sink, and mirror, the chrome coat hook on the door. A lifetime of rooms is what I was already dreaming of. A world of rooms shared with Julia. Losing count of them. Returning to them. Always returning.

I opened my eyes. Who would ever know that the lives of two young people had paused here, disturbing the molecules inside this small space? With the heat from our bodies rising through the cool air, I rested my palms against her hips and felt her shudder.

I WAS SITTING across the waiting room, staring at the door Julia had disappeared behind, while my mind raced ahead of me. I had no one to share the news with. No one in the world to invite to our wedding. But that was okay; we would get married in the chapel on campus and all of my students and my colleagues in the English department would be there. We'd have a reception after the ceremony, and everyone would see that we were in love, and that we were always going to be happy together. I would need a best man. Maybe Ed Mahoney, my student who had shopped for clothing with me. This is what I was thinking when the door opened and Julia slowly walked across the room. I stood up and waited for her. I think that she was smiling when I took her in my arms. I felt her lay her face on my shoulder. We stood very still for a long time while a woman came into the waiting room with a little red-haired girl in a pale blue cloth coat and a pleated plaid skirt with a matching cap. She must have been three or four. She climbed onto the seat beside her mother. Her thin legs in white tights hung down. She swung her feet back and forth while she stared at me. I smiled at her, and when she smiled back, I knew that Julia was pregnant and that I was going to be a father in this world.

"Julia?" I whispered.

"I'll need to buy some new clothes," she said.

I tried to move so I could see the expression on her face, but she held me too tightly.

"We'll buy all the clothes you want," I said.

"We'll drive home and tell my family," she said.

"Yes," I said, not wanting to remind her that we no longer had a car.

"Let's go back to the hotel now, Ross," she said. "I'm so tired."

TWENTY-THREE

LATER THAT AFTERNOON, while Julia took a nap, I walked to the jewelry shop and bought the ring I'd put a deposit on. Standing at the glass counter, my hand began to twitch again. I slid it into my coat pocket. The clerk wore a white linen suit. He told me I had made an excellent choice. "June wedding?" he said as he took my money.

"June," I said. "Yes." I could see into a back room. A workbench, a bright lamp, and a small television with two astronauts smiling on the screen.

"I need to buy some clothes," I said to him when he handed me my change. "Is there a store in town for women who are having babies?"

He dropped the ring, apologized, and then gave me directions.

THERE I WAS, following the pregnant mothers up and down the aisles. They walked behind their big bellies like women pushing wheelbarrows. Stopping to examine baby clothes so small they would have fit the dolls these mothers had played with when they were little girls. Though they smiled at me with generous expressions that seemed to imply we were all in this together, I could not have felt more out of place had I been walking along the bottom of the sea.

The owners of the store, identical twin sisters in their sixties dressed in matching gray flannel slacks and pale yellow cardigan sweaters, delighted in my inexperience and ushered me through a dazzling carnival of products, assuring me that I didn't need to buy everything right now because there was a practical chronology to the expanding needs of an expecting mother. "For example," one sister said patiently, "if your wife will be breast-feeding, then you certainly won't need to buy the bottles and the brushes to clean the bottles and the stainless-steel boiler to sterilize the bottles until she begins weaning the baby. Also, you could purchase the bassinet now and the crib much later." She and her sister shrugged their shoulders as if to say, *See, it's not that bad really*. Then they awaited my decision.

I bought everything. Happily. Joyfully. I bought so many things that I needed two taxis to transport it all to the hotel and then five trips in the elevator to carry it upstairs.

THE DOOR TO our room was locked when I returned. The shades were drawn and I could just make out the outline of Julia's body beneath the covers on the bed. I turned on the overhead light in the bathroom and pulled the door halfway closed, then eagerly set about reviewing my inventory in the narrow path of illumination that fell onto the red-and-blue-checked carpet. I ran my hands over everything, marveling at how beautiful it all was. The white wicker bassinet on brass wheels and the cream-colored satin liner. The wooden crib painted white with stenciled gold stars and spooled legs and an arched headboard like a church door. For the car, a bed in a box which you carried like a pocketbook. A changing table with a trapdoor that opened to reveal a bathtub. Baby's first seat in the shape of a miniature throne. A windup swing. A playpen with mesh sides and a mattress on its floor. A mobile of flying yellow duckies to hang above the crib. A stroller with whitewall tires and a fringed top to block the sun. A walking chair on wheels. A rocking horse, a tiny silver cup and spoon. Cotton nightgowns with a drawstring along the bottom and mittens so that baby wouldn't scratch its face while sleeping. Stacks of cloth diapers. A diaper pail. Silver rattles. Rubber pants. Teddy bears and a metal spinning top embossed with zebras. And dresses for Julia. Great, billowing cotton sundresses in pastel shades of blue, yellow, and lime green. And pants and Bermuda shorts with wide elastic waistbands.

There would be other things to buy as time went on, but this was a good start and I felt deeply satisfied as I opened the pages of baby's first book entitled *A Treasury of Days*, where Julia and I would record all the significant events during baby's first year of life. Somewhere near the middle of the book, between the pages set aside for describing our baby's first overnight trip, I slipped the list of Brother Martin's writers that I'd carried with me since I was thirteen years old. I set the book inside the crib. When I looked up the room was filled with moonlight.

I let Julia sleep for another hour or so. I was holding the ring when I laid my hand on her to wake her, and discovered that the bed was empty. What, in the dim light, I had taken to be the outline of Julia's body was nothing more than the pile of twisted blankets and sheets in the unmade bed.

I searched the hotel for her and walked around town until late that night. It was morning when I awoke in a chair and saw her standing inside the door to our room, holding her coat in her hands. Before I said anything I just looked at her there with all the baby things, and I saw those things for what they were: a barricade I had constructed on the road that led away from me.

"Don't say anything, Ross, please," she said. "There was a call for you yesterday while you were in town. I've written down the number. It's on the desk. I'm going home now for a few days."

I watched her touch the wicker bassinet before she turned away.

"How are you getting home?" I called to her.

"A friend's giving me a ride," she said as she closed the door behind her.

What kept me from running after her? I suppose I knew that I had no right to try to stop her from leaving, and a part of me wanted her to go home and tell her family that we were going to have a baby. There was that. And watching her walk out of the room was hard enough; I don't think I could have watched the elevator doors or the front door of the hotel close between us without breaking down.

Still, I would have gone after her if I had known that I would never see her again.

TWENTY-FOUR

THE TELEPHONE CALL had been from St. Luke's, with word that Brother Martin was dying. His sister had brought him back to the orphanage, where she was caring for him.

I finished my week of classes and office hours, hurrying back to the hotel each afternoon with the hope that Julia had called, and then I began my journey by Greyhound bus to Illinois to say goodbye to Brother Martin.

I left from Amherst, changed buses in Boston, and rode all night. Across the aisle from me a soldier in an army uniform never closed his eyes or looked out the window the whole time. Each time I awoke and looked at him he was still staring straight at the back of the seat in front of him. He spoke to me only once. "What state did we just go through, mister?" he asked. I told him Ohio, and I watched him write "Ohio" with a ballpoint pen across the palm of his hand.

ST. LUKE'S LOOKED exactly as I remembered, and this was reassuring. The driveway between two rows of maple trees. The slate-shingled roofs and the buildings of faded red brick. As I walked across the grounds a sense of well-being rose in me and I knew that this must be the way it felt for others to return home. When I crossed the walkway the younger boys swarmed around me just as I had whenever a visitor arrived.

Brother Martin's sister and a nun were caring for him in a small apartment in the eaves of the building where the Brothers lived. I'd never been inside that building, it was off limits for the boys. I sat beside Brother Martin's bed in the red light of a winter sunset. He looked a lot older. His hair had turned white. His green eyes had lost their sparkle, and the chiseled features of his face, which had given him the appearance of an athlete when I knew him, were now bloated from medication.

"Your trophies," I said, when he gestured across the room to a bureau where two of them stood. "I still have the one you gave me." He seemed to appreciate this. "And the club."

"How's your swing?" he asked faintly.

"Still working on it," I said.

He started to say something else, but then stopped and began breathing hard, shallow breaths. He raised his hand to me, gesturing for me to wait.

"There," he said. "The pain always passes, praise God. Tell me, Ross, what are you doing now?"

I told him that I was teaching. This seemed to please him. "That's fine work," he said. "And it gives you time for golf." He smiled at me. "I'm dying now, and when I lie here alone unable to sleep when the pain is bad, I close my eyes and I think back across my life to all the beauty I've seen. Big things, like the Grand Canyon and Yosemite National Park where I once hiked as a boy. I give thanks for the beauty I saw. And the little things, I remember them even more clearly. I still remember a certain four iron I once hit, a blind shot to the green from beyond a hill covered with trees. The white ball against the blue sky and the deep green shade of those trees."

He paused to allow another spasm of pain to pass, like someone stopping at a railroad crossing to wait for a freight train to go by.

"Did you par the hole?" I asked, to help draw him back.

He smiled. "I don't remember how it turned out. But the sight of it, that was the thing. Glorious. I was in my twenties then, I didn't appreciate the beauty of the shot until years later. It's not until your life slows down that you see things fully. That's the gift of growing old. God's gift. Remember this if you can."

"I will," I told him.

"Good," he said. "And don't miss the poetry of John Keats. That's a special kind of beauty."

"He's on the list you gave me," I said, and the thought of it in the baby book filled my mind with the vision of Julia's face and made me feel more alone in the world than I'd ever felt when I lived at St. Luke's.

"I'd forgotten that," he said.

"I've already read most of the writers."

"Very good," he said. "Very good, Ross."

I nodded and then I said, "I'm in a small boat at sea, Brother Martin."

His eyes had closed, but he opened them. There was a puzzled look on his face. I waited.

"You're in love," he said at last.

"Yes. And I have to confess that since I met her, I haven't really even swung a golf club."

"That's as it should be," he said with a smile. "I meant golf for when you're alone."

I thought of returning to the empty hotel room and I felt a cold wind blow through me. "I don't want to lose her," I said. "I don't want to think of myself alone again."

He looked into my eyes while I waited for him to tell me something reassuring. His eyes narrowed then, and after a moment, he asked me to move closer to his bed. When I was standing beside him he said, "That twitch in your hand, has it bothered you for a long time?"

"Not too long," I said, embarrassed.

He reached for my hand and took it in his. As he held it, he closed his eyes. Then he made the sign of the cross on my forehead. "Go and live well," he said to me. "Stay close to God."

HIS SISTER INSISTED that I stay for supper. She had made cold macaroni salad and chicken sandwiches. When she was walking back to the sink to get us both some water, I lifted the top piece of bread and found that there was only one tiny piece of skin from a chicken wing in the middle of the sandwich. The rest was mayonnaise. In the years that I had been away from here I had forgotten what it was like to be poor.

IT WAS A long trip back to Massachusetts. I was already looking at my watch fifteen minutes after we pulled onto I-70. In Cleveland four girls, the ages of my students, got on. I quickly ascertained that they had decided against going to college and were on their way to New York City where they were going to rent an apartment together in Manhattan and become famous models. For hours I watched them doing each other's hair and makeup, laughing as if they didn't have a care in the world.

When I slept that night while the bus rolled east, I drifted in and out of their conversation, the plans they were making, the dreams they had for what would happen to them once they began their new lives in New York. They talked for hours amid a cloud of hairspray, the air thick with the scent of perfume and nail polish. Without Julia, I felt lost and small, and their voices were comforting to me so far from home.

TWENTY-FIVE

WHEN I GOT back to the hotel room all of Julia's things were gone. I went through every drawer looking for something that would bring her back, but there was nothing. Even my half-knit sweater was gone. I had the eerie feeling that she had waited for me to leave, watching the hotel from a distance and then returning after I was gone.

I spent a week in that room, crying in bed and standing at the windows looking down into the street. Then, before I moved back into my apartment, I made arrangements for Catholic Charities to come take away the things I had purchased for Julia and the baby. I gave them everything except the baby book.

A few weeks passed. I was only going through the motions in class. It was driving me crazy not knowing what had become of her. Her hometown of Mount Carmel, Pennsylvania, was about a six-hour drive from Amherst. Donna, the department secretary, offered to drive me there one Saturday. Her husband was moonlighting on a weekend plumbing job and she was free.

It was a bitter-cold day, and we sat in the car with the motor running, watching the house for some sign of Julia.

"You need to go knock on the door and speak to someone," Donna said after a while.

I trusted her instincts but I didn't know what I would say to her parents. *I'm the man who got your daughter pregnant and now I don't know where she is.*

"I don't think it matters what you say," Donna told me. "You love this girl. You need to know that she's all right."

I looked into her eyes when she said this. It was precisely true; that was what I wanted to know. That Julia was okay.

"You can do it," Donna said to me.

I stared at the house for a while longer, getting up my courage. It was just a little split-level house that didn't seem large enough to hold Julia's big family. "Do you think I could just say that I was her friend?" I asked Donna.

"I think that would be fine," she said.

I walked slowly to the front door. One of Julia's brothers invited me inside but I stayed on the porch as he held open the storm door.

"We were good friends," I explained.

He told me that Julia was in California. "She moved out there and I guess she's going to start classes at Berkeley in the summer term," he said.

"So, she'll be in school then?" I said.

"Yeah."

"That's good," I said. I held the door frame tightly to keep from falling over.

"I wish she wasn't so far away," he said.

"I'm going to miss her too," I said.

I handed him a cardboard box wrapped in plain white paper. Inside was the ring and the baby book with Brother Martin's list folded into the middle pages. "Would you give this to her when she comes home?" I asked.

He took the box and said he would put it in her room. "She didn't say anything to you about transferring?" he asked me.

"No," I said, but I don't think he believed me.

When I got back to the car and told Donna, she put her hand on my knee and said, "I think we should go now."

THERE WAS A lot of news about Berkeley that spring as it became one of the first colleges where students and professors voted to go on strike after students at Kent State University were shot and killed. I became a devoted follower of the television news, feeling a little closer to Julia each time Berkeley was mentioned or a picture of the campus was on the screen.

I kept up with my classes. I was teaching *The Grapes of Wrath,* and losing myself in Steinbeck's sentences was the only way I ever stopped thinking about Julia and grieving for her.

IN EARLY MAY on a morning that felt like summer, I was sitting in the coffee shop where Julia and I used to go together. I was wearing short sleeves and the young man clearing tables stopped as he passed me. He had a red bandanna around his head and a silver cross hung from a chain around his neck. He pointed to the scar on my arm. "Hey, man," he said, "check this out."

He had an identical scar. "I got mine in a bet with a crazy marine," he said. "What about you?"

I lied and told him it was a scar from a childhood injury.

He nodded and turned to walk away with his tray of dirty dishes. "What did you bet the marine?" I asked him.

He turned back. "Ah, it was about some hot chick," he said, curling his lips. "I lost. He took her to Canada on the back of his bike."

I felt cold air blow through my lungs. "Canada?" I said.

He looked at me a moment as if he were trying to decide something. Then he shrugged it off. "The chick was knocked up," he said. "They went up to Canada to get an abortion."

I walked all the way from Northampton to Amherst that day and when I got to my apartment I couldn't remember where I'd been.

After that I spent a lot of days hitting golf balls behind the football stadium and nights reading Chekhov by candlelight, often reading the same page over and over again for hours.

Then, slowly, a numbness settled over me along with the feeling that I was returning, after a short journey, to a place I knew well, where everything was just as I had left it.

BOOK

II

ONE

YOU NEED TO buy a house," Donna said to me that summer. "There's a house for sale just down the road from my sister. Right next to the golf course."

If it hadn't been for Donna's company I would not have made it through the spring semester after I lost Julia. I told her everything and she listened patiently, always with a warm expression in her eyes. Having raised three sons, she knew when to listen and when to offer advice. Somehow, over the dismal weeks of May, she had persuaded me that Julia and I were not meant to be, that was all, and that if I did not give up, I would find the right person someday.

"I don't have anyone to live in a house with, Donna," I said to her.

"Someday you will," she said. "And you deserve a house of your own. Trust me."

I wanted to trust someone then. I needed to. So I bought the house. My first night I woke up calling Julia's name.

BY SUMMER I returned to my books and to golf. As long as I got off the first tee just as the sun was coming up, I could play eighteen holes, cut through the woods when I was finished, and get home without talking to anyone.

I did my morning exercises on the first tee. Twenty deep-knee bends. Fifty jumping jacks. Then I took the driver from my bag and began to swing it, slowly at first, going over the list of instructions . . . Left arm straight . . . Turn the shoulders and hips . . . Let gravity start the club down . . . Snap your hands down and through . . . Keep your head still . . . Follow through. I took my swings the way I always did, counting them out loud. I was back to my old ways, relying on numbers to mark the landscape of my solitary life.

I had reached seventeen swings one late-August morning when my sanctuary of silence was broken by the sound of a car pulling into the gravel parking lot on the far side of the clubhouse, and then the doors of the car opening and closing, and the voices of children, and a baby crying, and above it all a man whistling "The Battle Hymn of the Republic" with great enthusiasm.

I was so accustomed to being here alone that I had no idea what to make of this disturbance and I reacted quickly, grabbing my clubs and running off the tee like a frightened cat. At the clubhouse I stepped inside the dark screened-in porch and waited.

A man I guessed to be in his early thirties appeared a moment later. I saw him from behind. He was pushing a baby stroller and holding a small child in each arm. Over one shoulder hung his golf bag, over the other a baby blanket. He and the children were dressed in white, and when they reached the first tee the man set the children down then pushed the stroller off to the side. He put a finger to his lips and I heard him speaking.

"She's asleep. We have to be quiet or we'll get the human siren going again. Okay?"

Both children nodded earnestly and waited as he took his golf bag from his shoulder and laid it in the grass. Then he knelt down before them and began a complicated round of negotiations while I listened.

"Okay now," I heard him telling the children. "Here's your ball right here, Brady, and here's your club. Where's mine? It's right over here. Here's your ball, Sally, and here's your club. Now you have to let Daddy hit first. Why? You just do. Hold on. Let me put my ball on the tee like this. Why don't you get to use tees? Okay, that's a good question, you should get to use tees, Daddy just forgot."

He teed up the children's balls and then returned to his own. "Are we ready now?" Suddenly the baby let out a shriek. He stopped abruptly and slapped himself in the forehead with his open hand like a stand-up comedian. The children loved this; they laughed and danced around him, jumping up and down with joy. "You're okay, go back to sleep, Mr. Siren," he called to the baby. "Now you guys watch me tear the cover off this ball. Stand at attention right over here. That's good. Now watch. Keep your eyes on it, it's going all the way to China. And don't forget: this is our first time on a new golf course."

"In Massachusetts, right?" the little girl said.

"That's right, Pepsi. In the great state of Massachusetts, where we're going to live happily ever after. Now here goes."

And with that he took a swing that even Brother Martin would have envied. The sound that flew off his club when it struck the ball was solid and true; it carried its own echo and conveyed a form and dimension.

When he looked up to admire the shot, I realized it was Johnny Durocher, who had been hired to begin teaching in the fall.

"I don't see your ball, Daddy," the little girl said to him, gazing up into the sky.

"That's because it went too far!" he exclaimed happily. Then he helped the children hit their balls. This took some time, but soon they all headed down the first fairway, clubs and stroller and the baby blanket hanging from his pants pocket. A ragtag army. He was even more powerfully built and handsome than I remembered, and I imagined a beautiful wife still asleep in his bed this morning, awaiting his return.

I came out of the porch to watch them as they marched along through the low morning light. It seemed like years ago when he and I had met. During the winter, before my life fell apart. I knew the department had offered him the position, but I had been too absorbed in my own sadness for it to register in any meaningful way.

He began whistling again, and as I watched him with his children I felt the emotion that remains most enduring in an orphan. A longing for permanence.

TWO

THE PRESIDENT'S WHITE clapboard house stood on a small hill looking out over open fields, away from the university's buildings. Today its handsome gardens and verandas were lit up by the late-summer sunlight. Perennials were in bloom along the walkways. The cedar shingles on the roof blazed silver. And out in back, beyond the sliding glass doors off the living room, an enormous yellow-striped tent on poles and ropes had been erected on the lawn, trapping the rising scent of newly cut grass. At one end of the tent were two long tables covered in white linen for a bar. Nearby a quartet from the Northampton Symphony Orchestra played something by Chopin while the president and his wife and the dean of faculty and his wife mingled with the newly hired professors, just arrived on campus for their first semester, and the graybeards of the old faculty who were invited to give this event the feel of an ancient ritual.

I was supposed to be out there among them. Instead I was in a bathroom off the kitchen where the caterers were buzzing around a roast. I leaned over the marble sink, splashing cold water on my face, trying to breathe evenly and to make peace with the fact that for the past two months whenever I went anywhere in public I had to map out the route to all the bathrooms.

There was that, and my senseless counting. A number for each splash of water. One. Two. Three. Up to twelve. Then when I reached twelve, I made it twenty. Thirteen . . . fourteen. My preoccupation with numbers had grown more desperate, and I was hiding again. Like the drinker who requires less and less alcohol to become drunk, my tolerance for public appearances had declined rapidly. As a junior faculty member I was obligated to attend all official university functions, and they were always ordeals to be survived. It was as if some region of my mind had conjured the world as a giant high-school reunion where, at any moment, I might bump into somebody from the past who would see that my life, rather than expanding with time, had shrunk.

Bent over like a monkey, with water dripping from my face, I searched for a towel in the scrupulous bathroom. There were three of them folded neatly over a brass rod but they seemed too perfect to use, each bearing an identical insignia of a yacht-club pennant, or maybe it was the flag of a cruise-ship line. I knew that if I were to open one it would be like a road map that I wouldn't be able to refold properly. Half an hour earlier, walking across campus, I had composed the small talk that I would greet the president and his wife with. But now I couldn't recall any of it.

As I stood up I realized that I had somehow soaked my khaki pants across the fly. A dark gash across the dull white material. It filled me with disappointment. "Well," I said, "you're a fool, what do you expect? You shouldn't be permitted to go out in public."

AGAINST THE WALL, just beyond the tub, by a window with small square panes of old leaded glass, like the window of an English cottage, was where I stood, waiting for my pants to dry. I was watching the guests out on the back lawn beneath the yellow tent, when I was distracted by a couple just below me. Johnny Durocher and a woman I presumed was his wife were walking away from the yellow tent, holding hands. They walked slowly at first, and then after one last glance behind them at the party, sprinted across the back of the house to a high green hedge where they stopped, looked back once again, then fell laughing into each other's arms. Her tight dress rode up her thighs and I turned my head and looked away shyly. When I looked back, they were kissing passionately. His curly hair was the same shade of blond as hers. She lay in a beautiful surrender in his arms, her back arched as if she had fallen from a great height and he had caught her.

When their lips separated, he smiled at her as she took his hands in hers. Then she kissed him on the top of his head.

As I watched, it seemed to me that I had always known the world of men was divided this way, between those whom women desire and those who are invisible. For those of us who are invisible, the world of beauty is beyond reach. We stand outside, looking in. Sometimes staring the way I stared at this woman as she tipped her head back so he could kiss her throat.

IT WAS THE rain that sent them running back under the tent to join the others. A sudden shower presented me with the chance to leave the bathroom. Outside, I stood in the pouring rain until I was sufficiently soaked so that the splash on my pants no longer mattered. Everyone had lined up like spectators at a football game to watch the summer thunderstorm ricocheting off the hills north of campus. Bolts of lightning as bright as a welder's torch crisscrossed the sky. I stood beside two elderly women in housedresses who taught home economics in a department of just themselves, one of only five home economics departments left in the nation, it was said. These women fascinated me. They belonged to a lost time in America, it seemed. A time when women spent the final hours of the afternoon preparing themselves for their husbands returning home at the end of the workday. Putting on lipstick and perfume. Dusting the furniture with Pledge. I felt safe standing beside these ladies who, sagging with age, were as closed off from the world's beauty as I was. They were clearly not going to introduce themselves to me or ask me what department I taught in or where I had gone to graduate school or why I was still alone in the world, so I relaxed for a moment and watched a waiter in a red jacket glide through the crowd, wheeling a silver tray of shrimp above his shoulder. Off beyond the tent, Johnny and the woman who adored him were talking with another couple. Some of that fine morning light I had seen him standing in at the golf course seemed to surround him here, and the woman by his side, even under the gray gloom of the rainstorm.

THREE

THE FIRST DAY of classes in the fall semester always feels more to me like the beginning of a new year than New Year's Day. I am on the academic calendar, my internal systems are set by two fourteen-week semesters and by fifty-minute classes. You can set me at the podium in front of my students and tell me to speak for fifty minutes about any topic of your choice and I can do it. Start the meter running, and I will stop on time, just before my students begin to look up at the clock.

This year, my second, I was teaching all my classes in the afternoon. I had to beg for this, of course. I had presented my argument to the department chair, telling him that there were plenty of subjects students could take half asleep, but literature was not one of them. He seemed to buy this reasoning, though just after giving his approval he asked if I had ulterior motives for keeping my mornings free.

"It wouldn't be for your golf, would it, Professor Lansdale?" he asked with a sly grin.

"You've heard about my golf?"

"Always start off in the dark," he said. "Always walk the course alone."

"Well, I'm a lousy golfer," I told him. "I never know where the ball's going, so it's safer for me to be out there alone."

He just smiled knowingly at this. I hadn't convinced him of anything. But then, he hadn't guessed the other reason why I wanted to teach my classes in the afternoon. I was counting on losing myself in the literature and in my students so that both would transport me through that long, hard part of the day when I missed Julia most and felt unbearably vulnerable and lonely.

TODAY, THE FIRST day of the new semester, I looked out at my students. Their eager faces. Notebooks open. I stood before the tall floor-to-ceiling windows and let silence fill the room. I always began each literature course with a writing assignment, something that would challenge my students and bring them the beginning of an appreciation for what writers went through to put words on the page.

"How many of you," I asked today, "want to be farmers?"

Puzzled expressions. Eyes suddenly looking away from me as if I might be a madman who has wandered into their classroom.

Not one hand. "Not one farmer in the group? Who's going to feed us if we all become marketing managers and stockbrokers?" A few smiles now. "I'd like you to think about that and write a short essay, due on Thursday."

With this, they began writing down my instructions. "Three pages, please. Typed, of course. Double-spaced. Checked for spelling and grammar. Thank you. Now back to the farmers out there growing corn for the rest of us. How would you begin your piece?"

We were off and running.

"ANOTHER YEAR HAS begun," Donna said to me when I passed through the department office later that day. "Are you all right, Professor?"

"I think so, Donna. Thank you," I said. "Don't you think it would be satisfying to be a farmer?"

She smiled, then narrowed her eyes. "I don't like mud."

"Mud?"

"It seems to me you would have to spend an awful lot of time sloshing through the mud. But why do you ask? Are you thinking of a career change?"

"Do you think I should?"

"No. You stay right here where I can keep an eye on you," she said sincerely. "Our new writer in residence was asking for you this morning. Professor Durocher. He stopped in the office with his children. So adorable."

"Yes," I said.

"A little boy and girl, and a baby. His wife must have her hands full."

"Do you remember her name?"

"Linda."

"Linda," I said. I had never known a Linda before.

"He tells me his passion is golf," she said.

"Golf," I said. "Yes, I remember from his interview."

"I just thought you'd like to know," Donna said. She smiled at me again. "Maybe he'll be someone you can play with."

———

LATER THAT DAY in the campus mail, Johnny Durocher sent me a can of Guinness stout with a short note inviting me to join him and his family for dinner on Friday night.

"Can't wait to walk a few miles with you on the links," the note read. Signed, "Johnny."

F O U R

S O T H E R E I was in my bedroom in front of the only mirror I kept in my house, dressing like a teenage girl for a school dance. Trying on one sweater, taking it off, trying on another. Telling myself that I had to be careful tonight not to burden these beautiful people with my broken heart. I stepped closer to the mirror. "Can you do that, Professor Plum?" I asked myself. "Can you just be a human being tonight?"

I TRIED TO tell myself that I was just going off to class as I walked down University Drive. But the moment I stepped inside the foyer of the faculty apartments, my resolve vanished. Here was the phone booth where Julia had kissed me, and pretended to be my mother calling. Here were the stairs I'd hurried down to meet her. I hadn't been back since I'd moved into my house. And now the empty life that I had lived here before I met Julia seemed to be waiting for me, even more empty than it had been.

I ran up the stairs to the second floor to escape the loneliness. It was quiet in the carpeted corridors, easy to imagine a building full of boring professors hunched over their research. Then, the instant the

Durochers' door opened, a circus of noise hit me, like when you start your car, forgetting you've left the radio on full volume. Babies crying. Noise like you wouldn't believe. Pots and pans. Bells and whistles going off. Feet racing around the room. A parade. And there was Johnny with a wide smile, shaking my hand and telling me to come on in, come on in. He had the little girl and boy organized into a marching band with the pots and pans for drums and cymbals. "It's gets a little crazy around this time of the day," he told me, his voice rising above their noise. "They've got that last bit of energy to burn off before bed. We have to find a house before they toss us out of these faculty apartments. How are you? Glad you could come."

The new baby was sitting on his arm like a parrot, just out of the bath, a towel draped over his head. His deep blue eyes searching my face were full of wonder about me. And there were the other two, wild Indians in their footed pajamas. They were magnificent to behold.

"I have to show you something," Johnny said, handing me a bottle of beer. "Follow me."

IN A TINY bedroom, with the window shade pulled down, he said, "I'm all ready for you, Professor. Wait till you see this."

He had a slide projector set up on the bedside table. He turned it on, using the window shade as a screen.

"Take a look," he said.

I was staring at a golf green. The black-and-white-checked flagstick at the center. Behind and to the right, impressive old buildings from another century. Beyond that, I didn't have a clue.

"The eighteenth green of the Old Course at St. Andrews. Scotland," he said with a hushed, reverent voice.

"Yes," I said. "I remember you talking about St. Andrews when you came up for your interview. So you've been there?"

"Not me. These slides belonged to my father. He and I were always going to play there together, but we never got the chance. Isn't it something? Those hotels and shops, just a few feet from the edge of the green."

I looked at him, at the delight on his face, just as someone tugged on my pants. "That's Sally," Johnny said. "She loves to be held."

I didn't dare. Instead I patted her head. Her hair was still wet from her bedtime bath. She pressed her face against my knee as if she'd known me all her life.

Another image flew up onto the window shade. A stone bridge over a narrow river. "Swilken Bridge," I heard Johnny say. "Comes into play on the first and the eighteenth tees. You've got to know where it is on both fairways, exactly where it is, when the fog rolls in off the North Sea."

"You know this course," I said.

"Like my rosary. Take a look here."

It was an enormous hole in the earth with steep embankments leading up its sides.

"That's the Strath bunker on the par-three eleventh. The most celebrated par three in the world. With the winds over there, there's absolutely no safe way to play it. The green falls off so sharply, you can't get the ball to stop. And even if you do, the wind can sweep it off the green before you get there. Strath bunker is on the right, Hill bunker is on the left. They're so deep you can't see the flag when you're down in them. There are one hundred and twelve of those suckers on the course."

He stopped, knelt down in front of the little boy, and wiped his nose. Then he turned and looked at me as if he had just discovered I was in the room. "You probably already know all the stories about Bobby Jones."

"Actually I heard a few when I was a boy."

This pleased him. "Excellent," he said. "Do you know about his first British Open?"

When I told him that I did not, I saw the eagerness in his eyes. "Okay, it's 1921. Bobby is the most famous golfer in the world. He's like a rock star; wherever he goes people line up just to touch him. So he's playing in the British Open in 1921. He lands in the Hill bunker off the eleventh. He tries four times to get his ball out. Then he tears up his scorecard and quits. He had a fierce temper, and it got the best of him until he learned to control it. Six years later he returns to St. Andrews and wins the Open. The wind was blowing so hard for the last two days of the tournament that people in the gallery had to hold on to one another to keep from being knocked down. They carried him off the eighteenth on their shoulders. They loved him because of his flaws, you see? And he was so amazed by their affection for him that he told them the trophy would stay in St. Andrews. He wasn't bringing it home."

A new slide came up. "Come sit down over here," he said, motioning to the bed. It was a photograph of a young man with the face of a movie star. "That's Jones," he said, as if he were showing me a picture of his brother. "Two ticker-tape parades down Fifth Avenue. Here's another shot of him. Poor bastard was cut down in his forties. Some awful disease. He won the British Amateur at St. Andrews in 1930 on his way to taking the Open and Amateur titles of Britain and the United States."

"The Grand Slam of golf," I chimed in.

"That's right," he said eagerly. "People say it will never be done again. That it's the one record in the world of sports, all sports, that will never be equaled. When he learns that he's dying he returns to St. Andrews to play one last round on the Old Course. Somehow the local people found out, and when he stepped on the first tee the next morning there were five thousand townspeople there. Standing in the pouring rain. They followed him for all eighteen holes, then shook his hand when he finished his round. It must have been amazing."

I heard his voice fall off, but I'd lowered my eyes to look at Sally, who had laid her head in my lap and was fast asleep with her thumb in her mouth.

"She trusts you," Johnny said.

When I looked up at him, I saw that there were tears in his eyes.

He didn't try to hide this. "Hey," he said, "it won't be dark for another hour, should we go hit a few?"

Oh God, I thought, *from the sublime to the ridiculous.* I don't know how I would have gotten out of this if his wife hadn't rescued me.

"Not on your life," I heard her exclaim. I turned and there she was. Blue jeans and blond hair and a lit-up smile. As young as my students, I thought. "Johnny," she said with a soft but scolding tone of voice, "what are you doing? You're in here like the madman of golf. You haven't even introduced me to Professor Lansdale."

"Ross," I said, as I looked into her eyes. A pale, luminous shade of green. The little boy was suddenly all over her, in her arms, pulling at her hair, reaching inside her blouse, but she didn't seem to notice.

"Sometimes he tells me these golf stories while I'm trying to vacuum. I can't hear a word he's saying, but when I turn the vacuum off, he's still talking."

"The kids love my golf stories, Linda," he said with his big, open smile.

She looked down at Sally. "That's the one thing his golf stories are good for. What's the word there? There's a word for that," she said.

"I don't know," Johnny said.

"You should, you're the writer."

"Soporific," I said.

"That's it," Linda said. "Are you all right?" she asked me.

"Me? I'm fine."

"You don't feel like you've been standing in front of a machine gun?"

"No, really, this is great," I insisted.

"You know what it is, Ross?" I heard Johnny say. "American television is killing golf."

"Oh, Johnny," Linda said.

"It's true. Now golfers are just entertainers."

Linda placed her hand on the top of his head. She was smiling when she closed her eyes, looked up to the heavens, and said, "Dear God, you promised me that you'd slow him down a little. I'm still waiting."

"Ross and I hit golf balls in his barn when I was here for my interview last winter. You remember me telling you, honey."

"I do," she said, smiling at me.

"Did you spend a lot of time there over the winter?" Johnny asked.

"No," I said. "I sort of took some time off from golf last winter."

FIVE

I KEPT TO myself for the next few days, teaching my classes, walking back and forth to campus with my teacher's satchel. Though the weather was perfect I stayed away from the golf course, more for Johnny Durocher's sake than my own. I was afraid that he might show up while I was there and then have to lie his way out of joining me after seeing how terrible I was. Nothing could ruin a man's round of golf faster than a partner who couldn't keep his ball in the fairways. I still awoke with the birds and on one of those clement autumn mornings I discovered that from my bathroom window I could watch Johnny and his army make their way across the lower end of University Drive toward the course. He played every day, walking to the course with the baby in one arm and his golf clubs across his back in a dark blue Titlest bag. He was pushing a different baby carriage from the one I'd first seen him with. It looked like an antique. A big, boxy affair upholstered in blue-and-green plaid, which rode along like a small float in a parade on four oversized white-rimmed wheels. I could see the two little ones riding inside, and there looked to be plenty of room for the baby as well.

I let them have the course to themselves because I knew that I was no match for Johnny Durocher. I don't mean just the golf, though he certainly would have been astonished at my graceless game; men like him are far above me. Those men who need only six minutes to shower and dress for the day, and still look like a million bucks. Men with big, expansive lives, and beautiful people who relied upon them. Men in the supermarket who glance at me fitting my week's supply of groceries in just one bag. They watch a man like me shopping for food and they imagine I live with a cat, both of us eating out of the same tin of tuna. It's not a pretty picture. The beauty of the world is meant for lovers, as it should be. When Shakespeare wrote his sonnets he certainly never had me in mind. Me in my egg-stained bathrobe, staring into my empty refrigerator.

MY EVENING WITH Johnny and Linda lingered in my mind for days. And looking back now, I can see that as I walked home from their apartment, I was already giving myself away to the idea that they might adopt me into their beautiful family. After those few hours together, how could I help but be hopelessly and inevitably in love with them, though I knew that I had nothing to give them in return for the sweetness of their company.

I WAS DUSTING my living room one afternoon when Linda stopped by to say hello. She was holding the baby. "Just out for a walk," she said. She nodded to my dust cloth. "I admire a man who dusts. From my experience, you can get plenty of men to vacuum, but very few to dust."

I tried to improvise a response that would rescue me from the impression she might be forming. "Once a year," I said, and she might have fallen for this lie if I hadn't made the mistake of taking it one step further. "I wait until I can write my name on every flat surface, and then I get to work with a vengeance." I know she didn't believe this lie.

"It's the photographs that collect so much dust," she said.

First the dusting, and now the discovery that I didn't have a single photograph in my living room; somehow she had innocently found her way to the central empty corridor of my existence.

I tried too hard to recover and fell upon the most absurd defense. "Yes, the dusty pictures. I keep all of mine in albums now."

I was waiting for her to respond to this, unaware that I was staring at her baby and that she was waiting for me to look up at her. I almost apologized.

"Would you like to hold him for me?" she asked. "He's getting so big so quickly. Much too quickly. With each baby, time has accelerated."

She passed her son to me as if it was the most natural thing in the world to place him in the arms of a man who had never held a child. He was fast asleep but as she lifted him into the space between us his arms flew out to the sides like he was flying.

"Look," I exclaimed.

"All my babies did that," she said. "It makes me wonder if they flew here from their last world."

The baby settled his body against mine, a knee pushing on my ribs, a tiny fist opening and closing above my collarbone. His head came to rest beneath my chin and I took a deep breath of his fragrance. The scent of cotton sheets hung out to dry in a sunny breeze. Suddenly there was something like a far-off ringing of bells inside my head. I felt heat rush into my lungs. Outside the window just beyond the child's mother, I caught a glimpse of the sky plunging toward the ground as I was swept up in a violent storm of dizziness. I called her name. "Linda."

She took the child from my hands just in time, then steered me to my couch.

I apologized ten times to her. "Let me take your pulse," she said.

"I don't know what happened to me," I said, while she counted my heartbeats with her thumb and forefinger pressed against my wrist.

"You have an athlete's pulse," she said. "Slow and strong. When did you last see a doctor?"

"I can't remember."

"That's not good," she said, smiling with dismay. "If you have juice in the kitchen I'll get you some. I'll lay him down here." She put the baby on the couch beside me and drew his blue blanket around his narrow shoulders. I stared at him while she was gone. I wanted to touch him, but didn't dare.

When she returned I apologized again as I gazed at the baby. "I've never held a baby before," I said. "I thought that I'd do something wrong."

"You did fine," she said. "You grow into the job quickly."

"Are they very different—boys and girls?" I asked her.

"Different as night and day. Well, Johnny doesn't feel this way. He just wants all of them to be able to hit out of sand traps. But for me, from the moment I first saw this one, I felt the same responsibility I feel with his brother, to raise him to be the kind of man I would want to spend my life with. Sending men out into the world, you have to be careful."

She looked down at the baby. "I want them to be gentle most of all. The kind of men who couldn't hurt anyone."

Exactly, I thought. I watched her take her son's foot in her hand. Touching him brought her such pleasure.

"He's going to light up somebody's world someday, that's for sure," I told her. "Well, I guess he already has."

"That's sweet," she said. "And you, Ross, you said you'd never spent time around children?"

She was still staring down at her baby when she asked this.

"No," I said.

"You will someday," she said. "And you'll be a good father, I can tell."

I looked into her eyes after she said this. It took all my determination to change the subject. "I was wondering about something, Linda," I said. "I need to practice driving, so I can take my test. I've got my learner's permit. Could you teach me?"

"You're on," she said with a smile.

SIX

THE FIRST ENGLISH department meeting of the semester. The chair, Paul Speiss, holds his place at the head of the long oak table. Twelve of us sit facing him. Christ and the twelve apostles. Johnny is sitting next to me, on my right. "You've been missing some great mornings of golf, old sport," he whispers to me before we start.

Any lie will do here. "My back," I say. "I've got a bad back."

His eyes widen with skepticism. "I've got some scotch that will cure that," he tells me.

The Doan sisters, Margaret and Phyllis, jump in before the chair can declare the meeting open. They are in their late sixties, long-ago graduates of the classics department at Northwestern. Never married, they were hired together twenty-eight years ago by a department whose members at that time are now all buried.

Phyllis is upset with the dean's new request. "Here we are, a new year barely begun, and already the dean is placing more demands upon us. Someone in his office has had the bright idea that we should begin correspondence with the parents of our advisees." She groans, and her sister groans with her. "I personally want nothing to do with the parents of these underloved, overfed, spoiled . . ."

Paul cuts her off there. She is one to string together many adjectives. "Let's try to keep in mind that these students pay our salaries."

It's just another meeting. But whenever I look around the table, I see that all five women in the department are stealing glances at Johnny. Carol Fullerton appears to be undressing him with her eyes.

WHEN JOHNNY IS introduced, there is a pause. I turn to him and he is sleeping.

Paul speaks next. "Ross, why don't you give him a friendly little nudge."

He opens his eyes and sits up straight to a soft round of laughter. Martha Beckman goes on to ask him a question. She is blushing like a teenager. "I was wondering if the American Dream will figure into your writing assignments," she says.

Johnny smiles generously at her. She bows her head demurely.

"What *is* the American Dream?" Dan Crissfield says with exasperation. "I keep hearing references to it."

"Well," Johnny replies, and there is a hush of anticipation, "for me, with three little ones under the age of four, the American Dream is just a good night's sleep." He follows this with a Robert Redford smile. The audience collapses.

"YOU BOWLED THEM over," I told him later when he caught up with me as I walked home.

"Falling asleep? I'd say an inauspicious way to begin, wouldn't you?"

"An honest way to begin," I said.

We were walking beneath the great willow trees. Forty-six of them following the walkway across the front of the campus. Johnny remarked about them, how beautiful they were tossing in the wind above our heads. When he stopped to gaze up at them, I stopped too.

"I need this job," he said, his face still turned to the sky.

I caught some desperation in his voice and it made me feel uncomfortable, so I deflected it with my sorry attempt at humor. "It'll be a great opportunity for you to catch up on your sleep."

He didn't respond to this immediately. Then he said, "I imagine it must be tough meeting women up here."

"Oh, they're out there. But I've got high standards, you know?" He didn't seem to catch my sarcasm.

"That's good. Don't lower them."

"And what about you, why do you need this job?"

"Because Linda thinks this is the right place to raise the children. She's decided. And I don't want to disappoint her. I've done enough of that already. Other places where things didn't go so well for me."

"I'd say the only thing you have to keep in mind here is that everyone in the department is naturally jealous of any writer. You already know that, I'm sure."

"I'm not a real writer, Ross."

"I read your dossier. Remember?"

"Oh, that thing," he said disparagingly. "I paid somebody in grad school to put that together for me. No, I wrote one novel as a strategy. You see, I never would have been able to compete in the job market with the real academics. I hate research of any kind. It gives me cramps. So the only other route to becoming a professor was to present myself as a writer. One novel, my ticket is punched."

"It worked."

"So far." He said the real writers in the world were out there somewhere, writing, not holding down comfortable jobs. "It was too hard for me, writing," he went on. "Just one book, but it was like digging ditches, sitting there hunched over my typewriter. And that one book cost me time with Linda that I'll never get back. I had to dig the hole and then climb down into it until the book was finished. That wasn't for me. I like it out here too much."

"Still," I told him, "I'm looking forward to reading your novel."

"Now *that* is a good way to catch up on your sleep," he said. "I thought you read it before I was hired." He seemed a little troubled.

"Normally I would have," I said. "But last winter . . ." My voice trailed off, and then I stopped myself from dropping all the way to the basement. "I didn't have much stature on the hiring committee so they never passed your novel along to me. But the committee must have read your book and been sufficiently impressed."

"Do you think they actually read it?" he asked with some concern. "Because I've been told that at most colleges they only care that you have a book *published*. You know, they look at the jacket cover, make sure it's your name, and then pass on it."

I was ashamed to tell him that he was right. As a matter of fact when the department made its final decision on hires, we simply photocopied the covers of the candidate's published work and sent those copies to the dean of faculty for final approval. The assumption was that the dean couldn't tell the difference between good and bad writing anyway.

"Well, I for one will read your novel," I finished. "I'll find it in the office files and I'll read it. And by the way, I hope you don't mind, I've asked Linda if she can give me some driving lessons."

"Yeah, she mentioned that. That's great. You really don't have a license?"

"Not yet."

"Man, it must be rough getting women without any wheels," he said.

WE STOPPED AT my front door. "So, what do you say? Tomorrow morning?"

"Golf?"

He nodded.

"Have I told you that I'm terrible at golf?"

"I've seen your swing," he said, smiling.

"I'll tell you what. Because of my bad back, I'll push the kids around in the buggy and you play."

"Deal," he said.

I had already turned toward my door when he called my name. "Ross?"

"Yes."

"I was talking about something in class this morning. Do you ever think what it might be like to be a completely different person from the person you are?"

The question took me by surprise. I lied. "No, not really. Maybe I once did."

He nodded thoughtfully then said he thought about it all the time. "I'd like to be a quieter person," he said. "More thoughtful. And not afraid to be alone. A watcher of life. I've grown tired of the person I am."

As quickly as he had drifted off into this private thought, he returned and said with alacrity, "I'll swing by for you in the morning."

I WATCHED HIM walk away. I thought of Linda pressing against him, and of their children shouting with joy, running into his arms each time he returned home and stepped inside the door.

SEVEN

SO I PUSHED baby William in the plaid buggy that rode like a Cadillac while Sally and Brady played alongside their father with their sawed-off clubs. "Don't worry about where your ball goes, just have fun. Left arm straight," Johnny told them.

Left arm straight, I thought. Brother Martin's enduring instruction to me.

"You look good pushing a baby carriage," Johnny called to me. "Ever think of settling down?"

"If I settle down any more than I already am, I'll be underground," I said.

He hit a massive drive toward the sunrise beyond the first green.

"Amazing," I said. "If I could ever hit a ball that straight, I might take up this game."

"I can teach you to hit it straight," he said confidently. "Say, what was the gal's name who asked me about the American Dream at the meeting?"

"Martha Beckman."

"Should I be afraid of her?"

"Only if the idea of being tarred and feathered doesn't appeal to you."

He turned to watch Sally take a swing. "You're getting very close, sweetheart," he called to her. "Keep your eye on the ball. That bad, huh, this Miss Beckman?"

"Formidable," I said. "But I think you already have her eating out of your hand."

He walked over to Brady, teed up a ball for him, then put him between his legs and gave him a try with his driver. Their four hands on the club, swinging together. The ball took off like a rocket and Brady screeched with joy. "There!" Johnny exclaimed. "Go chase that one, tiger."

"See how long it takes me, Daddy!" the boy shouted.

"Okay. I'm counting. One. Two. Three. Four . . ."

When Johnny came back to my side of the fairway he said, "Have you tried banks?"

"Banks?"

"Single women stuck in those boring bank jobs?"

"You're serious," I said with a laugh.

"Not really. Come on."

———

WE WALKED FOUR or five holes and then stopped at a sand trap on number six. He took two plastic shovels from the carriage. "In my family these are known as sandboxes, not sand traps." We sat in the early sunlight, watching Sally and Brady play. "You might see this on the Old Course in St. Andrews," Johnny said. "Kids playing. People flying kites and walking their dogs. The Old Course belongs to the people of St. Andrews. It's still closed to golfers every Sunday by some ancient decree. A hundred years ago local women were allowed to dry their laundry across the first fairway. Imagine trying something like that at Pebble Beach."

"So," I said, "you and your father played a lot of golf together?"

"Early mornings he took me to the course just like this," Johnny said, nodding toward Sally and Brady. "He kept track of the yards that we walked together. I was in college, away from home for the first time, when he sent me a letter. It was the first letter he ever wrote to me. He told me that he'd added up all the miles and that by his count the two of us had walked from Connecticut to California and back."

"That's nice."

"I miss him every day. I want my kids to miss me when I'm gone. I don't think I want anything else as much as that. To be remembered, you know. Those two over there."

"They're beautiful children."

"I'm so lucky," he said. And then in the next moment he looked sad. "I want to do well for them, Ross. I want to provide for them."

"You will. You are."

"Yeah, but things didn't work out for me at the last two schools. I've got to learn to keep my mouth shut. Say, how about this: you sit beside me at every department meeting and step on my foot under the table if you think that I should shut up. My old man was always out of work. He was a boat rocker. Always taking on the establishment. Banging heads with the union bosses. He was a plumber. All he had to do was march, you know. Just march when they told him to march, and he would have had a very comfortable old age. My mom used to complain that he never stayed in one job long enough to be given a Thanksgiving turkey the way most fathers did."

"So he was a plumber?"

"A damned good one. But listen to me talking about myself. What about you?"

"Me? There's not much to talk about. This is the first real job I've ever had."

"How old are you?"

"Twenty-nine."

"Thirty-seven for me. Getting up there. Linda's ten years younger." He was silent for a moment as he watched his children pouring sand from their buckets. "I've got a lot of people depending on me doing well here," he said again. Then he called to the children. "Five more minutes, crew, and we're going home to wake up Sleeping Beauty."

EIGHT

HERE IS MY confession: sometimes I looked at Linda with her beautiful baby and I fantasized about the two of them belonging to me. When the baby cries in the night I awake and carry him into our bed and watch Linda place her breast to the little boy's lips. He looks up at me. My face, the last thing he sees before his eyes close. For the rest of my life, Linda will hold me in her arms. I will make love to her forever. Her body will rise above me and she will close her eyes and softly call my name, and tell me that she loves me. I will never be alone again.

———

"TONIGHT, YOU'RE READY to graduate from the parking lot," Linda said when she picked me up for my next driving lesson. We had been practicing in the parking lot behind the football stadium for several weeks, always at night after the children were in bed.

I told her that I wasn't sure.

"Trust me, Ross," she said. "My uncle Bud taught me how to drive. He'd always bring along a six-pack to fortify himself, and he'd send me right out on the highway." She was kneeling on the front seat, her legs tucked under her, her blond curls brushing her cheeks.

"I don't think your uncle Bud would have that kind of confidence in me," I said.

"Stop the car," she said sharply.

I THOUGHT A cat or dog had run in front of us and I hit the brake so hard that Linda flew off the seat, onto the floor.

"You stopped," she said as I helped her up.

"God, I'm sorry, Linda," I said.

She raised one finger in the air and shook it at me. "Stop saying you're sorry," she said. "That's why I told you to stop the car back there. So I could give you a lecture."

"I'm sorry."

"You did it again, Ross. Now stop! You don't have to be sorry all the time."

"All right."

"All right," she said softly, reaching into the glove compartment for her lipstick. "Now for my lecture. We've been driving in circles long enough, Ross. It's time to plot a course."

"A metaphor for my life," I said disconsolately.

She leaned back against her door, crossed her arms, and studied my face. "It doesn't have to be," she said. "You have just as much right to drive down Main Street as the next guy."

"I know."

"Only you don't believe that, do you?"

"No, I don't."

"Why not?"

"I don't know."

She put her hand on the dashboard and drummed her fingers for a moment. "Okay, none of my business," she said.

"No. I'm—" I caught myself before I apologized again.

She smiled at me and shook her head slowly.

"I appreciate it, Linda," I said.

"I care about you. Johnny and I both care about you. And Sally, you're her favorite person on earth right now. That's quite a compliment, you know. Children are an excellent judge of a person's heart."

I thanked her for that.

"So. How was your heart broken?" she asked.

When I looked at her, she shrugged her shoulders, as if to say, *Whenever you're ready, it's easy, just tell me.*

"Do you think I can make it from here to Smith College without a major accident?" I said. Then I sat up straight and put one hand on the gearshift.

"That's the spirit," Linda said.

"Here we go then," I said.

"Pull up the anchor!" she exclaimed.

"Blast off!" I said.

EXCEPT FOR THE baby and the abortion, I told Linda everything while we were parked in front of Julia's dorm beside a kind of shrine that some of the girls had made with photographs and candles for Jimi Hendrix and Janis Joplin, who had died a few weeks before.

"Have you thought of going to California to try and find her?" Linda asked me.

"Not really," I said.

"Why not?"

"I'm still letting go," I said.

"I see." She took my hand after she said this.

For a while we said nothing. Someone's stereo was playing "Bridge Over Troubled Water."

"Oh, I love this song," Linda said, rolling down her window. She listened for a while then asked me what I would say to Julia if I saw her again.

"I don't know," I said. "I've thought about it, but I don't really know. I don't think she loved me. How do you know? How do you know that Johnny loves you?"

I expected her to answer this question right away, but she thought for a long time. "His love for me has changed over time. All love does, I think. But he's always reached for me. In his sleep, or sitting across the table. Walking the kids. He reaches for me." She paused, then said, "Julia never said goodbye to you?"

"No. When I got back from St. Luke's, she was gone."

"Well, you'll have to find her then," she said. "Saying goodbye is very important. If I didn't have three kids, I'd drive out to California with you."

"That would be a trip."

"I've always wanted to see the Rocky Mountains," she told me.

Without realizing it, I had bowed my head and closed my eyes. "One night I jumped on a couch in the lobby and recited a poem for Julia," I said. "The dorm mother was not amused."

"Too bad for her."

"Julia used to sneak me into the coatroom. But, Linda?"

"Yes."

"I haven't told you everything." I looked up at her after I said this.

"You don't have to tell me everything," she said. "Or you can wait until our next driving lesson if you want to."

"No," I said. "I think I need to tell you now."

WE WERE WALKING to the front doors of the hotel when I stopped. "Maybe this is close enough," I said.

Linda took my hand again. "I think we should get in out of the cold, Ross," she said gently. "Don't you?"

I was looking up to the lighted rooms above us when she stepped closer to me, put her arm in mine, and said, "Let's go inside."

I WALKED BESIDE her across the carpeted lobby. If she hadn't been holding my arm, I would have turned and walked out or maybe fallen to the floor. "What was your room number?" she asked.

"It was 306."

She led the way to the desk and told the young woman on duty that we wanted to see a room.

"For tonight?" the woman asked.

"We'd like to *see* the room now, yes. But we won't be using it until Thanksgiving. We have company coming to visit over Thanksgiving."

The young woman turned to the key rack behind her. "Actually, we'd like to see room 306 if it's empty," Linda said.

WE RODE THE wooden elevator without saying a word. Down the narrow corridor with the brass wall lamps. It felt to me like years had passed since I was last here and I recalled the line from *Romeo and Juliet*. *In an hour there are many days.*

"It already feels like the past," I said to Linda when we reached the door.

She placed the key in my hand.

"Returning to the scene of the crime," I said.

"Is that what it was, a crime? A crime to love someone so much?"

I told her that I couldn't go inside.

"There are no rules in love, Ross," she said to me. "And if there are, they're made to be broken."

I thanked her for bringing me here. "But I can't go in," I said.

"Okay," she said. "Some other time then."

"Yes," I said. "Some other time."

NINE

I PLAYED SUCH lousy golf that fall that there were times when I could barely look Johnny in the eye. And to make matters worse, he was so terribly patient with me. Walking in the woods down the right side of every fairway, searching for my ball. "Forget it, Johnny," I would say. "I can buy more balls."

But he insisted on finding mine. "It's a two-stroke penalty if you lose your ball."

It was a rainy, cold autumn, too cold to bring the children along on most mornings. Wet, dead leaves blew down the fairways like litter in an alley. "Scotland weather," Johnny called it. "Perfect." Our faces and hands were always purple. Still he wouldn't hear of quitting. I would hit another terrible shot and he would pick up his bag, hoist it onto his shoulders, and say, "Carry on." And while we walked he would go through the litany again for me. "Keep the center of your body positioned over the ball. Left arm straight on the take back. Let the shoulders turn. At the top of the backswing, cock your wrists. Then snap the wrists through the ball and release the hands with the hips and shoulders uncoiling." As he grew colder, he would just nod and point, or step up next to me and move my club into position. I heard his instructions in my sleep where I sometimes held Linda in my dreams, desperate for the feel of her skin against my own.

"IT'S GOING TO snow tomorrow," Johnny said to me one morning as we were leaving the course. He had stopped and turned back to look down the first fairway. Something dark swept over his face. "I won't let my boys fight any wars for this government," he said. "I'll take them to Canada myself."

By now the war in Vietnam had spread to Cambodia, where American soldiers had been dying for almost a year and there didn't seem to be an end in sight. "I've just started thinking about that," Johnny said. "I've been thinking that I might write my next novel about that. A father who has a nice life going for him. A businessman with a big house. He's respected in the community, a deacon at his church. And he puts it all on the line in order to save his son. He takes him to Canada, someplace up in northern Ontario where no one will ever find them. He starts a new life there. A simple life compared to the one he's had."

A simple life, I thought. And I asked him the question Julia had asked me the day we met. "Do you think there's any such thing as a simple life, Johnny?"

"Maybe not," he conceded. "But some people seem to keep things in the right perspective. It's not easy in this country, where the whole system collapses if we're satisfied with what we have. '*I don't want a new car, thank you, I'm satisfied with the one I've got.*' Bingo, the end of America.

"No, I guess there's no simple life, but I hope that I can teach my kids the difference between pleasure and happiness. You can buy pleasure, but not happiness. And that doesn't mean happiness is free either."

I told him again that I wanted to read his novel, and I asked him what it was about.

"Not much," he said. "I started out thinking I was going to write the great American novel and all that, but in the end I was just trying to finish the damned thing. I can't remember what it's about. I know that sounds unlikely, but it's the truth."

EACH MORNING WHEN he left me at my door after golf, he promised he would remember to bring a copy of his book to my office before the day was through. I kept hounding him for it, but he never did and after a while I gave up.

Until Donna told me one day that she had been cleaning out some files and noticed that Professor Durocher's book was missing from his portfolio.

I was going to inquire around the department myself to see who had actually read Johnny's novel when his candidacy was under consideration and who was reading the book now, but something kept me from doing this. I guess it was that my colleagues were always so critical of everything. By now I considered Johnny a friend and I didn't want to give anyone in the department the satisfaction of putting down his book to my face.

TEN

PUT BABYSITTING ON the long list of things I might never have experienced if I hadn't met Johnny and Linda. Tonight I was on the living room floor in front of the couch, playing Chutes and Ladders. Candy Land. Apple juice in baby bottles. I thought about Julia. How I wished that she could have seen me here because I was doing well. Very well. I felt like I was something of a natural at this. I seemed to understand children. They loved surprises. They hadn't lived long enough to embrace adults' illusions, the things that we do and that we tell ourselves in order to live with the sadness of life. They cried when you left the room because they knew in some part of their minds that sometimes people leave and don't come back. Their demands were simple. *Stay with me. Hold my hand. Listen.*

Prince William fell asleep in his crib without shedding a tear. I made up a story about a basset hound who becomes a college professor while I lay between Sally and Brady on her bed. Their eyes grew heavy. Sally was brushing her cheek with the silk hem of her pale green blanket. The same part of her cheek, over and over. Comforting herself in her parents' absence, as she faced the long night alone in her dark room. I looked down at my right hand, at my fingers that hadn't twitched again since Brother Martin said his blessing for me.

Brady was asleep before I could wash his face and hands, which were so dirty you'd think he had spent the day digging ditches.

ALL WAS QUIET on the western front and I couldn't resist snooping around the apartment. The tiny rooms where Johnny and Linda seemed to linger. Their life defined by small things. A red button left on a windowsill. Dishes in the sink. A rust-colored seashell between the cushions on the couch. A grocery list on the counter by the telephone. All of these things were a fascination to me, coming from my world where nothing was ever out of place.

I had no idea that women kept so many pairs of shoes in their closet. Before I could stop myself I was lining them up in neat rows, the toes all pointing in the same direction. Oh, how wonderful it would be to clean this apartment, I thought. Top to bottom. Fill a whole day with cleaning. And start right here in this closet. On the shelf above my head were Johnny's neckties, a pile of them, their ends hanging down like party streamers. One with a golf green stenciled on it and the name of a country club. When I pulled it gently to get a better look at the name, I started an avalanche. Ties. Socks. A jock strap. Sweaters. And a motor-oil box which crashed to the floor spilling its contents onto the carpet, plastic containers of pills rolling across the bedroom. The noise woke the baby whose crib was on the other side of the wall. He began to cry as I was gathering up the pills, counting them despite myself. Sixteen. Seventeen. Reading Johnny's name on the labels. So many pills. "I'm coming, William. Don't cry. Please don't wake you brother and sister." Checking beneath the bed. Under the bureau. Eighteen. What if they came home now, walked in on me? I threw the pills into the box. "I'm coming, William." And there, at the bottom of the box, was Johnny's book. There was just enough light in the bedroom to read his name on the cover.

I CARRIED WILLIAM out of the faculty apartment building so that his shrieks wouldn't wake Sally and Brady. It was a warm night, more like spring than fall, and the moment William saw the moon, he stopped crying. "Good boy. Such a good little boy." In the moonlight I showed him his father's novel. "*Letters Home.* A novel by John Durocher. Here it is, William. Someday you'll read it. And take a look up there. See? That's where you live. That's your room right there. And over here, up the hill, that's the college where your father and I teach. See? All those buildings. I'm sorry I woke you. I shouldn't have been looking through your parents' closet. Making all that noise. I couldn't help it; I never got to do that as a kid. No closet. No parents. You're not going to fall back to sleep, are you? I can tell, you're wide awake now. So how am I going to explain this to your mother? Your beautiful mother. She loves you. And your daddy loves you. And Sally. And Brady. You have a lot of people who will always care about you. They'll never leave you. You're lucky. We're both lucky. And now I know why people love talking to babies; I can tell you anything and you won't repeat it. You're the perfect companion. It's wonderful, but we have to go inside now. Back inside to check on your sister and brother. Okay? Good. You don't have to cry any more. Everything's all right now."

Inside, I put Johnny's novel back in the box in the closet, then rocked William until he fell asleep.

"WE DECIDED TO let you sleep," Linda whispered to me in the morning when she brought me a cup of coffee. I had spent the night on Sally's bed. She and Brady were both still sleeping.

"I fell asleep on the job, Linda," I whispered.

"Good for you, and don't say you're sorry," she said. "I think you all needed a good night's sleep. I made pancakes."

"I don't think I've had pancakes since I was a kid," I said. I told her how much I had enjoyed last night. "I think they're getting to know me."

"You'll be friends for life," Linda said. Then she paused and smiled at me. "I was in here earlier, spying on the three of you. I was wondering if we live a good life, helping others, maybe we get to sleep beside our children again in heaven."

———————

WE SAT IN the kitchen and talked for a while. She rocked William to sleep in her arms.

"Johnny's out walking," she told me. "He's the early-morning maniac. I'm the sleeper. And he's been raising our children to be crack-of-dawn people. You know, 'It's five A.M., where are my Cheerios?' So I told him long ago that if he wanted bright-and-early, report-for-duty kids, then he was going to be in charge of them in the morning. Not me. I need my beauty sleep. In the morning all four of them buzz around my ears like mosquitoes."

She looked down at William who had awakened and was cooing at her. I watched her eyes catch the sunlight as she undid the top three buttons of her blouse and placed Will's lips at her breast. She did this as casually as if she were brushing her hair, while I quickly looked away. Wanting to look back. Wanting to stare at her.

"Could I talk with you about something?" she asked rather solemnly.

"Of course. Anything."

"It's about Johnny."

I thought about the pills rolling on the bedroom floor and I expected that she was going to tell me he was ill.

"He's awfully happy here," she said. "Do you think he's doing okay? I mean in class, and with the other professors in the department?"

"I'm sure he's doing fine," I said, though of course I didn't know.

She smiled. A nervous smile, I thought, meant to put me at ease. "Johnny used to tell me that being a college professor was the only job in the world you could hold down if you were a drunk and a slob. No clock to punch. No sales quotas to fill. He's always said he wouldn't last two weeks in a real job." She looked up at me and raised her hand to her mouth in embarrassment. "Oh, Ross, I didn't mean to imply—"

"Stop," I said. "Johnny's right."

Our eyes met briefly, then she seemed to be gathering her strength to go on. "He hasn't always been happy. When we met, I had just taken my first job out of college as a social worker. He was in the hospital, recuperating from an automobile accident and having a very difficult time. His sister was in the car with him. She was badly hurt and he wouldn't stop blaming himself. I spent hours talking with him, and I guess I believed that I could save him. My father says he always knew I would marry someone I thought I could save. I was the kid who kept bringing home sick animals. Sometimes they were already dead, but I brought them home anyway. And now I know that Johnny won't ever forgive himself for the accident. I shouldn't say this, but his sister hasn't helped. She's never gotten a job or tried to help herself. Johnny buys medication for her and every month it's the same thing; he drives to Connecticut and begs her to take it.

"It was an accident, an icy road. It could have happened to anyone. I think it's the accidents in life that determine the kind of people we become. Those things that happen that are not fair. Do you think?"

"Maybe you're right," I told her.

"No, I'm probably wrong, but would you keep an eye on Johnny for me, if you can? He lost his last two teaching jobs because he just couldn't function. He has days when he can't face anyone."

"I never would have guessed," I told her. "He has such energy. He's bigger than life, really."

"I imagine that's how he was all the time before the accident. People who knew him then tell me that he has never been the same. And I'm not asking for him to be the same. I love him the way he is. Broken. Do you know what I mean? If he weren't broken, he might not be such a caring father. I think about that a lot."

She looked down at her baby, then gently moved him to her other breast. She told me that Johnny didn't always tell her the truth about his work. "I mean, he doesn't want me to worry, I know that. But still. I just was hoping maybe you could let me know from time to time if people, other professors in the department, seem to be getting tired of my husband."

Now she looked up at me. She was blushing, which only made her more beautiful.

"Of course I can do that," I said. "And I will. Professors are terrific gossips, you know. Academic departments are snake pits. People looking to advance their own cause. I've only been teaching for a year, but I saw plenty of it in graduate school. I think the basic problem is that professors aren't kept busy enough, they have too much time off."

She laughed at this.

"It's true," I said. "Too much free time to cook up schemes. Don't worry about Johnny. He's doing fine. He's so charming, he has them all eating out of his hand."

Linda's expression didn't change when I told her this. I thought maybe she had heard it before from other people who later turned against Johnny.

"Well, thank you, Ross. If you look out for him, I'm sure everything will be fine here."

"I wonder," I said, "would you be able to give me a copy of Johnny's book?"

"He hasn't done that?"

"I've only asked a few dozen times."

"That's terrible," she said. "I'll get it for you."

IT WAS DEDICATED to Sara, and Linda explained that this was Johnny's sister. His kid sister, as Johnny referred to her. As I walked home that morning I stopped at the corner of University Drive and Maple Street, waiting for a truck to pass that was repainting the line down the center of the road. I opened Johnny's book to somewhere in the middle and turned so that sunlight fell on the pages. What I read, I knew at once I had read before. Beautiful, descriptive passages that Johnny had stolen from one of the writers on Brother Martin's list.

ELEVEN

NTIL THEN I had never been a big coffee drinker. One cup in the morning had always been enough for me. And I'd never had any trouble sleeping. But in what quickly became my obsession with finding the source of Johnny's plagiarism, I began pulling all-nighters, going through pots of coffee as I pillaged the college library and my own shelves, racking my memory to find the prose that Johnny had stolen. I knew that he was guilty. Somewhere in the thousand books I had read was the one he had copied. I was certain of this the way only a person who has no life but the invented life inside books could be.

As it turned out, I was not the only one on Johnny's trail.

"We have a problem here," the department chair said to me one November afternoon, handing me a stack of student evaluation forms as he closed the door to his office behind us. "Our writer. Your friend."

I looked down at the forms. "When you read these," he said, "you'll see that his students are quite fond of him, on the rare days when he comes to class. Did you know that he's spent much of the semester AWOL?"

The first three forms I read said the same thing. "No," I said. "I had no idea."

I don't think he believed me. "I see," he said. "The last two colleges where he was employed, has he spoken to you about any of that?" His tone suddenly annoyed me. "I've done some additional detective work," he said.

I surprised myself with my response. "Did you have his telephones tapped, Paul? Have you gone through his trash?"

"No need for that. It turns out there were plenty of people at the last two colleges who were willing to speak off the record. We're going to have to take some action."

"Well, have you spoken to him?"

"He's stood me up. Twice now. Two appointments."

I swore under my breath.

"I thought maybe since you two spend time together, you might want to speak to him first."

I looked at Paul and saw his genuine concern. Something rare in my profession. I thanked him and promised him that I would speak with Johnny. "I'm sorry, Paul," I said. "Give me a few days."

It could have been worse, I told myself. Paul, or anyone on the hiring committee, could have read Johnny's novel and been left with the same nagging suspicion I felt.

THERE WAS A marvelous snowfall just after Thanksgiving, and Johnny and his family fell in love with sledding down the hill in front of the president's house. They invited me to go along with them several times and I made excuses, trying to avoid the deep gnawing in my belly and the feeling of paralysis that overtook me every time I was reminded of my time with Julia. Then late one afternoon my doorbell rang. I was in the kitchen at the time, doing my compulsive dance around the counters with a yellow sponge. When I opened the front door there was just little Sally standing there with her sled, smiling up at me. "Mommy says you have to come sledding with me," she said. "I got you a pop." She reached into her pocket and pulled it out.

"Grape!" I exclaimed. "My favorite." Just then a snowball sailed across the street, whizzed right by Sally, and hit me on my right knee. I heard Johnny's laughter as he emerged from behind a snowbank and gave us a formal bow. Linda stood beside him with Brady and the baby. "That's my daddy and mommy," Sally said.

There was something in her voice when she said this; she knew that I knew they were her family, but she told me anyway with a declaration to herself and the world. I wondered if this was the way children reassured themselves, declaring what they knew to be true in a world where so much was unknown to them.

It delighted me that after every run Sally insisted I carry her in my arms back up the hill, dragging the sled behind us. She was wearing red puddle boots that were too big for her feet and kept falling off as we climbed the hill. We'd get nearly to the top only to discover that one boot had fallen off way behind us again. Down we would go to retrieve it, laughing all the way.

When it began to grow dark Linda went home with the baby to start supper, and Johnny and I took Brady and Sally on a few more runs, then stopped at the campus spa for hot chocolate.

He got their snowsuits off and set them free to race around the room. I watched him smiling at them, and then a great sadness came to his eyes. "They deserve better than me," he said without a trace of self-pity.

I could only try to make a joke of this, though I was stunned. "Well, let's hope they don't find that out," I said.

He nodded and then was silent. I wasn't going to talk to him with the children there, but I had to confront him, I knew that. "Would you want to hit a few balls tonight?" I asked.

"Night golf?"

"You want to?"

"The barn?"

"Yep."

"You've got lights in that barn?"

"Definitely."

WE WALKED HOME together. "I'll get the kids fed and into bed, then I'll swing by for you," he said as he took Sally from my arms. He put her in the sled with Brady and started pulling them down the street. I watched them for a long time as they made their way home. Why wouldn't it be enough for a man like Johnny to be a great father and nothing more? I wondered.

TWELVE

WE WERE PICKING up our first round of golf balls. I was in the hayloft above him and he was talking happily about St. Andrews, chattering away about how we were going to go over together when he got his invitation for the Christmas tournament. "It might be ten years from now," he said, "maybe twenty, but we'll get there."

"When did you say you applied?"

"My old man put my name in right after my twelfth birthday. I had just shot my first round of par."

"You were shooting par golf when you were twelve?"

"We were living in Ohio then. My father's brother was president of a bank in Toledo and one of his perks was membership at the local country club. He got my dad in somehow. A spectacular place called Inverness. They had a practice range there and that's where I lived. I'd pound balls until my hands were blistered. Dad said to me, 'When you can hit ten in a row that go exactly where you want them to go, come and find me, I'll take you out, we'll play a round together.' That was my dad. You set a goal and then you work your ass off to get there. You build a tunnel between you and the place you're trying to get to, and you plow straight ahead until you reach the end."

He paused. Something passed over his eyes, and then he smiled. "He got me a tuxedo the day he sent in my application to St. Andrews. That was my old man; he loved dramatic moments. He was great for celebrations. He threw a little party at Inverness and invited a bunch of his buddies. We went from the bar to the post office to mail off the application. Since then I've always thought in terms of twenty years: In twenty years, I'll be there. Twenty years from now I'll get my invitation."

"I'll be an old man in twenty years," I said to him.

"Me too, so what. We'll just be hitting our stride," he said. "God, in these next twenty years the kids will be grown up and gone. Sometimes I think it's going to go that fast."

I walked to the railing and watched him for a few minutes. I saw him step closer to one wall where I had written out my study notes years before. "I don't see any Thomas Wolfe here," he said.

"Over there under that beam," I said. He looked up at me and then followed my gesture. And I knew then. The passage was already in my head:

For all would come again and I would sit there on the stairs, in absence, absence, in the afternoon and try to get it back again. And it would come and go again, fading like cloud shadows in the hills, going like lost faces in a dream.

An obscure work of Wolfe's, a novella entitled *The Lost Boy*, in which the author wrote of his dead brother whom his mother longed for and memorialized throughout her life. I was sure of this, and certain that there were more borrowed passages as well. It was the perfect book for Johnny to steal from. Even scholars of Thomas Wolfe ignored *The Lost Boy*. And to my knowledge there had never been a modern publication of the work.

I gazed down at him as he read my old study notes on the wall. *Who would ever know?* I asked myself. I wondered if he had told Linda, and what circumstances had driven him to plagiarize. The accident? His sister's dependency? Weren't there always good reasons for this sort of transgression? I wouldn't judge him, I knew that. In fact, I thought poor Thomas Wolfe might be pleased, honored. But I realized that it had to be eating away at Johnny. It was one thing for an academic to cheat on a scholarly book. But for a writer, it was unpardonable. A writer with only words. I decided then that I would say nothing to anyone. But I would confront him about the classes he had skipped.

I called down to him. "I have to ask you about something," I said.

"Ask," he said, turning to look up at me.

"You've missed a lot of classes."

"Some," he said.

"Is there a problem that I can help you with?"

"Am I in trouble, Ross?" he asked.

"There's some concern," I told him, "that's all."

He walked across the floor and picked up a ball. "Does Linda know?" he asked, looking up at me again.

"I don't think so," I said.

"Who spoke with you?"

"Paul. He got your midsemester evaluations."

"My students," he said. "I've let them down."

"Actually, Johnny, your students adore you, they just want to see more of you," I said, trying to make him laugh.

He raked his fingers through his hair, first with the right hand, then the left. And he began pacing the floor below me. "I can't lose this job, Ross," he said. "You don't understand. There are too many people who need me. If I fuck this up . . ."

"You'll do fine," I said stupidly.

"Well, it's pretty clear that I'm not doing fine," he said. "I just can't face them some days. I get right to the door of my classroom and I can't go in. I feel like I'm this game-show host or something. *The Tonight*

Show starring Johnny Carson. And if they knew how uneducated I am. I just wrote a novel, that's all. And I'll probably never write another one."

I told him not to kick himself so hard. "Maybe you should sit down and explain things to Paul. He told me that he's set up two meetings with you."

"Yeah," he said, "I stood him up both times."

"You have to face him," I said. "Just tell him."

"Tell him what?"

"Look, Johnny, Linda told me about your sister. The car accident."

"Oh, she did?" There was an edge in this question.

"Yes."

He laughed sharply. "Why would she do that?" he said. He became even more agitated, raking his head again and walking in a tight circle, gesturing and talking to himself.

I climbed down the ladder and walked over to him. He was sweating though it wasn't more than forty degrees in the barn. His breathing was quick and shallow. He didn't seem to care that I was there. I reached out to touch his arm, but he pulled away.

"I have to get going," he said, turning for the door.

I called to him but he didn't stop.

I DETEST THE part of myself that couldn't just let go of it. The compulsive part of my mind that forced me to take a bus to Harvard that weekend. To spend two hours in the Houghton Library, matching the passages in Johnny's novel with the original in Wolfe's novella. When I finished, I had three pages of evidence. I folded the pages, and as I walked to Harvard Square to wait for my bus home, I nearly threw them away.

THIRTEEN

THE DAYS PASSED quickly as the semester ran to an end in an avalanche of papers, exams, and department meetings. Rain just before Christmas washed away the snow on Porter's Pond. And then, when the temperature fell below zero and a solid layer of ice formed, Johnny bought skates for Linda, the children, and me and insisted we play golf there. He was his old self again, as if nothing had come between us. He set up a course with fluorescent-orange stakes and flags anchored in buckets of sand. We hit the balls off mats of indoor-outdoor carpet. Never having skated before, I could only inch my way along with the children, but Linda and Johnny flew across the ice. Sally was talking a mile a minute about the things she had asked Santa to bring her for Christmas. And then she made her curious declaration again. "That's my mommy and daddy skating."

"Yes, it is," I said. "Your beautiful mommy and your handsome daddy."

"And you're my mommy's friend," she said.

This gave me a sick feeling in my stomach. I knelt down on the ice and looked into her eyes. "I'm your daddy's friend too," I said.

I DIDN'T LIKE the fact that our conversation in the barn that night had ended with Johnny walking away, and I was determined to talk with him again about his missed classes. I knew that he had finally met with Paul and I was waiting for him to tell me how the meeting had gone, but whenever I saw him he was always busy, too busy to talk or to spend time with me. He was working on something, he told me. Something he couldn't discuss with anyone. Often from my office windows I would see him dashing across the quad. He was full of nervous energy, he had a disheveled look, his shirttail out, his hair uncombed. Like a doomed Pied Piper, there were always students following him, rushing to catch up, drawn to whatever passion had taken possession of his mind.

HE WAS LIT up, practically dancing when he came into my office to tell me he had figured out what he needed to do. There was a wild exuberance in his eyes. He looked as if he hadn't shaved for days, like some mad scientist who had just emerged from his laboratory with the answer he'd long been searching for.

"Tell me," I said.

"I have a new novel." He pointed to his head. "It's all right here now."

"That's great, Johnny."

"Because, here's the thing, Ross; they can't fire me if I keep writing. I mean I might turn out to be a disappointment in the classroom, or, you know, doing committee work, but if I can pump out another novel, I'll be all right, don't you think?"

I agreed wholeheartedly. He stood in the threshold of my office, leaning his head against the door frame. "You don't have anything to worry about, Johnny," I said.

A moment passed. It seemed as if he hadn't heard me. But then, suddenly, as if he had been jolted by electricity, he leaped across the floor, clamped his hands on my shoulders, and thanked me. "I'm glad you agree," he said. "I'll make this book a damned hit, and we'll all live happily ever after."

And with that he was gone.

I'VE OFTEN THOUGHT that at the end of our lives, when we look back, we'll be hardest on ourselves for the times we failed to stand up to defend the people we love. Those times when we should have said something but didn't, hoping our silence passed for good manners. I failed to stand in Johnny's defense the next week at a special meeting of the dean of faculty's disciplinary committee. One member of the committee, Nigel Rushfield, argued vehemently that we dismiss Johnny at the end of the current academic year. "We don't want to strike the dangerous precedent of condoning sloth in our English department," he concluded, with what I interpreted as a measure of satisfaction.

I watched his mouth moving and tried to close out his words by picturing Johnny bounding along the fairways. I knew that in the days and weeks ahead I would recall this scene and my silence, going over and over in my head the honorable way I might have spoken to defend my friend, editing and revising in my imagination until I had sentences so perfectly constructed that they seemed more real to me than my cowardice.

I just sat there, thinking that if these people had been speaking about me instead of Johnny, I would have surrendered on the spot.

FOURTEEN

I KNOW IT must have been hard for Linda to come to me for help. She called me at around nine one night after the children were asleep and asked me if I could come over to their apartment.

"I can't reach him, Ross," she said as she handed me a cup of coffee. "And I don't know if you know this, but he's missed a lot of classes."

I didn't tell her what I knew; instead I tried to make light of this, telling her how professors in the English department frequently missed classes.

She wasn't really listening. "We're losing him," she said. "This is ruining our family. I can feel it coming. And the children can feel it too."

"Where is he now?" I asked her again.

She looked into my eyes, and then turned away. "I'm embarrassed to tell you this. He said he was going to New York to meet with his editor about an idea he has for a new novel. But I don't believe it. He can't be writing anything, Ross. I'm sure he isn't. He can't sit still for more than a few minutes. I know he's in Connecticut with his sister. She's gotten worse since we moved here. And Ross blames himself."

Linda walked across the room and looked out a window that faced the campus, which was lit up in the distance and from here looked more like a county fair than a college.

"He talks about an undertow that is pulling him down," she began slowly. "He tells me that all he can think about is what will become of his sister after he's gone. I can't make him stop talking that way. No one knows how much time they have together. We just want him to be with us now. That's all. Just be with us. We'll do the rest, but I feel like he's leaving me."

She put her head down and began to cry. I walked to her side, then hesitated before I pressed my face against her head. I closed my eyes and whispered to Linda that everything was going to turn out all right in the end. She didn't move or speak. I asked myself for the first time whether I was falling in love with her. I wondered how I could ever be forgiven for this and for the moments when I had imagined myself taking Johnny's place in her eyes.

I DON'T KNOW when it was that Johnny returned to campus. Maybe four days passed. I was coming down the hill from my office in Lawrence Hall when I saw him a good ways out in front of me. Rather than call to him, I stayed at a distance, planning to catch up once he had left the campus and was on University Drive. But at the student union, he turned right instead of left and began walking faster.

When he turned into the library I was still well behind him. Inside he disappeared down a stairway. By the time I got to the bottom and opened the fire door, I could see him at the far end of the stacks, entering one of the faculty carrels. It was very quiet. His door closing was the only sound.

I had always assumed that the library carrels were assigned by seniority and that professors waited years to get one. Johnny had certainly never told me that he had one. As I stood there, I realized he hadn't told me because he hadn't wanted me to know.

There was a low row of horizontal basement windows running along the west wall. That was the only natural light on the floor. Every two yards there was another long bank of gray metal floor-to-ceiling shelves stacked with periodicals and books that needed to be dusted.

I began walking slowly down the long center aisle. When I reached Johnny's carrel I saw light beneath the solid oak door. I could have knocked. If it had been him following me, he certainly would have knocked. Instead, I began looking absentmindedly at the titles of the books in the stacks across from his door, waiting for him. And after a while, I took down a heavy volume from the Warren Commission's report on the assassination of President Kennedy and sat on the floor reading it. I don't know how long I'd been sitting there when the sound of his door opening startled me. From the floor I saw his legs from the knees down, that was all. I listened to his footsteps walking away from me, down the corridor toward the men's room. I waited a few minutes and when he didn't return I walked into his carrel. The room was depressing, with just a desk and a straight-backed wooden chair and brown concrete walls. There was a sheet of glass covering the desk and beneath it Johnny had arranged colored photographs of his children in neat rows. I counted forty pictures. When I leaned closer, I saw that they were all of one child I had never seen.

I was paralyzed there when I heard his voice behind me.

"You've discovered my vault," he said flatly.

"I'm sorry, I . . ."

"That's okay," he said. He stepped closer to me so our shoulders touched. "That's Sara," he said, looking down at the photographs. "Isn't she adorable?"

147

"Another beautiful child," I said.

"My kid sister," he said. I watched him reach down and touch one photograph of the child on a new bicycle. "I don't have any pictures of her after she was seven or eight. She turned thirty last week. I went to Connecticut to see her. I've been trying to take care of her.

"Trying," he said again as he opened the desk drawer and took out a small bundle of letters in envelopes. "I've been writing her for months, ever since we moved here, and the letters are always returned."

He sat down in the chair and leaned back. He closed his eyes and took a deep breath. "I can't begin to tell you, Ross, how hard I've worked to get my life into some kind of damned shape so I could take care of the people in this world who need me. I've busted my ass. I've cheated and scraped. I need to get a house of my own. And a washer and dryer of my own. A decent car. You're not a man until you're settled that way."

I waited, not knowing what to tell him.

"I shouldn't have moved so far from my sister to take this job. She needs my help. She's angry at me for leaving."

"But you have to support your family."

"Right."

"She must understand."

"It's a sore spot between Linda and me," he said sadly. "Don't get me wrong, Linda's been wonderful to Sara. But she doesn't understand why our kids' welfare shouldn't come first. Priority number one. And she's right, of course, and that's why I took this job. It was the only damned job I could get that held the chance for some kind of permanence. A future, I mean. But before my father died I promised him that I would always look out for Sara."

He stopped and gazed into my eyes. "That's the deepest thing in me, Ross," he said. "Taking care of her. If I fuck that up, nothing else I ever do will mean anything. Do you understand?"

I told him that I did. "Why are you down here?" I asked.

"Here? Hiding, I guess. Trying to write, you know? If I could get some pages written, the start of a new book, maybe I can save my job here. You said so yourself."

I nodded.

"Well," he said, "I have to go home and help put the kids to bed."

He didn't move and neither of us spoke for a few moments. I thought about his *words—I've cheated and scraped.* I was sure he was referring to his novel, those lovely descriptive passages that he had taken from Wolfe.

"I'm sorry," he said suddenly, as if he had read my mind.

"Don't be," I told him.

"No, I am. I want to earn this," he said. "This job. This nice life of a college professor."

"You have," I said. "Let's go, I'll walk you home."

FIFTEEN

LINDA KEPT ME informed; he wasn't writing at all. The pages wouldn't come or he lacked the patience to wait for them to come. He was teaching, or at least showing up for his classes, which was good. The next time I saw him, all the light had drained from his eyes. He looked to me like I had looked back in the days after I lost Julia, when I was no longer curious about the world around me.

ONE NIGHT WHEN I was too worried about him to sleep, I went to his library carrel just to see if he might be there. I knocked softly on his door and when Linda opened it, I was amazed. She looked like she had just walked away from a plane crash, the only survivor. She swung the door open far enough for me to see that Johnny was asleep on the floor with Brady, Sally, and William. Sally's green blanket was draped over Johnny's chest, and I wondered if she had seen the fear in her father's eyes and placed it there in an effort to comfort him.

"He wouldn't come home," Linda whispered to me, "so we came here to be with him."

I suddenly felt vulnerable. "What can I do, Linda?" I asked.

She looked down at him. Then she asked me if I might be able to walk the golf course with him in the morning. "I heard it's supposed to be warm tomorrow," she said. "And Johnny loves it there."

IT WAS A warm February morning, like spring. The ground was frozen solid but the hard winter rains that had cleared the ice on Porter's Pond had washed away much of the snow on the course so that there were open areas of brown grass on all but the shaded fairways. I had been up late that night, too worried to even try to sleep. In my basement I spray painted a dozen balls bright orange while I tried to think my way through Johnny's predicament. Compared to the atrocities taking place in Vietnam and in so many Southern cities where Civil Rights marchers were being fire hosed and set upon by police dogs, Johnny's sin was small and meaningless. Maybe I could approach the dean this way so that Johnny could confess his plagiarism, be pardoned and set free from the guilt that I believed was crushing him. Or I could tell Paul Speiss in his capacity as department chair, and we could keep it between the two of us. But shouldn't I tell Linda first and ask her what she wanted me to do, if anything? No, I should talk with Johnny first. Let him decide what to do. And if he chose to do nothing but try to live with his guilt, then so be it. But by telling him that I knew of his plagiarism, wouldn't his guilt be even that much more insufferable? I felt cheap and disgusted with my-self for not being able to give it up completely.

I only wanted what was best for the family. The only family I had ever been a part of.

"So, what do you say?" I asked Johnny when I got him on the phone. "Maybe we should play eighteen this morning."

"Sure" was all he said.

STANDING ON THE first tree, I noticed that he had Sally's baby blan-ket hanging through a strap on his golf bag. He saw me looking at it. "She insisted that I bring it," he said, as he touched the silk hem. "She's worried about me."

"A daughter to worry about you," I said. "That's something, isn't it, Johnny?"

He nodded slowly, then looked down the first fairway. "We won't be able to walk on the greens," he said. "Why don't we just count strokes to the greens? Thirty-six is par."

I told him that was fine by me.

The sight of him looking so fit when he struck his ball made it diffi-cult for me to imagine him needing anything more in his life than he al-ready possessed. I took a couple of practice swings then stepped up to my ball. "Your shoulders," he said. "Turn them through hard." I tried on several more swings. "That's better," he said.

Into the woods on the right. "Damn it," I said. Johnny had already picked up his bag and was walking ahead of me. I watched him take the baby blanket from the strap and wrap it around his neck like a scarf.

It wasn't like him not to stop and help me search for my ball. But he just marched on, in his own world, until he reached his ball. I didn't have a chance of finding mine, so I dropped another one in play and called to him that I was going to hit. He glanced back at me but only for a moment. I called to him again to watch out, but he didn't turn around. Instead, he stepped up to his ball, looked once more down the fairway to pick his target, and swung. I watched his ball rise into the pale blue sky to a fantastic height, then drop into the snow on the green. I didn't bother to hit a second shot. I just ran down the fairway and caught up with him on the second tee. "I know that I was in bad form at times this first year," he said to me without looking up from his ball. "People in the department think I'm a slacker. But, you know, writers are sometimes. And I think the department will forgive me if I can just get on track, don't you?"

"Of course," I told him, though he seemed to be talking to himself, not me.

"I've got to write my way out of the trouble I've caused everyone," he said. "I've hurt Linda. I wonder if I've hurt her more times than I've made her feel loved. And I wonder if I'll hurt everyone in the end."

When he stopped, I wanted to reach for him. But I just stood there and watched him hit his drive. To my surprise he hooked it badly. When the ball disappeared into the trees along the left, he put his head down, grabbed his bag, and started walking without waiting for me to hit. I ran along beside him. "I think my sister's dying," he said without looking at me. "It should be me."

I stopped and watched him walk away. I felt sad and helpless, and scared for him, and then something inside me took over all these emotions and I ran after him and grabbed hold of his arm and turned him around to face me. And I was yelling at him. Telling him everything he had to live for.

"It shouldn't be you," I said. He looked at me as if he were trying to figure out who I was. His eyes were glazed over. And the first thing I thought, stupidly, was how does anyone who feels so awful hit such beautiful golf shots?

We just looked at each other in silence until he said something that I couldn't quite make out.

"I didn't hear you, Johnny," I said.

"So what?" he said.

I took hold of his arm again. "No, tell me what you said."

"I said they should be yours."

"Who, Johnny? Who are you talking about?"

He pulled away from me. "Linda and the kids," he said. "They deserve someone like you."

Suddenly I wanted to shake him, pull his hair, knock some sense into him. Before he could take a step I grabbed his golf bag and tore it off his shoulder. I took his driver first and flung it as far into the woods as I could. Then two irons in the same throw. "I lost somebody too!" I shouted at him. He didn't look at me. He just stood there with his shoulders slumped.

"I have people relying on me," he said slowly. "I needed to make something of myself so I could take care of them. How could you understand that?"

"Because I don't have anyone?" When he didn't answer me I pulled his putter from the bag and threw it into the branches of a towering cedar tree.

I was finished. The anger was gone. He left his bag on the ground and walked away. "I don't want to lose you," I called to him.

WHEN I GOT back to the clubhouse Linda was waiting there with the children. She asked me where Johnny was. "You didn't see him?" I said.

"No."

"He must have cut through the woods.

"You have my daddy's golf clubs, Ross," Sally said to me.

"I do. Would you like to hit a ball?"

"Yes, just one though," she said.

She hit it on the first try with the clubface perfectly square, snapping her wrists through the swing in an exact imitation of her father. "Look how far!" she shouted.

"So far," I said. "Such a beautiful shot. How did you do that, Sally?"

"Like my daddy," she said. "I just swing the way my daddy does."

SIXTEEN

I ALMOST TOLD Linda that day. Walking through the woods, searching for Johnny's golf clubs, I had decided that I would tell her about the plagiarism. This was the best thing to do: tell Linda and let her talk to Johnny, and then she and I would help him face the consequences so that he could put it behind him and move on.

But when I saw her at the clubhouse with the children, I couldn't do it. *Next time we're together*, I thought.

But then Johnny changed. Two days later he came into my office as lively and optimistic as the first time I saw him.

Linda had told him about Julia and he wanted permission to turn my story into his next novel.

"All I need is a story, Ross," he exclaimed. "If you let me, I'll write a beautiful novel, I swear to you."

It was the only thing of value I had to give him: my story of two young lovers together in an old hotel while the snow fell and their fate was decided. Johnny recognized its potential immediately. The turns of its narrative. The suspense lurking in the plot. He had already given himself away to the idea. I couldn't deny him.

————

TAKING NOTES IN the blue books we used for exams, he spent hours questioning me. He pushed me to remember the quality of light in the sky on the afternoon I first saw Julia. The scent of her hair when I held her. The texture of her skin. I yielded these details but told him nothing of the baby, or of Julia's journey to Canada with the ex-marine.

"Of course," Johnny explained to me, "until she met you she thought she knew the meaning of love. Then you ushered her into the garden, Ross."

We were sitting in his carrel. I told him I wasn't sure she had loved me at all. "I might have been nothing more than an experiment to her. She could test her love for Jack. Her resolve to keep her promise to him."

"That's not it," he said.

"Why did she leave me then?"

"That's easy to figure out. You got too close, and she got scared."

"Scared of what?"

"Scared of having to change her mind, I guess."

I couldn't answer all of his questions. But I was able to recall the feelings I had for Julia and the emotional moments we had shared. And he was certain he finally had the story that would comprise his novel. As difficult as it was for me to spend so much time talking about Julia, I found myself reliving the good times we had shared and feeling deeply grateful for them.

A WEEK LATER we were out walking the course again one morning when he said out of the blue, "I'm going to find her for you."

I was walking through a sand trap, trying to find a ball in the snow. I looked up at him and saw by his expression that he was perfectly serious. "You deserve to know why she took off," he said, shrugging his shoulders as if it were plain as day.

"You have to promise you won't do that," I said.

"Why?"

"Because if she wanted to see me, she knows where I am."

"Come on, Ross," he said.

"No, I mean it, Johnny."

He threw up his hands. "Fine," he said. "It's your life. But in my novel she comes back."

FOR LINDA'S SAKE I went along with them to a furniture store in Worcester the day Johnny picked out his red chair. A Queen Anne's chair, upholstered in cranberry-colored wool, with dark walnut legs. "Every novelist needs a good solid writing chair where he can park his butt," he said as he tried it out in the store.

"Every wife needs a chair with room enough for two," Linda said as she sat down on his lap. She kissed him briefly. "We'll call it your cuddle-bug chair, Johnny," she exclaimed. She turned to smile at him and he took her face in his hands and kissed her again, this time a long, passionate kiss. I watched his hand move up her thigh.

"Make love to me right here," he said.

"Oh, sure," she said, laughing at him.

"I'm serious," he told her. "I'm completely serious. I want you to pull up your skirt right here and—"

"Johnny," she protested, laughing again, but this time only for Johnny's sake. There was fear in her eyes and I was sure she knew that he was completely serious. She gave me a helpless and embarrassed look. I wanted to do something, but I just turned away.

IN THEIR APARTMENT, Johnny insisted that his novelist's chair be in the kitchen, close to his supply of coffee. At a window behind the low counter where Linda folded laundry. This is where he wrote the first chapters of his novel in longhand, on yellow legal pads, under a great burst of energy over spring break. He sent the pages to his former editor in New York on a Tuesday morning. He insisted that I accompany him to the post office. "Are you sure you don't want to read them first?" he asked me as we stood in line at the counter.

"Not until it's completely finished," I told him. He looked at me doubtfully. "What?" I said.

"You're afraid it's no good," he said grimly.

"Cut the crap," I said. "We both know it's great. Mail it off."

I watched him close his eyes and bow his head before he handed the manuscript in its manila envelope to the woman behind the counter. "That's my life, ma'am," he said to her. She smiled back.

My life too, I thought.

Empty-handed, we walked back to his apartment. Johnny talked all the way about how he was going to be able to be a better husband to Linda, a better father to their children, a better brother to his sister, a better teacher for his students, once this book was under contract. "A better friend also," he said to me. "And someday I'll persuade Sara to come up here and live with us. I know if she's around the children, she'll feel better about everything. It will all work out, and then I'll finally be able to rest."

"You don't have to be a better friend," I told him. "You're already the best friend I've ever had."

He took hold of my arm after I said that. "Did you ever find my putter in the woods?" he asked.

"Couldn't find it," I said.

"I hated that putter anyway. Hey, what's the name of the bunker in front of the seventeenth green?"

I thought he was testing me. "On the Old Course at St. Andrews?"

He stopped me on the sidewalk. And when I turned toward him I saw something dark in his eyes.

"I've forgotten," he said. "I can't believe it. I've told you all the names, Ross. Can't you remember?"

"I'm sorry. No."

We continued walking but he was silent after that, and he walked a step ahead of me as if I weren't there.

TO CELEBRATE WHAT Johnny was certain would be good news coming from New York any day, he insisted that Linda and the children and I join him in what he called his Red Chair Party. He filled the kitchen with balloons and paper streamers. He hired someone with a pony to give rides to all the kids in the apartment building. He made ice-cream sundaes and we drank champagne and danced. It was a great relief for me to see him smiling again.

It was late that night, after the children were asleep, when Johnny curled up in the red chair with a blanket. "I'm not leaving this chair until I get the call from my editor," he said.

"You're coming to bed, sweetheart," Linda told him.

"No, I can't," he said. He was quite drunk. "I have to keep a silent vigil here. I'm the night watchman standing sentinel. The shepherd keeping watch over his flock by night. I'm on duty, honey. I hope you'll understand."

Linda looked at me, her eyes pleading for me to do something.

"Johnny," I said, "once you've got your contract in hand you'll have to spend enough time in that damned chair writing the rest of the novel. I think you ought to sleep now while you can."

He bowed his head suddenly. "Ross?" he said.

"What is it?"

"Do you think I'm going to make it?"

"Of course you are," I said, though ever since he mailed the manuscript to his former editor I wondered if it was possible that this editor hadn't discovered by now the plagiarism in the first book.

"Why don't you sleep in my bed tonight?" he said to me. "Why don't you sleep with Linda tonight?"

"Johnny," Linda said.

"No, I want you to," he said to her. "Let him undress you, and then dress you in the morning the way he did Julia."

I felt betrayed. And then that feeling passed when I saw the humiliation on Linda's face. I wanted to help her, and Johnny. This was all that mattered to me.

SEVENTEEN

I HAVE DECIDED that we can't ever really know another human being. Not even the people who are closest to us. I can describe Johnny to you as precisely as I recall him, and yet it feels as if I have only invented him. And Julia as well. And Brother Martin. And Linda. Maybe I have invented myself too.

JOHNNY LEFT HOME a week later. He was going to check on his sister in Connecticut and then take a train into New York to find out what his editor thought of his chapters. The second day he was gone, Linda brought the children to my house and we baked bread together. A first for me. Bedlam in my kitchen. Flour all over the children and in their footprints on the floor. "My mother used to say, 'Show me a wife with flour under her fingernails and I'll show you a happy family,'" Linda said. "I don't know about that. A happy family, but maybe an unhappy wife." We baked four extra loaves and took them to the group home along with some board games I bought in town for the children.

Frankie shook my hand and then Linda's with great ceremony, a proud smile on his face. While we watched the kids play with Sally and Brady, she told me Johnny's pages had come in Saturday's mail with a short rejection letter.

I drove the car back to Amherst with Linda and the baby beside me. In the rearview mirror I watched both children fall asleep in the backseat. "I don't know how I'm going to tell Johnny," she said. She turned her face to the side window. "All his hope was in those pages, Ross."

"I know."

"How will I tell him?" she asked me again, this time as she turned toward me.

I wanted to comfort her. I wanted to give her some hope. "When Johnny gets back," I said, "we'll go over his pages together. We'll just keep working on them until they're so good that no one can turn them down." Even as I said this I knew that there would never be any redemption for Johnny. If, somehow, this book turned out to be a masterpiece, and then if he were to write ten more masterpieces, or fifty, each one more brilliant than the one before it, nothing could cancel out the plagiarism. He had crossed a line and would never be allowed to cross back.

TWO WEEKS PASSED with no word from him. Linda called his sister every day to see if he had shown up there. And I stopped by the apartment each night to see if Linda had heard anything. One night she asked me if I would sit on the bed beside her until she fell asleep. I held her hand while she talked about the births of her children. "Johnny was always frightened about bringing each baby home. He never slept when they were newborns. I came home one afternoon and found him taping old photographs of our dead relatives to the wall beside the crib. My great-grandfather. His grandmother. In case the baby died he would have some faces to look for in heaven, he told me."

That night in Johnny's chair I awoke in terror from a dream about Julia. Linda was already awake. "I heard you talking to someone," she said.

I was breathing hard and feeling colder than I had ever felt before, because in my dream Julia had asked me why I hadn't been satisfied just to be her friend, why I had insisted on being more than that. If we had been friends then we could have spent our lives living in the same town and seeing one another every day.

When I told Linda, she said, "A friend who stays by you through everything, what could be better than that?"

I looked into her eyes. "I'll stay by you, Linda," I told her. "You can count on that."

She thanked me, then asked me to lie beside her on the bed. "I just need to feel you next to me," she said.

We lay in moonlight, our arms at our sides, touching, both of us silent when the baby began to cry. Linda started to get up, but I stopped her. "You go back to sleep," I said. "Let me go."

When I lifted William from his crib, my head bumped the mobile that hung from the ceiling and a few notes of the Brahm's lullaby played. This made him smile. I smiled back. "You are the world's most handsome little boy," I said to him.

WHEN I LOOKED out at the faces of my students it took all my determination to keep from telling them to forget everything I had ever taught them about literature, to put aside all of that and everything else they had ever been taught, and to concentrate only upon finding the person they could spend their lives with, someone they could talk with and play Scrabble with and grow old beside.

At the same hour Johnny died, I was teaching Hawthorne's *Scarlet Letter*, reading aloud the scene where Hester speaks of her sin to the man with whom she has committed adultery, trying to convince herself of their essential goodness, despite their guilt. Donna appeared in the hallway outside the classroom, motioning to me.

LINDA TOLD ME at the door to the apartment, before I could step inside. I reached for her, but she turned away. "There's still enough snow for us to go sledding," she proclaimed as I followed her into the living room where she was dressing the children. "I can't find Brady's mittens," I heard her say. I walked in behind her and knelt beside her while she searched the floor of a closet. "I'm looking for red mittens," she said. I watched her turning over shoes, her eyes wide and darting wildly. "You'll have to help me tell Sally," she whispered to me.

I WAITED UNTIL we had taken our first run and I was carrying Sally up the hill, pulling her red sled behind us. "You know that we will be friends forever, right, Sally?"

"Yep," she said happily.

"We'll go sledding every winter, and when I get old, you'll pull me up the hill, right?"

"Because your legs will be tired."

"That's right. You're such a smart girl. And you know that someday I will die, right?"

"Yep. But not for a long, long, long, long time."

"That's right. Only sometimes people die before they get old. Do you know that, Sally?"

"You're squishing me," she said.

I hadn't realized that I was holding her so tightly. "I'm sorry," I said to her.

"That's okay," she said. "My daddy won't go sledding with us, will he?"

I stopped and looked into her eyes. "No, Sally. He can't go sledding with us anymore. I'm sorry. I'm so sorry." I paused and looked up at the top of the hill where Linda was sitting on a sled with Brady between her legs and the baby on her lap.

"Your daddy has gone to heaven," I told Sally. She didn't say anything in return. She just tipped her head back and looked up at the darkening sky.

EIGHTEEN

I WENT IN Linda's place to identify Johnny and to make arrangements for his body to be sent home. It was my first time driving her car alone with my new license. The officer in charge of investigating the accident met me at the morgue in Darien, Connecticut, then graciously agreed to take me to the place on the Merritt Parkway where Johnny had died. We stood along the shoulder of the highway while he went over the details as he remembered them. "In single-car crashes like this, with no tire marks," he explained, "we tend to conclude that the operator of the vehicle was asleep at the wheel. In the case of elderly operators, there is the possibility of heart attack. But without tire marks, we concluded that the vehicle struck the abutment at top speed, with the operator making no attempt to either slow the vehicle or change its direction."

I knew at once what he was not saying. I knew that he was protecting me from the other possibility, that Johnny had crashed his car intentionally. "I'll get back in the cruiser," he said, "so you can have some time here alone."

I bowed my head and heard Linda's voice when she told me that Johnny was dead. "We're all orphans now, Ross."

Johnny had visited his sister in her converted garage apartment in Madison, Connecticut, which is where I went next to tell Sara that her brother was dead. It took me a while to find her place. The sun was already going down and I decided it would be better to wait until morning to see her. I checked into a motel on a side road next to a playground, took a long shower, and got into bed. I was about to turn off the light when, in the mirror across the room, I caught the reflection of the little glass shelf above the bathroom sink where I had set my razor and toothpaste, deodorant and toothbrush. I had the momentary impression that I had moved into this room for good and was destined to spend the rest of my life here. It was crazy, and frightening. I got up, put all my things into the car, and slept on the bed in my clothes.

I HAD NO idea what I was going to say to Sara, but the moment I saw her slumped in a wheelchair, I knew that I would not tell her what I suspected was the truth; her brother had looked at her and he had lost hope of ever being able to take care of the people who needed him.

"It was a car accident," I told her as I knelt beside her. She wept like a child and we held each other and cried together.

When she leaned forward in my arms I saw that she had taped on old black-and-white photograph of Bob Dylan to the seat back of her wheelchair.

"Do you like Dylan?" I asked through my tears.

"Johnny took me to see him in concert once," she told me, drying her eyes on her sleeves. "It was the best night of my life."

IT WASN'T UNTIL I had said goodbye and was outside walking toward my car that I realized Johnny was gone from my life. This made it terribly difficult for me to leave. I leaned against the car and looked back at Sara's apartment, wondering what it was like to have a sister, and trying to imagine the sense of responsibility for her that Johnny had felt.

Before I got into the car, a man came up to me from the house across the street. He gestured to me and I waved back. When he was standing right in front of me, I realized that he was deaf. He took a small notebook from his back pocket and began to write in it.

That was how he told me that he was Sara's landlord. I spoke slowly while he read my lips and nodded that he understood. I told him that I was a friend of her brother's. His eyes brightened and he wrote Johnny across one page in his notebook. He smiled.

I told him that Johnny had died in a car accident, and this made him bow his head and then look up at me with such sadness in his eyes you would have thought he had lost his own brother.

Before I left I wrote down my address and telephone number and asked him to please contact me if there was anything Sara needed. He nodded eagerly, and wouldn't let me leave without meeting his wife.

She was a pleasant woman in a flowered housedress. There were photographs of their five children above the fireplace. "All grown up," she said.

"Well," I said, "you'll have grandchildren someday."

"I can't wait," she said. "And I hope my husband didn't impose on you?"

"I don't understand," I said.

"He's very protective of Sara. He didn't recognize your car."

"Please," I said, "that's fine. I'm glad he cares."

"Her brother used to park his car right there where you're parked now. The last time I saw him, when I got up to make breakfast, he was there, just sitting in his car. I wish I'd invited him in. I almost did. I make a very nice coffee cake, and I almost went out to the car to ask him if he wanted a piece."

I looked out the window to the place where Johnny must have decided to end his life. I wondered if a piece of coffee cake from a woman in a dime-store dress might have kept him alive, and what more I could have done for him.

NINETEEN

SOMEHOW WE GOT through this together. Linda and the children and I. In one corner of the living room of their apartment there was a small plywood table with legs maybe fifteen inches high and tiny chairs for Brady and Sally. I spent most of the summer there on my knees, with glue and construction paper and scissors with blunted ends, making things. Cards and houses. Valentines and paper chains that we hung on the walls. Anything the kids wanted to make. Red-and-pink hearts with glitter were Sally's favorite. On the days when Linda couldn't come out of her bedroom we slid cards under her door. "Mommy's tired," Sally would say. "Someday she won't be tired anymore."

ONE NIGHT AFTER I had Brady and the baby asleep, I lay beside Sally waiting for her to close her eyes, feeling privileged and also deeply sad to be establishing myself in Johnny's place. "Your brothers fell right to sleep," I said. "What about you, you're not sleepy?" She had her eyes open and was staring at the ceiling. She shook her head.

"Hey," I said, "where's your green blanket?"

"I don't need it anymore," she said. "I'm growing big now."

I pulled her closer. "Yes, you are," I said.

"I'm going to be Toto in my dance recital."

"That's wonderful, Sally. You'll be the best Toto."

"Toto is a dog," she said.

"Yes, I know."

She took a deep breath. "Sometimes I see my daddy up there," she said.

"Where?" I asked.

"Up there," she said, pointing to the ceiling. "He checks on me, my mommy said."

"Yes," I whispered as I kissed her cheek. "He'll always be there checking up on you."

"But what if I live in a different house?"

"He'll follow you," I said. "He'll always follow you." I looked into her deep blue eyes and thought how far from this room, this little bed, she would go in her life. How far from this night, to another night when she might gaze up at the ceiling as she held a boy in her arms for the first time, floating in the holy silence between lovers. In a hospital bed with her own baby. And at the end of her days, as an old woman. It would happen that quickly. And it made me unspeakably sad to think that I would be gone long before her, unable to console her in hard times. In the normal run of life it is only the children and the very old who sleep alone. But I had this in common with Sally, and for the first time I wondered if the reason she had taken to me from the beginning was because she sensed that I was unaccompanied like her, spending my long nights alone.

THAT SUMMER I spent my nights on Johnny's red chair. Always checking on each of the children and Linda before I closed my eyes. Sometimes staying awake until morning. Once, when Linda's grief seemed as if it might drown her, I held her through the night in the chair. Just before she fell asleep she brought her hands to her lips. "He did it because he thought he had failed us," she said.

"It was an accident," I reminded her.

"He did it because he gave up on himself."

"There's no way of knowing that," I said.

"Oh, Ross," she said, "if I keep trying to know the answer, I think that I'll go mad."

All I could do was hold her.

Another night I read Johnny's novel aloud to her, the way I had read to Julia in the time we had together. *Your life appears to be a straight line,* I thought, *until you live long enough to see it begin to bend.*

Staring at Linda, I suddenly remembered the first time I saw her with Johnny. And I told her about this.

"Making out behind the bushes?" she said. "Are you sure that was us?"

"It was you."

"It seems like another life."

"It was, Linda. It was another life for you."

She looked down at Johnny's photograph on the jacket of his book. She asked me if I would tell the children someday about that first time I saw her with Johnny.

"Of course, I will."

"I want them to know that they were brought into this world by a love story," she said.

ONE NIGHT AFTER the children were asleep, Linda and I went through Johnny's clothes. Each time we put something in the box she had marked for the Salvation Army, I reconsidered and kept it for myself. "I can't see you wearing that tie, Ross," she said.

"Oh yes, I'll wear it."

"And these shoes, they're way too big for you."

"No, no, they'll be perfect." I just couldn't let any of it go to strangers.

I carried everything out to my car so the children wouldn't see the boxes. There were still a few stars visible in the rising light of dawn. I gazed up at them. Inside, on the dining room table, Linda had one more box.

"Johnny's Scotland box," she said when I stood beside her. There were his slides and photographs of the Old Course. "He never got to St. Andrews."

"Maybe he's there now," I said. "Playing eighteen. In peace."

WINTER CAME ON so quickly that year. By mid-October all the trees had been stripped and by Thanksgiving the rivers and lakes were frozen solid and there was a layer of hard snow on the ground that looked like it would last until spring. I spent hours standing at the windows in my office in Lawrence Hall looking out at the whitened fields. Whole mornings and afternoons passed by me this way across those windows. I saw dawn and dusk and darkness there, and a startling blue cast of light above the hillsides where the snow lay evenly.

On one of the first days in December I spray painted a dozen golf balls Day-Glo orange, and I began walking the golf course wearing boots insulated with felt liners and carrying a driver and a little strip of green indoor-outdoor carpet Johnny had given me the time we hit golf balls on the frozen lake. I hit each shot off this mat, aiming in the direction of the greens where they lay buried beneath the snow, and I cried openly while I walked. I cried through my backswing and while I followed the flight of my ball above the trees that rattled in the wind. I cried like a boy for the beauty that had once marked my life. The beauty of Julia's smile when she desired me and the way she walked beside me down the hotel corridors, stopping to lean against the wall and pull me close to her. I cried for the memory I had of time spent with Johnny and his children on this course on the gold mornings of summer. I cried for those things and for the day Linda had told me that Johnny was dead. I had felt that day that *I* was disappearing from the world, not him, vanishing into the dark shadows of myself.

LINDA MOVED AWAY before Christmas, back to Delaware to live with her parents. I told her that I didn't know how I could go on without her. We cried in each other's arms. "I think you should stay here, live with me in my house so I can take care of all of you," I said.

She kissed my forehead. "That sounds wonderful, Ross," she said. "But I think we need to be with my mother for a while."

I watched her drive away and then I walked to the golf course. I stood on the first tee and looked out over the Cathance River. It was frozen, and irresistible in a way I cannot explain. I faced it as I laid the strip of carpet on the snow. I placed a ball at my feet and then stood up straight and calculated the distance. A hundred and eighty yards, maybe one ninety. A three iron for Johnny. A fairway wood for me. Give yourself an extra club length or two, Johnny had always counseled me. That way you can take an easy swing. I adjusted the club in my hands. I cocked my wrists at the top of my take back. Two practice swings, carefully turning the wrists over, releasing my hands, when the clubhead reached the position of the ball. A deep breath. Then another. A long look, imagining the path that the ball would take. Picturing a nice straight line from my feet to the winding river. Head down. Strong left arm. A moment of stillness. Silence while I waited for life's complexities to be transformed into simple geometry. The sky, the snow, the trees, the river, a cathedral of silence. I was almost thirty years old now, a man alone on a snow-covered golf course, trying to let go of old dreams and to take hold of what I suddenly knew was the great truth of life: that all we hold in common are the ways we can be broken.

That was my last thought before I brought the club back for real and then swung down and through the ball as hard as I could. When my head came up I was already looking to the right, prepared to watch the ball veer off insanely. But there was no ball there. This time the ball was flying straight. It had happened maybe fifty times in all the golf I had played; my hips and shoulders had turned in perfect timing with my wrists breaking so that the ball had no choice but to fly straight.

I barely caught sight of it as it cleared the trees on the near shore. It was still rising, still gaining speed and altitude, as it crossed the river, heading for Main Street. And for once I begged the ball to turn right before it killed someone. "Turn right!" I yelled, just before the ball cracked against the roof of a truck. At first I couldn't move. I saw the truck's tail-lights flash red. The driver's door flew open and a man jumped out, already looking up at the sky. I threw myself flat against the snow.

I waited, wanting in the worst way to pick up my head and see what was happening down in the street, but I didn't dare. I heard a car horn, and off in the distance the whistle of a freight train running south. And then I laughed. I laughed out loud. The first time I had laughed since before Johnny's death. I felt my right cheek going numb in the snow as I closed my eyes.

ONE

I FINISHED THAT year at the university and one more, passing my fourth-year review and winning tenure, which meant a comfortable job for life, before I resigned and returned to St. Luke's to teach literature and composition as Brother Martin had. That was eleven years ago. At the time I was still driving to Delaware once a month to visit Linda and the children. I was in love with her, I knew. But I couldn't bring myself to step toward her. And when I moved back to Illinois and the distance became too great, we wrote and called each other often. I remember a call from her on the day when William started kindergarten. She was feeling blue, she told me, now that all of her children were in school, and she wished that she could go back and have them all small again. "Just for a few days," she said. "Then I'd let them go."

That day when Linda called I reminded her that she was just thirty-two years old. "You're still a girl," I told her.

"I don't feel like one, Ross," she said.

We vowed then to always stay close, but somehow we lost touch and drifted apart the way people do. It was neither her fault nor mine, and I missed her the way I missed Johnny and Julia and Brother Martin. Those people who had blessed my life and then were gone.

THOSE ELEVEN YEARS passed at St. Luke's, and then came a Thanksgiving morning. A day when all of us awaken early and prepare the big meal in the kitchen of my youth. My specialty is freshly baked bread:

molasses, wheat, and raisin bread from Linda's recipes. The children love the mess we make at the long table. Dough in their hair. Flour footprints on the floor. That morning when the telephone rang, my hands were busy kneading dough and the boy who answered the telephone held it to my ear for me. I thought it was Linda's voice but I was wrong.

"It's Sally," she said. "Happy Thanksgiving."

"Oh, no," I said, "this isn't Sally: Sally is just a little girl."

"I'm seventeen," she said. "I have a boyfriend."

"Don't say that," I teased her.

"I'm sorry," she said, "but I'm growing up. Mom wants to tell you something."

It was about Johnny. His invitation from St. Andrews had finally come. "It doesn't seem fair," Linda said. "I don't know whether to laugh or cry."

"It's not fair, Linda," I told her.

"Do you know," she said, "his father sent in his name when Johnny was twelve? He would be fifty-one now."

Fifty-one, I thought. I asked her if she was okay.

"I'm all right," she said. "The kids are thriving."

"Growing up," I said. "I want to see them."

"Yes, we have to get together."

"We will, Linda," I said.

"When?" she asked. But she did not wait for me to answer. "Ross," she said. "I thought maybe you might go for Johnny."

"To St. Andrews?"

"It must be beautiful there," she said.

IT HAPPENED THAT I was grading papers late one night after Linda's call when one of the boys on my floor woke up crying. He was five years old, one of those kids you love so much because he tries so hard to be good and ends up being bad most of the time. I carried him back to my room so he wouldn't wake the others. He had a high fever and as I sat by his side through the night watching over him, he drifted in and out of sleep. In his fever dreams he kept his hands in tight little fists at his sides as if he were ready for a fight. He looked like such a brave and stoic traveler, and as I gazed at his face I realized that in my life I had never fought for anything. I had lived carefully. I had walked a narrow road. Now there was gray in my hair, and soon I would begin to age quickly. But did this mean that I could not still become something I had never been? Was it too late for me to change?

In the early morning when the boy's fever broke, I wrapped him in blankets and carried him down to the kitchen to a wicker chair I had pushed in front of the window that looked out to the field where Brother Martin had hit golf balls. I went up to the storage closet above the laundry room and brought down my golf clubs, which I had not seen in eleven years. "I want you to watch something," I said to the boy. "Just look out this window."

It was cold outside and some of my resolve began at once to drain away. "Kick yourself in the butt and get to work," I said below my breath. Then I swung as hard as I could at every ball and when I looked in the window, the boy had risen onto his knees in the chair and his eyes were open wide.

IN THE DAYS waiting for my passport to arrive I wore as my street shoes the spiked golf shoes Linda sent when I told her that I had decided to go to Scotland. She had bought them for Johnny just before his death. I wore them everywhere, trying to break them in, and for a week I had an army of boys out back chasing balls for me.

I FLEW FROM Chicago on the fourth day of December. The last thing I said to Linda when I called her from the airport was that I wished she were going with me. She had just been promoted in her job as a social worker and couldn't get the time off. "I'll be with you though," she said. "I feel like I'm standing right next to you now."

TWO

HURTLING THROUGH THE dark night over a black sea at thirty-three thousand feet, I convinced myself there was nothing to be afraid of. And after two gin and tonics and a bottle of wine with dinner, I felt like I was just riding on a bus. I told the stewardess who brought me a blanket and pillow that this was my first flight. "Well," she said, "there's a first time for everything."

FIVE A.M. IN Gatwick Airport outside London, far from home for the first time in my life, and the world was a fascination to me. I was a child among the dignified tea vendors with their wooden carts and the old, proper British gentlemen in tweed coats. I stared at the strange money in my hand.

At a broad window, watching daylight burn off the night stars, I looked down and saw that I was still wearing Johnny's golf shoes. The only shoes I'd brought. *All this way without my shoes, Johnny*, I said to myself. But I was not complaining; I was too happy to complain.

THE TRAIN ACROSS England and Scotland moved slowly through a world of slanting green fields and great stone churches that were black with age. Pastures marked off by ancient rock walls covered in emerald-green moss. Tan-and-white sheep grazed beyond the simple cottages. In the distance the gray North Sea heaved beneath its white-capped swells.

I can't explain it really, but through this world a straight path seemed to be opening to me as if I were an actor on a movie set, so that the man selling coffee on the train turned to take my order just as I approached him. And the taxi driver in a dull green waxed raincoat put down his newspaper as if it were only a prop and rose to his feet to greet me when I arrived in Leuchars.

"Are you here for the Christmas tournament?" he asked as he hoisted my bags into his trunk.

"Yes, the tournament," I said, a little nervous, now that I was so close to St. Andrews where I would *become* Johnny Durocher and leave myself behind.

"Aye," he said. "How long have you waited?"

I thought a moment. "Since I was twelve."

"That's long enough," he said. "I hope the weather improves for you. It's been wet since October."

INSIDE THE TALL church doors of the Rusacks Hotel, I looked up at the stained-glass window above the threshold where the last of the afternoon light was coloring the broad ceiling. The muted shades of blue and gold seemed more beautiful and vivid than any colors I had ever seen, and I gazed at the light like a man in a trance. When I turned, a tall woman with short black hair and red lipstick was smiling at me.

"You must be Mr. Durocher from America," she said pleasantly.

"Yes," I said. "That's me."

We shook hands. "And how was your trip then?"

"Fine," I said, as I took in the rest of the lobby. The antique rugs, the enormous brick fireplace. The mahogany furniture and pale yellow pillars. "This is a beautiful hotel," I said.

"Lovely, yes, isn't it?" she agreed. She glanced down at some paperwork and I saw her expression change. "You'll be staying for twenty days, is that right?" she said slowly.

"Yes, ma'am," I told her.

"Yes. It seems here that you were going to furnish us with a credit card, but we don't have one." Now she looked up at me, with a slightly apologetic expression. "I'll have to see your passport as well, Mr. Durocher."

"My passport. Right," I said, trying to sound confident. I had anticipated this moment; there was nothing I could do but tell the truth and then beg for understanding if I had to. She looked into my eyes while I explained that my name was not Johnny Durocher, and when I had finished telling her my story she tilted her head in an amused way that instantly reassured me.

"My lips are sealed," she said. "Tell me, did your friend wait a long time for his invitation?"

"Since he was a boy."

"Right then," she said, handing me back my passport and credit card. "We'll be watching you. My family never misses. If it stays this wet though, we'll be watching you from inside."

I thanked her. "The Old Course," I said. "Can you tell me how to get there?"

She smiled at me again, then raised her hand and said. "Just out that door, Mr. Durocher."

THREE

I WALKED DOWN the nine stone steps from the back door of the hotel into a shadowy mist at the edge of Johnny's dream, where the pull of time paused and all the sound fell out of the world. In this inexplicable ground of silence I stood breathless, certain to the center of my bones that it was *meant* for me to come here. No . . . more than that, I felt like I had been returning here since the beginning of my time, before Johnny and Linda, before Julia and Brother Martin. Before the people who brought me into the world had released me from their embrace. We all have moments like that, when everything that has ever happened to us, our finest achievements and failings, even our exquisite longing, *all of that,* seems to have carried us to a still point where our lives begin to turn onto their intended course.

A light rain was falling from a heavy gray sky. I heard it ticking against the nylon sleeves of my jacket, and this was enough to break the spell.

SEVEN STEPS TO cross the narrow paved street behind the hotel. One more step over a low wooden rail and I was standing on the Old Course, at its far corner where the final fifty yards of the eighteenth fairway rose to a pale green with a red flag blowing stiff in the wind. I knew this land. This deep ditch guarding the green was the Valley of Sin. Just beyond the green, the Royal and Ancient Golf Club stood its ground, striking a stately pose, like the country home of a baron or the customs house in Hawthorne's *Scarlet Letter.* Forbidding and elegant. A magnificent stone ship of a building that the sea seemed to have heaved upon this shore centuries ago. Beside it, the old Grand Hotel, a ragged pink structure, rising five stories beneath a peaked roof and a silver dome that looked out over the sea. Waves pounded the shore as I walked to the starter's box.

I was greeted by a tall man about my age with jet-black hair, blue eyes, and a dark green scarf tucked into his V-neck sweater. He stood behind a counter and nodded his head as I stepped inside. "You look as if you've come a long way," he said. His name was Andrew and there was a kind of music in his voice.

"I have, yes."

"You'd be our American, then. The only Yank in the tournament this year." He shook my hand. "Durocher, is it? Johnny Durocher?"

Without hesitating, I said I was. We shook hands. "Tell me," I said. "These shops behind the green, would they be some of the shops that closed the day Bobby Jones returned to play his last round?"

"Aye, they would," he said proudly.

"You know the story."

"Everyone in Scotland knows the story."

We looked at each other in silence and the moment passed.

"Are you here early to practice?"

"I am."

"You've got two weeks. Will you need a caddie?"

"No, thank you."

"Very good. Have you got your letter?"

Johnny's letter. This moment I had worried about. But as I handed him Johnny's letter, I felt confident and sure of my purpose here.

He looked it over, then our eyes met. "Very good," he said again, placing the letter in a drawer.

"Can I get out today, Andrew?"

Another smile. "You'd rather play than sleep for a while first?"

"I've got a lot to learn," I told him.

He looked past me, up at the black sky where the rain had turned to sleet.

"My clubs are in the hotel," I said eagerly.

"Rusacks?"

"Yes."

"And you're ready to go out now?"

"Five minutes. I already have my shoes on."

He glanced down at them. "So you do. All right then."

I had stepped out into the sleet when he called to me. "You'll be the only one on the course."

———

I RAN BACK to the hotel like a boy. I didn't feel the sleet on my face or the water soaking my feet. I ran up the back steps, inside past the bar and the dining room, through the library where people were reading and drinking tea. In the front lobby I changed out of my wet socks, stuffing them in my golf bag. I waved to the desk clerk and called to her that I was going out to play.

"Enjoy your game," she called back.

FOUR

I STOOD ON the first tee of the Old Course at St. Andrews with my history: Johnny's shoes and name, and Julia's clubs. I pulled out my driver and began to swing it through the air, first in slow methodical arcs as I visualized Johnny's swing in my mind. I stopped and dried my hands inside the pockets of my pants. That was when I noticed men in blazers and ties standing in the front windows of the Royal and Ancient Golf Club. They were watching me. I pretended not to notice them, but suddenly I began to feel light-headed and unsure of myself. My feet seemed to have vanished beneath me. In all of Johnny's glorious descriptions of this place, he had never mentioned that an audience of real Scottish golfers would assemble to watch me slice my ball into the sea.

I was losing my resolve. Just off the eighteenth green, in the big windows of the shops and hotels, more people stood watching. I had already set my ball on the tee though I didn't remember doing this. I looked down at it and wondered if I should pick it up, go sleep off my jet lag in the hotel, and return here in the morning, before anyone else in St. Andrews was awake.

Then I remembered Johnny telling me the account of Bobby Jones's first appearance here. How his knees and hands shook as he stood on the first tee, right here where I was standing. Right here . . . Bobby Jones stood right here, afraid that he would duff his first shot. The great Bobby Jones. *All right*, I thought. I took a deep breath, exhaling slowly. I walked up to my ball and took my stance. Then one last, long look down the fairway. Out in front of me was the widest fairway on the course, a broad-double fairway shared with the eighteenth hole, benign as a park. Along the left side, the hotels and shops. Down the right, beyond the low white rail, the sea. Up ahead no bunkers between me and the white flag waving on the first green, 370 yards away. Just the meandering river, the Swilken Burn, no wider than a sidewalk, protecting the green. I dried my hands again inside my pockets, then gripped the club. "Pick out a target," Johnny always told me. "And visualize a corridor running from that target to you." I found a cottage roof off in the distance and took aim.

I'm playing golf in Scotland, Johnny, I said to myself. Like a mantra, I repeated it in a whisper: "I'm playing golf in Scotland."

I was concentrating so deeply that I saw the clubface strike the ball. When I looked up the ball was flying straight and high like it would never come down. *Straight and far!* I said to myself. Toward the end of its flight it faded slightly to the right, but landed well in bounds. I watched it roll forward across the wet grass. It was the first golf ball I had ever hit in front of an audience, and I was ecstatic. I marched to my ball like a soldier returning home from battle, taking in the landscape as if I were just out for a pleasant walk. Up ahead a father and son were flying a kite. I heard a car behind me and turned to see a Rolls-Royce crossing the fairway on the narrow tarred road known as Granny Clark's Wynd. Sometime during my preparation to hit my drive, the sun had burst through the overcast sky and I was no longer alone; people had appeared from every direction. They were old people walking dogs and parents pushing babies in prams and young people jogging all around me. It was as if the golf course I had stood on at the first tee had been transformed into a public park.

This put me at ease. I reached my ball and waited for the kite fliers to turn and acknowledge me with a wave. They stood off to the side and watched. I felt confident as I waved back. My drive had traveled maybe 240 yards. A long drive for me.

I took a while considering my second shot, enjoying the moment, luxuriating in the achievement of my first shot. Jack Nicklaus, Arnold Palmer, even Bobby Jones would take that shot any day. Just far enough from the first flag to take a full wedge into the green. The wonder of the game of golf revolves around the unlikely fact that anyone can hit an ideal shot out of the blue like this.

In front of me were 130 yards of flat green ground with only the narrow river at the front of the green to worry about. I chose a six iron, at least three club lengths more than I would need, but I wanted to be sure to clear the river, and I planned to hit the shot softly with a half backswing. A punched shot. *I'm playing golf in Scotland, Johnny,* I said to myself as I stood over my ball. *Easy swing. Nothing hard. Head still. Don't pull up. See the club strike the ball.*

I hit the ball so cleanly that I never felt the impact, and when I looked up it was streaking high and straight for the pin. I watched it all the way until it fell from the sky, safely beyond the river, something that Nicklaus, Palmer, and Lee Trevino had failed to do in tournaments here. Johnny had told me many times how difficult this second shot could be if the prevailing wind from the west was blowing hard. Without the wind, a fine golfer could hit a wedge. When the wind was high, even a well-hit fairway wood might fail to carry the river.

But I was over safely and for that moment golf seemed like a simple game. I thought the ball had struck the green maybe twenty feet behind the pin. I rejoiced, and kept right on rejoicing even as I watched it roll off the back edge and disappear.

I walked left toward the Swilken Bridge, waited for a lovely Oriental girl to take a picture of her boyfriend, then crossed triumphantly.

The green as I approached it turned out to be humped and slanted and larger than any I'd ever seen. My ball must have hit twenty yards behind the flag stick, not twenty feet. I stopped to search for a flat landing zone near the pin, then discovered that just behind the green, where my ball had disappeared, the rough was a maze of spike-leafed bushes and tall yellow grass so thick I couldn't sweep them aside with my pitching wedge as I searched for my ball.

Within five minutes I had found two balls, neither of them mine, and after a few more minutes of looking, I gave up and dropped a second ball into play.

I gazed at the green, then back up the lovely fairway to the city of St. Andrews rising brilliantly in the plum light of late afternoon, its ancient rooftops and steeples outlined against the sea-colored horizon. Who would know that this wasn't the ball I had hit? Who had seen me drop the second ball into play? With a good wedge perhaps I would draw close enough to the pin to make it in one putt for my par four. I looked down at the ball and felt silence enclose me again. Sooner or later everyone who cares to play good golf has to be honest about himself. I had never listened to Johnny talk about the two of us going to Scotland together to play golf without picturing myself stumbling around the course, embarrassing both of us. Knocking balls out of bounds, hacking great divots from the fairways, endangering other golfers with my wildly errant shots. Playing so terribly here on the Old Course, the final destination for every true pilgrim of the game, would be insufferable. It was one thing to knock over a glass display case of diamond rings in a jewelry story; it was something worse to do this in Tiffany's. On a normal course I would have to struggle to break one hundred, bogeying half the holes and double-bogeying the rest. On this course with 112 pothole bunkers ahead, and greens you could barely keep your ball from rolling off, it would take a string of miraculous shots and the hand of God to bring me in with a score of eighty-nine in the tournament. Which is what I wanted. To play an honorable round for Johnny meant breaking ninety.

I looked down at my ball again. I could pretend that one of the balls I just found in the rough was mine. Or I could cut my dishonor in half by pretending I had found my ball, taking a one-shot penalty to move it from the rough, and make bogey five from here. Doing this on seventeen holes and making one legitimate par would bring me in with a score of eighty-nine. But this would be the furthest thing from an honorable round, and over time, five years from now, or ten, when all I would recall of this journey were the ways I had cheated, I would have nothing. Nothing at all.

Standing there in rough so thick I could not see my shoes, I made my decision. No cheating. In every practice round, and in the tournament, I would play each ball where it lay and take my penalty strokes like a man. Which meant I was hitting my fifth shot when I dropped my new ball into play instead of my third. I got into my stance. No practice swing. Any delay and I might change my mind. I struck the ball squarely. It flew up and landed perfectly on the edge of the green. It rolled up one hill, down the other side, then up and down another into a hollow just as it broke left, then sharply right before bumping hard into the iron flag stick and dropping into the hole. Call it dumb luck. Or maybe a reward for being honest. I had flown all night across the Atlantic Ocean, I hadn't been in Scotland long enough to unpack my suitcase. I had been on the Old Course for twenty minutes, hitting my ball with twenty-year-old straight-up-and-down Ben Hogan blades, and already I had been blessed with a shot that surely rivaled the best ever struck in the five hundred years the game had been played here.

FIVE

OMEHOW IT BECAME the longest afternoon of my life. I never hit another decent shot after holing that wedge. I spent hours searching the rough for my balls. I landed in nine pothole bunkers and took a total of seventeen strokes just to get out. They are sinister creations, like sandy-bottomed graves, a few of them so deep that you can only see the sky when you look out. Somewhere around the sixth hole I became confused by the layout of the two golf courses that run the length of the Old Course on either side. I played two holes on the New Course and one on the Eden Course before I realized my mistakes. The beautiful green fairway shared by the first hole and the eighteenth gave way on the second hole to a landscape suited to mountain goats, craters and humps and acres of those spiked thickets called gorse that I had encountered behind the first green. Most discouraging of all was my stupid slice that haunted nearly every shot and forced me to walk far, far off line across the hostile terrain. By dusk when I turned around to make my way back to the hotel, I had such horrible blisters on my heels that I had to walk barefoot.

Coming down the seventeenth fairway along the Road hole I began to hear people singing. Up ahead at the eighteenth green a Christmas tree was lit and I could make out a crowd of people in the street. They would all see me stepping over the rail and walking across the narrow lane to the hotel with my shoes in hand, the perfect portrait of a defeated American golfer.

This was in my mind as I stood over the ball for my second shot on eighteen after duffing a drive that merely rolled out in front of me maybe 150 yards, never leaving the ground. I had a five iron in my hand. By now my bare feet were so cold they felt like shapeless blocks of wood beneath me.

A deep breath. Then two slow practice swings, turning the shoulders and swinging down at the ball. Left arm straight on take back. Head down. Shoulders rotating right. My target was a man's hat just behind the green.

The take back felt perfect. But when I began to swing I failed to turn my shoulders and brought the club forward with just my arms. Stiff-arming the shot so that at impact it felt like I had swung my club into the side of a car. And worse, I felt my body jerk up sharply like some pathetic imitation of a jack-in-the-box. I wasn't looking down at the ball when I struck it; instead my eyes were on the people singing carols behind the green. And by now, several of them, including the man whose hat I had picked for my target, were looking up into the sky at my ball.

Up and left. Their left. *My right.* And there it was sailing straight for the hotel. I couldn't bear to watch. I bowed my head and waited for the sound of windows shattering and glass showering into the street below.

Instead, there was a crack, like a gunshot. I looked then and saw one slate roof shingle sailing through the sky.

I grabbed my bag and scurried across the fairway toward the North Sea, running with my head down. I didn't stop until I was on the beach, where I dropped my clubs and sat down in the sand, determined to wait there as darkness fell so no one would see me walking to the hotel.

AFTER A WHILE, stars appeared. I stretched out with my head against my golf bag and gazed up at them until I fell asleep.

I slept an hour or so and then awoke to the sound of waves crashing onto the beach in the advancing tide. My body was numb with cold and the heels of both feet were sore from Johnny's shoes. To the world I looked like someone washed ashore.

Walking across the first fairway, I looked in the direction of the first green where I had been so hopeful. I could still picture my drive. The majestic flight of the ball. And my second shot as it carried the river. And the little wedge shot that set the ball onto the green, rolling toward the hole.

At the steps of the hotel I paused, then turned and faced the course, which looked lovely and benign. *Tomorrow,* I thought dramatically. *I'll be back tomorrow.*

IN MY ROOM I placed my golf bag in front of a window, in a band of moonlight that caught the faces of my irons. From this window I could see the Christmas tree at the eighteenth green lit up against the dark ocean beyond it.

I filled the bathroom sink with warm water and washed the sand out of the raw, pink skin on my heels. For a while I stood at the window. Dinner was just finishing at St. Luke's, six hours behind. The boys would be going off to study now. I pictured their faces and said their names just below my breath. The names of all forty-two boys. I pictured the Christmas tree in the foyer and I began to feel homesick. I laid my head down and fell asleep to the sound of the floorboards creaking in the hallway outside my door like those in the old hotel in Northampton where I had been young and in love.

SIX

IN THE MORNING I awoke to George Harrison's guitar on the radio, playing that old song "While My Guitar Gently Weeps." I sat up and surveyed the room. A wonderful room with high plaster walls painted pale yellow. Three tall windows, one looking out over the Old Course and the sea. The others facing a handsome stone building four stories high. Chimney pots on the roof. There was a cherry red carpet on my floor. Mahogany desk and bedside tables. White lace curtains with drapes tied back. Triple-crown molding bordering the high ceiling.

I saw people in the windows across the street. Pairs of people living in separate apartments. I watched an elderly lady bringing tea to her husband. Another woman watering plants on a windowsill.

I wondered what it would be like to live here, to awaken in this room every day for the rest of my life. A little food each day. A walk. Some books on my shelves. That's all I would need.

Framed photographs were hung on the pale yellow walls. All scenes of golf from past British Opens. Long ago when the golfers played in cardigan sweaters and ties, or Harris tweed coats. Like they'd just walked to the course from the bank where they worked. I stared at one photograph on the wall directly across the room. An old black-and-white picture showing thousands of spectators circled, fifty deep, around the outline of the eighteenth green. In the center of the green, four men spaced apart. From my bed they looked like four skaters on a frozen pond.

A gust of wind rattled one window. I looked up and thought of Johnny. Would his energetic soul, which never rested at home, have been at peace here? I thought about the round of golf I had played yesterday. My drive on the second hole that had sliced so badly I had to walk off the Old Course and across two fairways of the New Course to retrieve it. Everything had fallen apart quickly after that, but now I wished that I had finished the round anyway. My first round on the Old Course at St. Andrews. I was discouraged about that. *Today will be better*, I thought. *Some breakfast and then back at it.*

But something was wrong. When I swung my legs out of bed, the sheet was twisted around my feet and stuck to my bloody heels. I hobbled into the bathroom dragging it behind me, then stood in the tub, soaking the sheet until I could slowly peel it off my heels. The skin was completely gone.

I spent the day wrapped in a down comforter, sitting at the window looking out over the course, with my feet in a wastebasket filled with warm water. I watched the golfers teeing off for the first hole and those making their way up the eighteenth fairway. After a while I could identify the same foursomes I'd watched teeing off on the first hole finishing up their round, and my day fell into a restful pattern. I could tell that it was cold outside by the heavy clothing the golfers wore, but the sun was bright all day and I counted 148 golfers. Very few of them hit better drives from the first tee than I had, and each time one of them hit his second shot into the Swilken Burn I was filled with an unreasonable hope.

As the hours passed I grew impatient merely watching the golfers and began to analyze their swings. The guy in the red pants who lifted his front foot off the ground before he swung. The fellow who smoked his pipe and opened up too quickly. A big man with a caddie, who stiff-armed the ball miserably, the way I had hit my six iron on eighteen, sending the ball to the roof of the hotel. These strangers became my students of the game and I caught myself muttering advice to them. After a while I convinced myself that my own demise the day before had resulted from the simple, straightforward fact that I had forgotten to make myself keep my head down and actually see the club strike the ball. A lack of concentration perhaps attributable to my excitement. Sitting at the window, I managed to convince myself that if I had done that one thing, I would have played a good round.

Next time, I thought. *Next time*. And as the day wore on I couldn't wait to play again.

SEVEN

I LOST THREE days of practice sitting at the window, eating room-service sandwiches and waiting for my feet to heal. I watched the golfers go out and come back. The first day I was impatient. But then I accepted my fate and spent my time reading and exploring the hotel. When I discovered a bronze plaque on the door to my room with KEL NAGLE engraved on it along with 1960 OPEN CHAMPION, I set out barefoot to read the plaques on every door. It took a few hours and in the process I saw what a magnificent hotel this was, like an old ocean liner, with its wide, grand stairways and marble pillars. I loved the slow wooden elevator that was just big enough to accommodate two grown men, each with a bag of golf clubs. And the chandeliers. There were rubber hoses on each floor that predated a sprinkler system for fighting fires, and the great hall of a library with its wheeled ladder for reaching the highest shelves.

Each morning on the table in front of the window that I left open just an inch or so during the night there was sand that had blown in through the screen. Just a few grains of sand each morning, fine as sugar. I gathered them with the flat of my hand and brushed them into a glass, to take home for Linda to put on Johnny's grave.

I KNEW THAT I had to get moving. I had allotted myself twelve days to prepare for the tournament, and I had lost three to my blisters. On the fourth I put down my book and slipped my feet into Johnny's golf shoes, pushing my toes as far forward as I could before gently bringing down my heels. Then I headed into town.

Baby steps all the way up North Street and across to Market. At Boots the Chemist the employees were wearing Santa hats and decorating a Christmas tree. I bought some Band-Aids and got directions to a shoe store a few blocks away where I found exactly what I needed. Soft slippers with hard soles made of some kind of indestructible plastic. They were gray-and-black and bore a king's crown about the size of a nickel in gold-and-red exactly like the big clock on the Royal and Ancient Golf Club.

My king's slippers, I thought as I dressed in my room, where the windows were streaked with sleet and the wind sounded like thunder. Long johns, top and bottom. Corduroy pants. Plastic wind pants. Turtleneck. Wool sweater. Plastic rain jacket. Scarf. Ski hat pulled down over my ears. Walking to the elevator I had no pain at all in my heels. I was elated.

I STEPPED OUTSIDE into a gale-force wind. Wind that was blowing so hard I had to walk with my head down, and for every two or three steps forward, I was blown a step back. On the first tee, my golf bag was yanked into the air and swept thirty feet down the fairway by a gust of wind that ripped its legs off. I was shouting at the top of my lungs, "I'M PLAYING GOLF IN SCOTLAND!" but the words sounded faint, as if they were coming from far, far away. My balls were blown off the greens before I could get there to putt. Blown off the tees also. On the sixth my ski hat flew off my head. It was a hundred feet away before I could start running after it. The metal flag sticks were bent into U's, with the flag brushing the grass. I couldn't feel my fingers on the club. At the eleventh hole par three, I hit a seven iron high into the air and then, five seconds later, turned and sprinted out of the way to keep from getting hit by it as the wind drove it back at me. Blown all the way back, like a boomerang!

It took me almost six hours to play seventeen holes. Coming up the eighteenth fairway I was using my two iron as a walking stick, a cane to lean on. In the front windows of the hotel people were having their tea. A few waved to me and I gave a little salute. Scott returning from the South Pole. I was proud of myself for finishing. I had counted only two golfers on the course all day.

INSIDE THE CHARIOTS pub just up from the shore, the bartender poured me a pint of Guinness then took my wet clothes and hung them to dry in front of a space heater behind the bar.

I sat at a small table in front of a coal fire, adding up my scorecard. Two over. Two over. Par. Three over. Two over. One over. Par. One over. One over. Par. Par.

Three double bogies and a triple were unacceptable. *Pathetic,* I thought. And then I tried to find hope in the fact that I had finished with four pars.

The bartender waited until I looked up, then spoke to me from behind the bar. "Without the wind," he said, "you'll do better."

"I'm not sure," I said disconsolately.

"Aye, you will," he insisted. "Was this your first time out?"

"Second."

He came around the bar and sat down at my table, taking a pencil out of his shirt pocket so he could write on a bar napkin. "Here, then," he began. "Number one, 370 yards. Easy par four. Number three, 352, par four. Easy. Number five, 514 yards, par five. That's not that long for a par five. Number six, 374 yards. Seven is only 359. Number nine, 307. With the wind at your back even a duffer could drive the green. Number ten, only 318. Twelve is 316. Sixteen is 381 and eighteen is a gift at 354. So, that's . . . how many holes? Ten holes that any man can par if he can hit the ball straight and keep out of the pothole bunkers."

"I'm not sure I can do that."

"Sure you can. You just need to learn the course. You're playing in the tournament?"

"I am, yes."

"Well, then, hire one of the old lads to walk around with you once or twice and then you'll have it."

I thanked him. "My name's Durocher," I said. "Johnny Durocher."

"Joe," he told me.

"I missed three days because of blisters on my feet," I explained. I lifted up one foot. "I played in these today."

He marveled at this. "Maybe you're the first American ever to play the Old in bedroom slippers," he said.

EIGHT

THEY WERE HANGING colored Christmas lights on the lampposts along North and Market streets the next morning when I walked to town. There was a beautiful sunlit sky of blue and only a trace of breeze off the sea. I was going to buy a few things I needed and then head right out to play eighteen holes in reasonable weather for the first time. I was already looking forward to how nice it was going to feel to play with hands that weren't frozen.

I bought some jam doughnuts to keep in my room, a loaf of bread, and a bottle of wine before I walked on a few blocks looking in the storefront windows. I was standing outside a small shop with a red door, beside the cathedral looking at a nativity scene in the window, when suddenly rain began to pour out of the blue sky. It was so improbable that I looked up at the sun in disbelief and searched the sky for clouds. I began to feel weightless and vulnerable. I don't know how long I stood there, but I was soaked when a young woman called to me.

"Come inside."

I turned and saw her holding open the red door, beckoning me inside the shop.

As she closed the door behind me, I heard a pennywhistle playing a shrill and solitary sound that seemed to be coming from far away. I felt myself turning slowly, enclosed within a windy silence. I watched the woman walk toward me. She was young, thirty perhaps, and wore a pale blue sweater that matched her eyes. "Have you walked a long way?" she asked me. A simple question that I answered only inside my mind. "Sir?" she said. "Why don't you sit down?"

She led me to a black stool beside a chrome cash register that seemed to be ringing.

"May I call someone for you?" she asked softly.

I watched her lips moving, forming more words, but without sound.

I apologized. "I'm feeling dizzy," I said. I tried to remember how I had gotten here, which direction I had turned from the hotel, but it was all a blank.

"Shall I get you some tea?" she asked.

My eyes fell upon rows of richly colored kilts and scarves behind her. "Did you make those?" I asked.

She nodded, and asked, "Are you shopping?"

Before I could answer her, the windy silence filled my head again. But this time I heard myself speaking just below the silence. "It's strange," I said. "I've just been wondering if maybe there is a place, some far-off place, a different place in the world for each of us, and if we ever reach our place, we find the people we've lost." I paused.

"I know what you mean," I heard her say.

"It's so strange," I said. "But I was thinking, that if we find this place that's meant for us, we walk down a street there and turn a corner and everyone we've ever lost in our life is waiting for us."

I saw her looking down at my slippers. "I'm sorry," I told her. "It's just a thought."

"A beautiful thought," she said. "Does everyone find their place?"

"I'm not sure," I replied.

"Have you?"

I looked into her eyes. "Yes, I think so," I said.

She nodded slowly. "Are you here on holiday?" she asked.

I looked into her eyes. "I'm here for someone I lost," I said. "A friend."

"I see."

I knew then what I wanted to do. "May I tell you a story?" I said. For some reason I felt no reluctance asking her this. And as I began, her expression remained so serene that I found it easy to tell her everything.

When I finished she said, "You need to meet my brother, Peter. We live just outside town. You can catch a number ninety-five bus right in front of the hotel. Four miles out of town you'll see a massive big hotel they've built on the left side of the road. Get off at that stop and walk down the next dirt road on your right that you come to. You'll end up at my front door. I'll be working until four, but I'll phone Peter now and tell him you're on your way, if you'd like?"

"Yes," I said, "of course," though I didn't quite understand.

"Number ninety-five bus," she said again. "They run past your hotel every twenty minutes."

I thanked her and walked to the door.

"Mr. Lansdale?" she called to me.

I stopped and turned back. "Bring a few of your sticks," she said.

I didn't know what she meant. "I'm sorry?"

"Your clubs. Bring a few of your clubs."

"All right," I said.

"Bring the ones you want to break in half," she said with a grin. "Not the ones you're fond of."

NINE

I GOT THERE just after noon in the worst weather imaginable. A cold, lashing rain, driven sideways by a ferocious wind from off the sea. My slippers were soaked by the time I reached the farm about half a mile down a dirt road. There was a low stone wall, blackened with age, that ran in front of the whitewashed cottage with a bright green roof. Built into the wall was a red iron mailbox with Queen Elizabeth's profile stamped in relief. I was walking to the front door when someone whistled sharply.

Off to my right up a hill I saw a man standing in front of a small barn that was leaning badly to one side.

"You brought your sticks," he said as I approached. He had thick red hair and narrow shoulders that were slightly pitched forward.

"You're Peter," I said.

"And you're Ross. My sister told me to expect you."

"I brought my dreaded irons," I said. "Two, three, and four."

"Aye, the long irons," he said. "Come in out of the wet."

We stood just inside the open barn doors out of the rain, looking over a beautiful valley that ran up to a steep hill, maybe a mile in the distance.

"I've spent a lot of time in a barn like this," I said, looking around us.

This farm, Peter told me, had belonged to his father and his father's father. "Now there's just me and my sister and two hundred sheep," he said wistfully.

"Sheep?"

"They're out there in the rain. You'll hear them when we start hitting balls. They don't care for golf. But my sister's boys love the game."

"How old are they?"

"Seven. Twins. You can't tell them apart. They're at school now."

"Their father?"

"He's off in Edinburgh at the present time," he said, shaking his head slowly. "Chasing after something. He'll be back when he gets hungry and cold. I don't care much for the man, myself. In fact, I don't like him at all. But he's my sister's husband, so when he's around I hide my whiskey and try to be a gentleman."

"I understand," I said.

"It's my own fault. He and I were best pals growing up. I'm the one who told him to ask Mary to dance. Oh, you should see the two of them dance." He shook his head. "It's true love, I'm afraid. And when they start dancing I start singing, I can't help myself. I see the way he looks into Mary's eyes, and I forget that I can't stand the man."

He shook his head again then asked me if I wanted to hit a few balls.

"I forgot to bring balls," I said. "I'm sorry."

"Don't be sorry," he said. "I've got a thousand of them here."

There were three barrels standing under a workbench, each of them filled with balls. "I have Mary's boys pick them up for me when I start to run low," Peter said.

"I was sure you played," I said.

"No, not anymore," he said. "I hit them out into the field with the boys, that's all for me now. I played a fair game when I was younger though."

He paused, considered something. "Have you got a temper?" he asked.

"A temper? No, not me."

"You should. It's a good thing to get angry every so often when you play this game. If you ask me, too many men approach it like they're going to confession. Then the wind blows them down."

"The wind is amazing," I said.

"Sky's clearing a bit," he said. "Why don't we take a walk? You can tell me about your friend."

THE CHANCE TO talk about Johnny, first to Mary in her shop and now to Peter, made the years since his death disappear. When we finished walking we sat inside the cottage. Mary had been waiting for us and I told her how grateful I was.

"I needed to talk with someone, and there you were," I said to her.

She stood at the coal stove heating water. "Your Johnny would be very pleased that you're here. And he knows. He's watching you."

"Oh, no," Peter said with a smile. "Here comes the sermon. My sister is trying to reform me," he said jokingly.

"I'm not trying to do anything of the sort," Mary said. "I gave up on you years ago. But you believe what I'm saying, don't you, Ross?"

They both looked at me while I thought for a moment. "I do," I said. "I feel Johnny here."

WHEN MARY'S BOYS came home from school she made them model the kilts that she had just finished making them for a Christmas pageant. They were beautiful little boys, all arms and legs in constant motion, with bright red hair and freckles like their mother.

"Mr. Lansdale teaches in an orphanage," Mary told them.

"And he's going to take you two back with him if you don't learn to behave yourselves," Peter chimed in.

LATER I HIT golf balls, then watched the boys scatter into the valley to gather them in burlap sacks. I paid them ten pence for each ball and told them how I had chased golf balls for Brother Martin.

Before I left, Peter said I was welcome to come back in the morning.

"Are you sure?"

"Of course. We'll get to work."

"I only have a week," I said.

"Then that's all the time we'll need," he said, shaking my hand.

He sent me home on a bicycle with the boys chasing after me all the way to the main road. "I want one of those kilts," I yelled to them as they waved goodbye.

"I'm riding a bike in Scotland," I said, pedaling back to the hotel in my slippers with my irons resting on the handlebars. Past the green hills and the lovely fields drowsing in the late-afternoon light. Sheep with black faces looked up at me, and way out ahead the steeples of the city marked the skyline.

TEN

BRIGHT AND EARLY the next morning at Peter's farm. I'm hitting the last of fifty-three balls. He has counted them out carefully. Fifty-three. Sixteen with my driver. Two with a seven iron. Sixteen with my wedge. The rest with middle irons except for two shots with my fairway woods for the two par fives on the Old Course. And each shot aimed at a tree in the valley. Fifty-three strokes, plus two putts on each hole, would make a score of eighty-nine. That will be my goal in the tournament, to break ninety.

After I have hit my fifty-third shot, he calls to me to start over.

"You were counting?"

"Yes, I was," he says.

"I only hit three cleanly."

"I know. But that round is over. Start again."

———————

HE HAS ME hitting the balls while standing in the threshold of the barn door. He has shortened my backswing to a more compact arc, and if I hold the plane of this arc while swinging down and through the ball there is only the sound of the clubface striking the ball. If my club strays on the way back or the way down, I strike the door frame with a loud cracking sound, which prompts Peter to call to me from his workbench where he is making something for the twins.

"You missed that one," he calls out each time I don't hit a ball cleanly.

WE SAT IN the barn drinking tea after I finished. "Let's do some mathematics," he said as he took a piece of paper and a pencil from his coat pocket. "To shoot an eighty-nine on the Old Course, after you give yourself two putts on each green, you're left with fifty-three strokes. Sixteen are from the tees with your driver. Two are drives with a seven iron on the par threes. That leaves sixteen wedges to the green after you get close. Two fairway woods on the par fives. So, how many does that leave?"

He wrote down seventeen before I could finish the math in my head.

"I can't hit the ball straight though, Peter," I said.

"I know that," he replied as he turned over the sheet of paper. He drew a map of the Old Course, and to my amazement, he marked out every one of the one hundred and twelve pothole bunkers. The out-of-bounds markers. Everything.

"If you'd grown up on the course, you'd know it by heart too. It hasn't changed in the fifty-four years I've been alive."

He had a strategy for me and I listened as he went through each hole. "Burn is an easy four. Play it as a bogey so you don't put too much pressure on yourself at the start. Here's where you want your drive to land. You've got plenty of room there for your slice."

"I want to get rid of my slice, Peter."

"You will. Now here on number two. Dyke. Aim way left here, almost to the Old Course Hotel. Don't worry about people coming up the seventh. Just shout if you hook it by accident. But you won't hook it. Not from what I've seen." He smiled until I smiled back at him.

"Thank you for your confidence," I said.

"Not at all. You play two as a bogey also. Three, another bogey. Four—Ginger Beer—another five. Hole O' Cross, the par five—you can par this hole. I'm going to show you how. That's your first par. Six you par. The fairway opens up nicely right there for your drive. Seven, bogey. Eight, you par this par three. Nine, you must par this four. It's the only flat approach on the course, you can run a low five iron from anywhere. Ten is a par. Eleven, another par three, you give yourself a bogey. Don't try to reach the green between the Hill and Strath bunkers. It's not worth the gamble. Twelve and thirteen are bogey fives. Fourteen is the second par five and I'll show you how to par it. This is your toughest test. But to shoot an eighty-nine you'll have to hit par here. Fifteen and sixteen, bogeys again. Seventeen, the Road hole. Give yourself a double bogey here. You may need it." He smiled again.

"That leaves the hotel windows on eighteen," I said.

"Don't worry about the windows. You'll make par on eighteen. You've got that big open fairway. The only one on the course."

He leaned back and looked at me.

"If I do this, I'm going to insist that you sing for me," I said.

He nodded, then leaned forward over his map. "Now, let's go over this again," he said.

We were still working when the boys came home from school. They raced around the barn trying to be quiet every time Peter told them to hush. Finally he yelled at them. "Boys! For the love of Jesus! If I give you my leg to play with, will you leave us alone?"

They promised they would and to my astonishment Peter drew up the right leg of his trousers and unhinged his wooden leg. He handed it to the boys and they ran off shrieking with delight.

"Compliments of the Falklands," he said. "Those two love the leg, so it's useful from time to time."

"You played golf before you lost your leg," I said.

"That's right."

"You were good."

"Fair. Now let's get back to work here."

BEFORE I LEFT that day he placed one of my clubs in my left hand. He closed my fingers around the grip. "Strong left hand," he said. "As strong as you can, so you pull the club through the swing, into the follow-through." Then he placed my right hand below the left and gently closed my fingers. "This one has to be soft. It's this right hand that is killing you. Just lay it over the grip so that it's barely there. Just like this. That's it. Now swing. Again. Now watch. With the soft right hand, you're releasing the club at impact. Can you see? Watch my hands. Take the club back. Gently. Gravity brings it down this far, to here. Then my wrists break through the ball, here. Here. This is where you generate your power with your wrists breaking. Can you see?"

"Yes."

"You break your wrists just as your shoulders and hips are turning left. So the clubface is square at impact, and then it quickly releases down."

I told him that I remembered Johnny telling me a thousand times that someday he was going to teach me how to hit down on the ball. "That's what he meant, isn't it?"

"It is," he said. "Pretend you're trying to hit the ball under a table. Now, go back to your hotel and swing each club tonight. Don't just swing them, though; go through each hole. What do you swing on the first hole?"

"Driver. Seven. Wedge. Two putts."

He smiled and nodded his head. "You were paying attention. Now go and let me get my leg back before the lads lose it."

ELEVEN

LOVERS ON THE beach. From my window I can see them, walking hand in hand or with their arms around each other. The wind blowing their scarves behind them. By their physical touch they distinguish themselves from the rest of us, the grown-up bankers, professors, janitors, and cooks who have learned to live without it, and to conceal our longing for it. And that man in the blue cap walking alone; he could be me. How clumsy compared to the lovers whose bodies move as one. The rest of us are separated by the space that lovers cannot tolerate. Someday, if we live long enough, we will all tell our love stories to a stranger from down the hall.

AT PETER'S SUGGESTION I bought new grips for my clubs at a shop in town. "The softest grips you have," I said to the clerk.

As I followed him to a corner of the store he said, "Are you the American who plays in his slippers?"

"That's me," I said.

"Are your blisters better?"

"I'm going out today in my golf shoes for the first time."

THERE WAS A different starter at the Old Course today. He introduced himself when I stepped up to the box. "George," he said, as we shook hands. "You're playing in the tournament," he said.

"I am. Any tips for me on the first tee?" I asked.

"No negative thoughts in your mind," he said.

It was good advice and I ripped my drive down the center of the broad fairway. A beautiful shot that reached nearly 260 yards after a long roll, duplicating the first drive I'd hit on number one. I kept my head down so long that I had a hard time spotting the ball when I looked up. And my right hand was so soft on the club that I didn't even feel the impact in it.

The wind for once was low and so I took a gamble on my second shot. Rather than play long with a seven iron to be sure to carry Swilken Burn, I hit a full nine from the soft grass. I will remember this for the rest of my life, the sound the ball made as it jumped from the ground. I had consciously released my hands at impact the way Peter had instructed me. I must have hit down on the ball at just the precise moment my wrists were breaking, striking the ball and the earth simultaneously. A big grassy divot flew out ahead of me and I could hear the ball sizzling as it shot up into the sky. I carried Swilken Burn easily and landed on the back right corner of the green.

I made par. *An easy par!* I said to myself as I marched toward the second tee. Then a slight setback as my drive sliced moderately before it came to land. When I reached it I found that it had come to rest at about 180 yards, only twenty yards short of two pothole bunkers and just a few feet inside some terrible rough that ran along the right edge. I had been lucky. In my excitement I had gripped the club too tightly with my right hand. I had two hundred yards to go and I still couldn't see the green, only the outline of Cheape's bunker, a massive hole in the ground just under a hundred yards ahead of me. I couldn't remember from Peter's map what was beyond that bunker and the ground was so hilly I couldn't see anything. I took out my fairway wood. *Soft right hand. Head down. Don't swing hard. Just motion. Turn the shoulders. Turn the hips through.*

I made solid contact and when I looked up, the ball was flying perfectly. And far. I raced after it, my clubs rattling against my back.

At first I couldn't spot the ball anywhere, so I began looking to the right of the green, thinking maybe the shot had sliced as it was falling. No sign of it to the right. I walked left and found it lying in one of the shallower pothole bunkers, forty yards in front of the green. I took four strokes from there for a double bogey six, wrote a note on my scorecard to remember these little bunkers on the left front of the green, and kept going.

"Number three, Cartgate, 352 yards," I said as I set my ball on the tee. I remembered Peter telling me that this was a drive where a slice would kill me. Heavy rough down that side of the field in front of me. All I wanted to do here was swing softly without bearing down with my right hand or using my arms at all. All the power I needed would be generated by turning my hips and shoulders and snapping my wrists through the ball at impact. "Relax," I said. "Soft hands."

I aimed left just to be safe and hooked the drive right into the Principal's Nose pothole at about 200 yards. I saw the sand fly up from where I stood on the tee. "Well," I said, "you've got your work cut out for you now."

In the bunker I laid my wedge flat and swung through as hard as I could. The ball flew up, hit the top ridge of the pothole, and dropped down at my feet in a worse position than before.

Two more swings and no dice. Finally I turned around and hit the ball out the back of the bunker. This time I hit it squarely and it flew about eighty yards in the wrong direction back toward the tee. I took a ten on the hole, and with it lost any chance I might have had for a decent score.

I made peace with that, however, and bogeyed number four, Ginger Beer, with a fine drive and second shot that covered all but the final twenty yards of the 419 yards to the green. When I fought for and made my par on number five, the 514 yard Hole O' Cross, I yelled my battle cry at the seagulls circling overhead: "I'm playing golf in Scotland!"

At the end of nine holes I was rolling. The bunkers had killed my score, but I had four pars and a birdie and, best of all, only three sliced shots, and even those hadn't gotten me into any real trouble.

I was heading to the tee at number ten when I saw two golfers walking toward me. I waved to be friendly but they didn't wave back. When they got closer one of them called to me in a very proper British accent: "Have you permission to play as a single?" They drew closer to me. I saw that they were young men, in their twenties, and dressed impeccably in beautiful golf clothes.

I waited until they were ten yards away and then I told them that I had permission from George the porter.

"Very good then," one of them said.

I don't know why I felt like I had to win their affection, but I went on to tell them that I was practicing for the tournament. They didn't seem to care, though they invited me to join them.

That was my mistake. They were both magnificent golfers, making par or birdie on every hole. When I asked if they were from St. Andrews, one of them explained that they were students at Cambridge and they drove up once a week if the weather forecast was good to play the Old Course.

I never hit another decent shot in their presence. My slice returned worse than ever. I lost balls. I fell into the rough and sliced open my right cheek on the gorse. They were very well mannered, exceedingly well mannered, so that each time I hit a ball that didn't disappear out of bounds or wasn't an outright laughable duff, they would both say in unison, "Good swing! Spot on!"

These boys—tall, lean women killers, handsome as movie stars with heartbreakingly beautiful black hair—were the prefect representatives of the English aristocracy who by some awful luck found themselves playing golf on the most famous course in the world with an utter fool. With their striped Cambridge scarves tucked into matching baby-blue V-neck sweaters, they gave new meaning to perfection. I kept thinking that if one of them were to hit an ugly shot like any of mine, their parents and grandparents would suddenly look up from their tea three hundred miles from here as if a gun had been fired at them, and all the gold-framed paintings of their ancestors would fall from the walls of their country houses.

By number sixteen, I was so humiliated I just wandered off into the rough like a lost child separated from his parents at a shopping mall. I sat down in the high bushes and gave up. I had been playing so far behind them and so far from the middle of the fairway where they were playing that it would take two or three holes before they realized I had disappeared.

TWELVE

A CLERK AT the front desk of the hotel lent me a flashlight and I rode the bicycle out to Peter and Mary's cottage. I don't know what time it was when I got there, after nine though, and everyone was asleep.

"I woke you, I'm sorry," I told Peter when he opened the door.

He squinted at me in the porch light. "You look like hell," he said. "Come in."

"FUCKING ENGLISH," HE said after I told him about my afternoon. "We should have our own country. We've got nothing in common with the British."

He poured the whiskey. "But you were going all right on the front nine."

"Yes."

"Not slicing the ball."

"It was amazing."

"If you had stayed out of the bunkers you would have shot in the mid-forties."

"I know."

"Do as well on the back nine and there's your round."

"I know."

"You're close!" He shouted happily.

"I don't feel close," I said.

"Have another drink and you won't feel anything. A swing, you know, can come and go. Your friend Johnny surely told you that. It's not like Mary's recipe for bread. You let those Cambridge fellows unnerve you. You started pressing, right here, with that damned right hand of yours."

"My curse," I said forlornly.

"No such thing as a curse," he said. "You're going to have to make a better map than the one I drew for you."

"I don't understand."

He used the whiskey bottle, our glasses, and an ashtray to show me what he wanted me to do. "You have to find a safe landing spot for each shot. Every shot on every hole. Give yourself a comfortable distance, nothing you have to swing hard to reach. How far on each drive?"

"Two hundred?"

"Make it one eighty. And for your long irons, say one forty. How does that seem to you?"

"Fine."

"It will take you two days, maybe three, pacing out each shot from the spot where you'd hit the ball to the safe place where you want it to land. And on the blind shots you'll have to mark something on the horizon. That'll be easy after the turn, with the city up ahead of you. But going out will be more difficult. Do you understand all this?"

"I think so. I only have three days though."

"I know that. Don't worry. This will work. How are your feet holding up?"

"Fine."

"Another drink, then we'll go out to the barn."

———————

WITH HIS CAR headlights on, I hit balls for him that night. I apologized for the first three shots, which were terrible. But I never got any better. "It's gone," I said.

"It is," he said. "But it will come back. You're still tense. You're stiff-arming the ball. It's motion, remember, not force. And remember this too, Ross: too many Americans take far too long standing over each shot before they hit the ball. Your body gets stiffer and stiffer. It's like putting yourself into a cast before you swing. Do all your thinking before you get into your stance, then just hit the damned ball."

LATER HE DROVE me back to the city. When we passed the university I asked him if he knew which building it was where Bobby Jones was honored the night he stood up from his wheelchair.

"I'll take you there," he said, turning sharply left.

WE SAT OUTSIDE the hall with the car windows down, talking about what it must have been like that night. He had been told the story a thousand times, he said, beginning when he was just a boy.

"A man sang that night," I said. "I watched a tape. It was amazing. This voice, this beautiful tenor voice just rose up out of the crowd and there was absolute silence."

"Aye. I've been told I'm related to that fellow somehow."

"Really?"

"No. Pulling your leg. But it's something, isn't it, how a man can be remembered. I mean, golf in America in Bobby Jones's days was nothing anybody today would want to defend. Only for rich men. White men. You see?"

"I do."

"But everyone loves Bobby in St. Andrews. And your friend Johnny dreamed of coming over here to walk in his footsteps on the Old Course."

"Johnny always said it was because Jones was an amateur. He never was paid for playing golf."

"Could be. You and I will never know, I suppose."

There was a silence as we both watched the moon break through the clouds.

"The song," I said.

" 'Will Ye No' Come Back Again.' "

"You know it?"

" 'Will Ye No' Come Back Again?' " He began to sing with a voice so beautiful, it startled me.

"Bonnie Charlie's noo awa',
Safely owre the friendly main.
Mony a he'rt will break in twa,
Should he ne'er come back again.
Will ye no' come back again?
Will ye no' come back again?
Better lo'ed ye canna be,
Will ye no' come back again?"

He stopped and rolled his window up. "Every Scot knows that song," he said. "Do you think you can sleep now?"

UNDER THE MOONLIGHT that night I walked all the holes again, counting out the steps and writing notes as I went. Even in the darkness I felt the land becoming familiar to me, this land that Johnny had dreamed all his life of walking.

THIRTEEN

WHEN I WENT into the dining room for breakfast the next morning all the waitresses were standing at the windows watching the snow fall. "It's a real snow blizzard," one of them announced when she saw me. "We don't see this very often, where the snow stays on the ground."

It was beautiful and I quickly ate a bowl of cornflakes then put on all the warm clothes I had in my room and began walking the course in the storm. I got as far as the fourth hole when the wind turned to the north very suddenly and tripled its ferocity. In an instant I couldn't see a thing, and like a boat at sea that fails to take its bearings before the fog rolls in, I had no idea which direction I had been facing at the moment I was blinded by the driving snow. It was strange how the fear came upon me. First with a metallic taste in my mouth as I walked a few steps in one direction, then turned and walked in a different direction. There was no city in the distance. No cars running along the streets. No sound at all but the howling wind. Then I was out of breath and my feet were so cold I couldn't feel them.

I walked around aimlessly for almost an hour without a clue as to where I was or how to get back to the hotel. I cursed myself, a man who had lived through enough winters to know better than to wander outside alone in blizzard conditions. Then I started to sing "Will Ye No' Come Back Again." Of course I knew none of the lyrics; I just made them up, crazy, ridiculous lyrics about Scottish girls and Americans playing golf in their slippers, anything to occupy my mind. I was singing as loud as I could when the earth fell away from my feet and I dropped straight down into a pothole bunker.

———

THE DOCTOR IN the emergency room told me that my right arm was very seriously sprained—any worse and it would have been broken. He scolded me for my ignorance, told me that three toes on my left foot were only half an hour away from frostbite, and stared hard at an X ray of my right shoulder. "You've done some damage here as well," he said flatly.

He put my arm in a sling and prescribed a painkiller that knocked me out. When I awoke it was evening. I had slept through the day, the night, and the next day. Dusk on the twenty-second of December. I awoke feeling that I had missed my plane home.

BY THEN THE snow was gone and there was a peaceful rain falling. People were out walking under umbrellas, and there were golfers on the course moving along methodically while I watched.

Finally I looked down at my arm in the sling. It was the moment of truth; if I couldn't move my arm, I wouldn't be able to play the tournament. I closed my eyes as I lifted the sling over my head. I felt it drop to the floor. I opened my arms and gazed down at my right arm, bent across my chest. I pulled my seven iron out of my bag with my left hand. I placed the grip of the club in my right hand, then straightened my arm.

I couldn't straighten it completely, and I didn't have enough strength to grip the club tightly. But to my surprise the pain was not overbearing. I took one slow swing. Then another. Then I quickly dressed and caught the bus to Peter and Mary's.

"Which bunker was it?" Peter asked.

"Road," I said miserably. "But I'm going to make it, I can play with the pain. It's not that bad."

Suddenly Peter's expression changed. "Follow me," he said.

Outside the barn he set some balls on the ground then helped me take my arm out of the sling and lay my right hand on the grip of the club. "Go on now," he said. "See how you do." He shrugged his shoulders calmly, and nodded to the ball. "Go on," he said again.

I took my stance and swung a four iron hopelessly. I didn't even bother to pick up my head to see where the ball went.

"Another," I heard Peter say.

I hit the second ball the same as the first.

"You might want to watch this one," he said.

I looked at him and his eyes were lit up.

I hit the third ball and it flew as straight as a ball can fly. And far.

"You hit the first two so far I didn't see them come down," Peter said with delight.

"I can't understand."

"Sure you can, Ross," he said.

With no resistance from my right side, I was finally able to release my hands and turn my shoulders cleanly through each swing.

"I'll stay here all afternoon if you want me to," Peter said. "You're a joy to watch."

I hit another shot long and straight. "Did you see that one, Peter?" I said.

I MADE MY notes on hotel postcards and walked the course in the morning, writing down directions for each shot to land safely. Giving myself easy distances to reach—180 yards for each drive, 140 for my middle irons, and inside 80 yards for my wedges. I was on number sixteen when the wind ripped the cards from my hand and scattered them across the fields. After I had chased them all down I walked back to the hotel and called Linda.

"We're getting snow right now," she said. "Just in time for Christmas. The kids are happy. And how are you, Ross?"

"I'm a long way from home, Linda," I said.

"All of us are thinking about you."

"I would have called before. I mean, I've wanted to call you every day, from the minute I arrived. Johnny's here, Linda."

There was a brief silence.

"You're together again," she said.

I tried to find the words. I raised my hand to my face and closed my eyes. Outside a church bell rang the time. I didn't know what I wanted to ask her until I was asking her. "If it's all right, Linda, I thought I'd come see you and the children."

"For Christmas?" she asked eagerly.

I hesitated. "I get home on Christmas day. But we have a break coming up in February. Would that be a good time?"

"Yes," she said. Some of the music was gone from her voice.

"Tell the children, Linda."

She hesitated, then when she asked if I was sure, I sensed her reluctance. I thought she was just protecting the children in case I didn't make it. "I'm coming," I said. "You can count on it."

FOURTEEN

MARY HAD DRESSED the boys in their kilts for our big night out. We met at a restaurant across from the university library. I was surprised that Peter hadn't come.

"He's busy doing something," Mary said. "But he told me to tell you that he'll see you tomorrow on the first tee at nine, before you go out. How's your arm?"

"Dead," I said. I showed her that I couldn't make a fist.

"Wonderful," she said with a grin.

"After all the years of suffering with a slice, I fall into a hole and it's gone."

"God works in mysterious ways, we like to say."

WHEN WE FINISHED dinner Mary took me up into the tower at the cathedral with the boys.

"St. Rule's Tower," Mary said. "My favorite place."

We looked out over the twinkling lights of the city. Far out in the North Sea there was a slow procession of tankers and container ships moving across the dark horizon.

"Lovely, isn't it?" Mary said.

She lifted the boys so they could see over the tower walls.

"This is where I fell in love with my Donald," Mary said wistfully. "We came here on our second date. I was down below and he was up here. He hollered to me. I looked up, and thought, 'I'm going to marry him.' "

She paused and took one of the boys into her arms. "Peter doesn't care much for Donald, but to me there's no one finer in the world," she said.

"That's wonderful, Mary," I said.

She smiled shyly. "And you," she said. "You're a lovely man, if you don't mind me saying. You should find someone to walk beside you."

It brought tears to my eyes. "When I was a boy," I said slowly, "a man told me that every love story is a small boat set upon the open sea." I looked at Mary.

"That's a poetic way of saying it."

"He was a wonderful man," I said.

"I shouldn't ask," she said.

"That's all right."

"Have you been alone all your life, Ross?"

"Not alone, no. I'm a teacher so I have my students," I said.

"You don't deserve to be alone. You should have someone at your side," she said again.

"I did once," I said.

She just looked at me and nodded as if she understood.

WE SAID GOOD night in front of the hotel. "Think about me tomorrow and say your prayers," I said.

"We'll see you after. I'll bring the boys."

They were in the backseat of the car. I stuck my head inside. "I'm going to hit a home run for you guys tomorrow," I joked.

They looked at each other. "What's a home run?"

"I meant a hole in one," I said.

"Peter instructed me to tell you to lay up short on every putt tomorrow," Mary said. "Stay below the hole. And play for bogeys." She smiled at me. "You'll do fine, Ross."

FIFTEEN

I GUESS THE first sign that I recognized, now as I look back, was the smile on my waitress's face at breakfast the next morning. Each time I looked up from my porridge she was smiling and blushing.

Then when I was walking out of the dining room I noticed that all of the staff were watching me.

I went back up to my room, dressed for a long cold day with three layers that had become my standard uniform, and grabbed my clubs. I went out the back door of the hotel into the rain and stopped at the first golf shop I came to where I was going to buy some presents for Linda and the children. When I tried the door, it was locked. Christmas Eve, I thought. Then I saw the hand-printed sign on the window: CLOSED IN HONOR OF JOHNNY DUROCHER. "Peter," I said.

At the next shop there was the same note in the window. And in all the shops up the eighteenth fairway. Then when I looked across to the first tee there were people standing in the rain, a gallery under black umbrellas. I felt my legs weaken. I counted thirty-eight people standing there in the rain, and when I got closer, they all nodded and smiled at me, and began to clap their hands.

At first I couldn't talk, but then I thanked them. "I'm just going to pay my greens fee and then I'll par this first hole," I said. There was laughter as I walked to the starter's box. George was waiting at the door, shaking his head.

"I won't take your credit card today, sir," he said. "Your round has already been covered."

"I don't understand," I said. "I don't understand any of this."

He shook my hand. "No negative thoughts in your head when you strike your first ball. Remember?"

I WAS DOWN on one knee taking a handful of tees from the front pocket on my golf bag when someone stepped in front of me. When I looked up it was Peter. "I'm going to follow you as far as my leg will allow me to," he said.

I shook his hand and tried to thank him.

"Don't have to say a word," he said. He looked at the people gathered to watch. "I think Johnny would be pleased, don't you?"

"I'll never forget this, Peter."

"Good," he said. "Now, before each shot take two of your heavy irons and swing them through the air, breaking your wrists on each swing. Do you understand?"

"I understand."

"And keep your putts below the hole. Coming downhill is deadly."

"Right."

"Will you remember that?"

"I will."

"Good then."

I WAS IN a threesome with a fellow from Germany and a retired RAF pilot who lived outside London. Neither had ever played the course.

We shook hands and I won the toss to take the honors.

I SWUNG TOO hard, and in my eagerness to see how far the ball was going I'd caught it with the heel of my club and pushed it way left. *Left,* I thought.

My opponents both drove down the middle of the fairway. *It's going to be a long day for you if you don't keep your head on the ball,* I said to myself as I started walking. When I turned back I saw that the gallery was following us.

MY DRIVE WAS still 150 yards from Swilken Burn, but I didn't even think about playing up to it safely. I took my four iron and swung from my heels. The ball never left the ground. It rolled all the way to the edge of the river, paused, then fell in.

The others were safely on in two when I took my stroke penalty and pitched my ball onto the green.

Peter stepped up next to me. "What are you lying?" he asked as I lined up my putt.

"Four from here," I said.

"You're away," he said. "Don't go past the hole."

My hands were shaking and I struck the ball too heavily. I watched it roll thirty feet downhill of the hole. I took a six to my opponents' pars. I knew as we stood on the second tee that my chance of breaking ninety with a six on my card was almost impossible. Peter read my mind. "Don't count strokes," he said to me. "Fight for each shot."

I watched both men hit beautiful drives, then I took out my notes and put my mind to what was at hand.

I hit a decent drive to the left, maybe two hundred yards to the safe landing zone I'd mapped out, well short of Cheape's bunker and left of the fierce rough on the right. I could see my ball sitting on the top of a small rise. *That's an easy bogey from there*, I told myself confidently.

I saw Peter nodding his head as he walked out in front of me.

"Ladies and gentlemen," I said to the gallery, "that's as good as I can hit a drive." I bowed dramatically and tipped my hat the way Johnny would have.

THERE WASN'T any such thing as not counting strokes. After seven holes I knew I had two double bogeys and the rest bogeys. I was counting, but I was also concentrating as hard as I could on keeping my head down. I had my dead right arm and hand to thank for the fact that as we approached the eighth hole I hadn't sliced a single ball.

THE WIND WAS howling by the time we stood on the tee facing the 166-yard par-three eighth, Short. I heard the gallery's umbrellas flapping behind me. After my opponents both watched their drives sail right of the green in the wind, I took out my driver and hit one of those low stingers that Peter had taught me. My ball left the ground only for about a hundred yards before it hit and rolled straight onto the green, stopping six feet short of the cup. *This hole is mine, Johnny,* I said to myself. I knocked the ball hard into the cup for a birdie while the shopkeepers applauded generously. I bowed to them again.

The ninth hole, End, is a very short par four. Only 307 yards but over a fairway that dips low and runs through a minefield of bunkers. Kruger. Mrs. Kruger. Boase's. And another half dozen that have no names. On my postcard I had written, "Hit a soft drive here. Stay right and short of Boase's bunker at 217. Left off fairway is all bad. You can safely run second shot onto green which is quite flat. Danger is trying to kill the drive."

I put the card in my pocket and told myself to go for it. With the wind blowing so hard from behind, I figured if I could just get the ball high and out there a ways, it might fly all the way to the green.

I laid my dead right hand on the club and took three painful practice swings, telling myself, *Stay down, stay down low, and break your wrists.* Then I remembered a story Johnny had told me about Jack Nicklaus playing in the Open here. Standing on the eighteenth tee, about to hit his drive, he suddenly stopped, handed his caddie his club, and took off his pullover sweater. Then he proceeded to drive the 354 yards onto the green.

I dropped my driver on the ground in front of me, took off my jacket, and threw it down the hill. I heard the gallery buzz. I bent my knees slightly. Stay down. Stay down. I drew the club back, hesitated, took a deep breath, then let my club fall slowly with gravity until it reached the point where my wrists began to break. There I snapped my wrists as powerfully as I could, keeping my head still. When I heard someone in the gallery say "Perfect," I looked up in time to see the ball racing onto the green, straight for the flag.

Two putts and I won the hole. "I'm playing golf in Scotland for Johnny," I whispered to Peter as I walked past him.

"And you're making birdies," he said to me. "Don't let up."

———

THAT WAS THE only time through the whole round that I varied from the notes on my postcards.

NUMBER ELEVEN, HIGH, is the most celebrated par three in the world. From an elevated tee, you hit across a valley to a treacherously sloping green set right on the edge of the Eden River and protected in front by three enormous bunkers. Strath and Shell on the right, and Hill on the left, ten feet deep. The narrow passageway between them is no wider than a hallway.

Someone in the gallery wished me good luck as I teed my ball. When I stood up, the ball blew off the tee in a ferocious gust of wind that came in so hard from off the river, I could feel the salt spray on my face. When I glanced back at the spectators, all of them had their heads bowed to get out of the driving rain. They looked like they were praying for me.

In a gale like this one I knew the only smart play was to hit a driver or a two iron low through the valley and bring it to a stop well short of the bunkers and the green. From there if I had managed to keep the ball in line with the passageway, I could run the ball on the ground the rest of the way up the slope, two putt, and gratefully take my bogey.

I looked up into the cold, stinging rain, out to the water beyond the green. I followed my notes, lining up my shot with the tower at the air force base in the distance. After my ball blew off the tee two more times, I decided to hit it from the ground.

I swung easily with a two iron. The ball started off well but then hit the side of a knoll and kicked to the left, landing right up against the thick gorse from where it took me two more strokes to reach my opponents' balls, which were lying just a few yards apart between the bunkers, the spot I had wanted to reach on my drive.

When Peter came up to me, I could see that he was in pain. "I can't walk any farther," he said to me. "I'm sorry." He smiled and shook his head. "Just play to the end the way you're playing now and you'll have it. I'll be on the eighteenth."

SIXTEEN

I FLIRTED WITH disaster on number thirteen, Hole O' Cross, where there is no safe second shot with the wind in your face. Trying to steer clear of the Coffins' bunkers, I pulled my drive left into heavy rough. After five minutes without finding it, I was going to give up and take the two-stroke penalty when the gallery joined me in my search until we discovered it resting among the gnarled roots of a bush. All I could do from there was knock the ball into the open field, then set up for my third shot with 245 yards standing between me and the green. I hit a driver with a punch swing that covered all but the remaining 100 yards, then checked my cards again.

I had written, "From one hundred you must be in line with the middle of the green. Aim for tallest steeple. Lion's Mouth and Cat's Trap bunkers must be carried. Heavy gorse. Can't see green at all until you come down over the final hill."

I put the cards back in my pocket and when I looked out to find the tallest steeple on the horizon, everything had disappeared in fog. I felt a wave of desperation pass through my mind and I just stood there, unable to move, for the longest time. I turned to glance at the gallery. One man caught my eye and frowned in sympathy.

I went through my cards. "Number fourteen, totally blind on tee, aim for tallest steeple. Must stay out of Hell bunker in center. Second shot, aim for the little steeple on far right of horizon. Fifteen, drive directly on church steeple between two prominent humps in field . . . must stay well clear of enormous Cottage bunker at 170 yards. Sixteen you can see principal's Nose bunker and you must stay out of it on drive!!!"

With the fairway being so narrow, never more than sixty or seventy yards wide all the way in until the eighteenth, and with so many bunkers strewn across that narrow path, there was no way for me to stay clear of the bunkers ahead of me unless I could see them or at least mark my shots by the steeples and towers on the horizon.

I started praying that the fog would lift.

But it grew worse. On sixteen I hit my wedge right into Grant's bunker, which I couldn't even see until I was five feet from it. After taking three strokes to get out I couldn't afford to play Road hole, number seventeen, conservatively as I had planned. A 461-yard par four, I was supposed to play it like a par five and be grateful to take bogey. But now, after losing so many strokes, I couldn't afford anything but par.

I stood on the tee with the wind flapping my wet jacket. My pants were soaked. My feet were soaked. My hands were red with cold and I couldn't feel my fingertips. Out ahead the dark green drying sheds behind the massive Old Course Hotel were lost in fog. Johnny had talked so often about this hole that I knew by heart that a perfect drive could be accomplished if you aimed for the second O in Old Course Hotel, which was painted across the wooden sheds. I couldn't see any of that. The two-hundred-yard-long hotel had vanished like the *Titanic*. It was gone. Nothing but a wall of misty fog was ahead of me.

My drive felt perfect through my hands, the best I'd hit all day. I walked straight ahead, believing that I would find the ball. I had the whole gallery searching with me and I was growing discouraged when someone shouted through the fog, "Got one!" I yelled back asking what brand of ball. "Titlest three!" he called. I was using a Strata. I wanted to lie, believe me; a two-stroke penalty for a ball lost because of the fog, and my chances would be over.

"Not mine," I told him. I took the penalty, walked back to the tee, and hit another drive without even taking a practice swing. I was defeated now; if there had been a chair anywhere nearby, I would have sat down and hung my head.

As I walked in the direction where I thought the green would appear, a man in a blue beret and a ragged green coat caught up with me and held out a silver flask, offering me a drink.

I thanked him and declined.

"I love your old Ben Hogan blades," he said, as he fell into step alongside me.

"I think they need a new owner," I said miserably.

"You've played a scrappy round," he said. "Nothing to be ashamed of."

I was about to ask him his name when he said, "I'm Donald Hannah. Mary's husband. I'm the vagabond you've been hearing about from Mary's brother." He smiled sadly. "I'm to make sure you get to the eighteenth green."

We shook hands. He told me that Mary and the boys would be waiting for us when I finished. "I saw the signs on the shops in town," he said. "Very nice."

His sad face and his humble demeanor made me feel comfortable at his side, and we had walked only a little ways when I began pouring out my heart to him, a stranger. My round of golf for Johnny was ending now and with it my hope of playing well to honor him. Despair churned inside me, along with the depthless sorrow I felt for Linda and the children. I had held this inside from the time I arrived in Scotland, but now it rushed out of me in words that I'm sure made little sense to the man striding beside me through the fog. "I wanted to break ninety," I said. "I wanted to do this for my friend, but I can't do it now. I've lost my chance. I guess I never really had much of a chance. And I was just thinking how unfair it is that this fog came in and made everything more difficult for me. But that's life, isn't it?"

"I'm afraid it is," he calmly. "I think your friend would be happy that you remembered him this way."

I ended up recording an eight at the Road hole. But on the eighteenth tee when I looked out ahead and saw that the shops and the hotel with the intimidating windows had vanished in the fog, I felt relieved. I teed up my ball just as the Holy Trinity church bells began tolling the hour. Waiting for the last bell, I thought again of Jack Nicklaus ripping off his sweater and belting his drive here. That's exactly what I wanted to do now; I wanted to swing from my heels for all I was worth at one ball, for all the times I had stood in amazement watching Johnny hit his drives out of sight. I wanted to swing hard enough to get out all the anger I had not acknowledged before. My anger at him for not making this journey with me.

I took off my rain jacket, and then my sweater. "I'll hold those for you, Mr. Lansdale," I heard Donald say. When I turned around he was holding out his hand. Behind him all the people who had followed me around the course stood waiting silently. Rain was pouring off their umbrellas. I could see the cold in their faces. Without thinking what I would say to them, I told them the truth. "I'm not Johnny Durocher," I began. I told them how Johnny had dreamed of playing here. "He was a player," I said. "And I always thought that when I came to St. Andrews, it would be with him beside me." I told these lovely strangers how Johnny and I had met, and how he given up his life so tragically, believing that he was not able to care for the people who needed him. "I wish I could have made him see how much we needed him to stay with us," I said.

Then, just as I finished, the rain stopped and a shaft of yellow sunlight broke through the fog. I watched the umbrellas come down in unison and the people turn their cold faces into the warm light. Then I drove my ball spectacularly off into the mist and began walking the last fairway. *I'm going to finish with a par for you, Johnny*, I said to myself.

UP AHEAD, WITH the fog lifting, a man told me he had seen the ball hit the narrow crossing road and ricochet straight ahead toward the green.

"Straight?" I said. "Are you sure?"

"Oh, I'm sure," he said. "Straight and powerful."

I walked on, daring myself to think that maybe the ball had bounced hard enough off the tarred roadway to carry up the 130 yards to the green.

The hotel windows were turning gold in the sunlight by the time I approached them. People were standing in the light in the hotel library and I waved to them as I passed, feeling confident this time and unafraid of my next shot. I pulled my shoulders back and marched straight ahead toward the flag that waved gently in the distance where a crowd of people had gathered behind the green.

My drive had come to rest just over a hundred yards from the hole. *Well,* I thought, as I came upon it, *not quite a Jack Nicklaus drive. But good enough. Good enough.* I took out a six iron and, after one practice swing, hit a low shot from the inside of my back foot that hit softly in the Valley of Sin and skidded up the side of the hill and onto the green. *That's it,* I said to myself. *That's perfect.*

I holed my putt for my third birdie of the day, shook my opponents' hands, and then as my gallery began applauding, I turned to them.

"No chance on a day like today, laddie," an elderly man said to me as he took my hand and shook it. I thanked him and the others; one by one, each person who had walked the round with me came up and wished me luck and happy Christmas.

At last Mary and the two boys stepped out of the fog. "Can I have your ball?" one boy asked.

"Thomas!" Mary scolded him. "You have a thousand balls at home."

I opened my bag and gave them every ball I had. They couldn't have been any more pleased if I had given them silver.

Donald put his arms around the boys while Mary stood beside me as I added up my score. I didn't have to say anything. She could tell. She took my arm. "Come on now," she said. "Peter's waiting for us in the pub."

SEVENTEEN

THAT DAY RETURNS to me like something from a dream. I ended up hitting a ninety-two on the Old Course in St. Andrews. Without the penalty for the lost ball, and with just one more putt dropping, I would have had my round in the eighties that I had set out to achieve. I won't tell you that it doesn't matter to me that I fell short, because it does. I can remember as if it were just an hour ago how awful I felt walking across the street to the pub. I was discouraged, muttering to myself that I deserved the loneliness and the sorrow in my life, and that I would always lose everything that mattered to me. The game of golf can make you beat yourself up this way.

But there is always the next shot when you might sail the ball up close to the pin with the grace of Bobby Jones. Or the next hole you might birdie with a dead-center putt. Or the next time out when the grass will strike you as never having been quite so green before or the sky such a heartbreaking shade of blue, and that is the reason I still play.

I no longer play alone, however, because that Christmas Eve in Scotland my life turned. I drank a few pints of beer with people I felt I had known forever, and then someone called for quiet and the pub was transformed into a church by Peter's lovely tenor voice as he sang the Scottish ballad that had been sung for Bobby Jones. I was fighting tears when Mary's husband came up to me. The room was noisy then with people ordering drinks, but I heard his voice above all the others as he called my name. I watched as he turned and gestured across the crowded room to a woman with long, lovely silver hair who was standing beside a lighted Christmas wreath, smiling at us. "She says she's an old friend," I heard Donald say to me in a low voice. I felt the breath rush through my lungs.

IN MY MEMORY now is a pale sickle of moon laying on its back as Julia and I walked along the shore in the last light of that afternoon, talking about the paths our lives had taken over the years since we were together. She told me that Linda had contacted her through Smith College and asked if she would come to Scotland to see me. The moment she had heard Linda's voice, she knew that the time had come for us to see each other again, she said.

"I can't believe you're here," I said to her. I would tell her this three times as she walked beside me.

The third time she stopped, and when I turned to her, she placed her hand on my arm and told me that she was glad I'd had Johnny and Linda in my life. "Such close friends," she said. "I've never had that."

My intention was to say nothing that would dredge up painful memories of our shared past. But I couldn't help myself. I told her that Johnny and Linda had given me something to live for after I'd lost her.

Her eyes filled with tears when I said this. She gripped my arm tightly and then let go. We stood on sand turned hard as cement by the cold. "Your parents," I said to change the subject.

"They patched things up the way people do," she said with a sad smile. "They decided to look forward instead of back. I did the same. I married Jack when he came home from the war."

Suddenly I didn't want her to tell me any more. After all the times I'd wondered what had transpired in her life, now I wanted to spare her having to explain anything. "It's so beautiful here, isn't it?" I said, turning away from her to gaze at the breaking waves. "I think I'll come here to grow old."

She spoke my name. Her smile was gone when I turned to look at her. "I almost came to see you," she said softly. "Before Jack came home. I think I was going to ask if you would take me back. I'd done some crazy things."

I brushed her hair off her face to stop her. "It turned silver like your grandmother's," I said.

She smiled at this. "You remember?"

"Everything, yes."

She nodded. And then, to my surprise, she said there were little things that always reminded her of me. "That time you told me about the man at the orphanage who said we are made of stardust, do you remember?"

"Brother Martin," I said.

"Yes. Well, there was this children's book I read to my sister's daughter when she was little. An angel sprinkled stardust on everyone."

When she laughed, I remembered how I had always loved the sound of her laughter. She looked into my eyes for a moment, then reached across the space between us and took my hand in hers. I was looking down at her wedding ring when she began to speak again. "This has been quite a trip for you, Ross, hasn't it? I'm sorry you lost your friend. Linda must be a marvelous person."

I raised my eyes at that word. *Marvelous*, I thought, a grown-up word. I told her that there was still a part of me that hadn't accepted Johnny's death. "Some days when I'm teaching, I think I hear his voice in the classroom across the hall."

Just then two fighter jets from the air force base across the river at Leuchars took off and filled the sky with thunder. We both looked up and followed them as they raced through the clouds. When they had vanished, she said that she had told her sisters all about us. "I wanted them to know about the time we shared in that wonderful old hotel."

I asked her if it seemed like a long time ago. She looked up at my face. "Fourteen years ago, Ross. It was another life," she said with a slow voice. "The time has gone very fast though. If anyone had ever told me back then how fast the time would pass . . ." Her voice trailed off for a moment.

I waited, then told her about the times when I had longed to be near her. "There were thousands of days and nights when all I could do was think of you," I said. "I wouldn't be able to make you believe this."

"I do believe it, Ross," she said. "I do."

I guess I was waiting for her to tell me that she had done the same. But there was just a silence that persuaded me to stop speaking about things that were not right there in front of us.

"We could have some tea," I heard myself say. And she smiled at this.

"Tea and a cigarette maybe?" she said.

WE WERE HALFWAY back to the hotel when the rain returned. Great sheets of rain blowing in fiercely off the gray sea. She began running and laughing. "I don't smoke," I called to her. "I'm sorry."

"That's okay. Next time we meet, let's make it southern California!" she shrieked happily as she charged through a deep mud puddle and splashed us both. She hollered back to me, "Do you have a bathtub where you're staying?"

"I do. Up there, straight ahead."

"And hot water?"

"Absolutely. As much as you want."

"Heaven," she cried out.

EIGHTEEN

I DREW THE bath for her while she took off her clothes in the
other room and got into my robe. "I never knew you to wear a
robe," I heard her say.

"Well, I'm a grown-up now," I called back to her. When I stood up I
was light-headed and dizzy from the hot steam. I steadied myself
against the sink and then looked at my face in the mirror. For all the
times I had imagined us together again, I had never pictured myself
looking any older than I had when I knew her. She was right, the time
had passed quickly.

Her voice startled me. I turned and she was standing in the threshold. "Sometimes the face looking back at me has this confused expression," she said, smiling. "It's like, 'Who are you? Where did you come
from?' "

I made an effort to move away from the mirror, but didn't quite
manage it. She had pulled back her hair and I saw that she was wearing
small pearl earrings. Around her neck a tiny silver cross hung from a
thin, black ribbon.

When I turned to face her, she was looking at the books I had stacked
on my bedside table. "You're still a reader," she said as if she were telling
herself this.

"I read the same books over and over," I said. "The ones I already
know by heart." I watched her thinking about this. Then she looked past
me to where the rain was lashing the windows. She said that she had always known she would see me again.

"I used to write down things I wanted to tell you in case we ever ran
into each other," she said. Then she smiled brightly. "Do you remember

the time we talked about how we were going to grow old together? You said the nursing homes would be exactly like colleges by the time we were old. Coed dorms, of course. And I'd finally have the time to actually *read* the books. We'd all swim in the pool with those little floaties on our arms," she said, laughing. "I can still close my eyes and see my dorm mother."

"She looked just like George Washington."

"No dorm mothers where we're going next," she said. "No rules of any kind."

I should have waited, but I filled the next silence by asking her awkwardly if she was happy. After all the years, this is what I needed to know.

"I've had a good life, Ross," she said. "I've been fortunate. I've been loved." She held out her hands and showed me there was dirt under her fingernails. "I've worked beside my father all these years. We just put a new engine in a 1955 TBird before I came over here."

"Amazing," I said. "I'm so glad you've been happy." I meant this. I suddenly felt relaxed, at ease in Julia's presence, in a way I had never been when we were young.

"But you were right, Ross," she said. "You told me once that no one would ever love me the way you did."

She looked away for a moment, then said, "That was true. No one ever has."

In her eyes just then I saw something vanishing. I knew by the way she changed the subject so quickly that I was not entitled to ask her why she had left me so suddenly and how she had decided to go to Canada for the abortion. "Your golf clubs," she exclaimed with slightly too much enthusiasm. "They're the ones I gave you?"

"The only ones I've ever owned." I was looking at her and for a moment I thought about how close we had been, how I had touched her and she had touched me, and here we were, close enough to reach for one another as we had so many times in the past. Despite that, I would not ask her if she and Jack had children. Not because I wasn't interested—I was—but it didn't seem to matter now. I was looking at Julia, but what passed through my mind was how nice it would have been if Linda could have come to Scotland and seen this beautiful place.

She took a deep breath as if she had just run down a long road to reach me. "My bath," she said.

"Yes, don't let it get cold," I said.

BEFORE I LEFT the room I stood outside the bathroom door and told her that I was going downstairs to see about drying her clothes.

"Please don't go to any trouble," she said.

"It's no trouble."

She thanked me, then said, "Ross?"

"Yes?"

"I'm glad you're well," she said.

A CHAMBERMAID IN housekeeping put Julia's clothes in the drier while I waited upstairs in the library. As difficult as it had been for me to believe that Johnny was gone forever and would not be returning, it was now even harder for me to believe that Julia was in my room, just above me. I closed my eyes, only for a moment it seemed, before the chambermaid was standing in front of me, handing me Julia's things, which she had folded neatly. I thanked her, then climbed the carpeted stairs to my room with the clothes still warm in my hands. A gray sweater. Navy blue woolen tights. A long blue-denim skirt, three times longer, it seemed, than any of the skirts she had worn in college. A white blouse with a high round collar embroidered with tiny blue flowers. Clothing meant to conceal rather than reveal. The clothing of a woman who has reached a turn in the road.

———

I KNOCKED AT my door and waited for her to call me in. She stood in my robe, facing the rain-streaked windows. Light from the desk lamp lay across her throat. She said something to me without turning to face me. "It was just that I met Jack first," she said. "And I had promised myself to him."

I didn't move. "I know," I said. "I understand." I stepped toward her, holding out her clothes. "They're still warm," I said, trying to smile.

While she was looking into my eyes, she slowly took them from me. "Thank you," she said.

I WAITED DOWN in the lobby while she was dressing. I called a taxi for her and as we said goodbye, she told me that she was glad she had come to see me. We just looked at each other a moment. "Linda talked with me," she began.

She gazed out into the street for a moment. Then she turned back and glanced quickly at me. "What we had together was a gift," she said. "And we've honored that gift by becoming the people we are, don't you think?"

We walked outside then, with her question still floating somewhere above our heads. And I felt an easing in my chest. A small weight lifted.

The taxi had already pulled to the sidewalk. I kissed her goodbye. "We won't lose touch again," she said. One friendly kiss on the cheek. She quickly turned away. She was opening the back door when she suddenly paused, still holding the door handle, and asked me if Amherst, Massachusetts, was still a beautiful college town.

"I don't live there anymore," I said. "Didn't Linda tell you?"

She looked surprised. I told her that I had left eleven years ago and returned to St. Luke's. I saw something in her eyes. An expression, part fear, part disbelief, seized her face. Her eyes lowered then, and she got into the taxi and closed the door. Her head was bowed when the car pulled away.

NINETEEN

A s I WRITE this now I am waiting for morning classes to begin, sitting behind the desk that I pushed up close to the windows eleven years ago when I returned to St. Luke's. From where I sit I can see the courtyard below, and signs of an early spring. The brick walkways reappearing through the melting snow. Brother Kelly's hatless head. Often on a morning like this in the stillness before the boys come thundering up the wooden stairs for class I think back to my own boyhood here, to those days I spent searching for someone to love me the way one searches for a path that leads home in the darkness. I was always hoping to be touched, longing for the benediction of love.

And now love has come to me in the most unexpected way. It was waiting for me when I returned from Scotland on Christmas day. I opened the door to my room and found Linda sitting in the yellow chair at the foot of my bed. She had moved the books from the chair to the floor. A small thing, I suppose, but to me it signified the beginning of a new life.

"I had to come," she said as I sat beside her.

"The children?" I asked.

"I know, I'll make it up to them. I won't stay."

"No," I said. "I want you to stay."

THIS IS LOVE then, isn't it? Someone's glasses folded on the table by your bed, the morning's first light glancing off their gold rims. Someone's clothing draped over the arm of a chair with your own. This is the confirmation of life's order and holiness. And beside you, a face on the pillow. We see who a person is in the world if we watch them waking, those first seconds as they are returning from sleep, before they remember where they are in the universe. This is someone who asks for nothing except that you never withdraw your love. A pledge you cannot imagine breaking. Sometime in the night an ache you have carried inside and learned to accommodate disappears, replaced by a marvelous lightness.

I said good morning to Linda when she opened her eyes. "Make love to me again," she said.

LATER SHE WALKED to the window and turned back to face me. "We can do this, Ross, can't we? Love each other well, I mean."

"Yes," I said.

She smiled and nodded her head and said there was something that she had to tell me. She walked back to the bed and held my hand as she began to speak. Julia had called her just after she left my hotel. "She was pregnant," she said softly.

"I know," I said.

"No, Ross," she said. "I don't think you can know this."

Startled, I looked into her eyes, waiting for the next thing she would say to me.

"You remember how crazy everything was back then. Julia told me that her life went off the rails for a while. She got in with a bad crowd. She spent a winter living in a school bus, lost in drugs like so many people were. And there was a child. Your child. She couldn't go through with an abortion, and she wasn't ready to be a mother, so she made arrangements to give it up."

Linda paused for a moment, looking away from me and then back. "It was a boy, Ross. She and her father brought him here."

WE WALKED TO the administration building in the first light of the new day and searched the files together. It didn't take long to find the paperwork. In a folder there was a copy of the birth certificate stamped with the state seal of Pennsylvania, along with a notation on a lined sheet of paper: "Normal delivery at full-term" beside a space for the mother's name left blank. And a legal document naming the adopting parents when the boy was three years old. At the back of the folder was a copy of Brother Martin's list of writers. A copy, not the original, and I like to imagine that Julia had left instructions for the original to go along with her son so that a part of me would accompany him through life.

I COMPOSED a long letter to the boy over several days of writing and quitting and starting over, then placed it in the folder so that if his mother and father decided some day to tell him he was adopted, there would be a place where he could begin to piece together his history. The letter was really the story of my life. I wrote about my boyhood at St. Luke's, and the influence of Brother Martin on my life. I wrote about my friendship with Johnny, and in great detail I recounted my time with Julia so that he would know the love story that had preceded him into the world. When I was finished I had written thirty-one pages, and I felt for the first time that I knew who I was.

THE BOYS I have taught here at St. Luke's will tell you how I often bring the game of golf into my lectures as I try to prepare them for their lives, for the rise and fall of hope that they all face. Sometimes they roll their eyes and smile up at me like children, and I try to remember that is what they are. *Children.* So young. So young, though they have already lived through hard times. By the time they arrived here they were already the brave survivors of unspeakable betrayals and disillusionment. I catch a glimpse of weariness in their eyes from time to time, an emptiness. The same emptiness that marked me as a boy. Still, there are days when I am able to reach through all that separates us and touch them. This happened just the other day. I had finished my lecture on T. S. Eliot and was about to dismiss class when I glanced out the windows and saw that Linda and the children were down below, standing in the sunlight, waiting for me to walk them to supper. We had been married for three months by then and as I watched them, Sally was dancing her younger brother in circles as I had seen Johnny do to her so long before. It made me smile.

"Put your pens down," I called excitedly to my students. "Put away your notebooks and come see this."

And as they gathered around me and gazed down at the people who have blessed my life, I told them that one day they would have families of their own and then they would see how this journey we take together in our small boats upon the open sea, this life of difficulty and disappointment, can surprise us at any moment with its beauty.

ACKNOWLEDGMENTS

Thanks to Jim Sullivan, James Robinson, Jim White, and my brother David, who all played golf with me Stateside to get me ready for Scotland, and then to ease my longing for that beautiful country once I had returned home. And to my son, Jack, who took time from his busy teenager's life to play eighty-four rounds with me while I was working on this book. Thanks to Richard LeBlond for opening the doors in St. Andrews. On the courses there, Jim Brown, George Wilkinson, and Mike Kinnear granted me solitude as I walked. I am indebted to them and to the marvelous staff at the Rusacks Hotel. In Scotland I made the acquaintance of the lovely Pat Ciesla and her husband, Mike, who soundly beat me one clement afternoon out on the Eden course. I am especially grateful to Bryce Roberts, one of America's finest teaching pros and a generous, thoughtful friend.

And thanks as well to my agents, Lynn Nesbit, Richard Morris, and Brian Siberell, and to my editor, Jason Kaufman.

For the rest of my life, in my dreams I will be walking the fairways of the inimitable Algonquin golf course in New Brunswick, Canada, in a foursome made up of the boys who work there: Marc Gelinas, Gary Bernard, Tim McCullum, Robert Riva, Andy LePage, Marty Mitchell, Caleb Martin, Michael and Jim Cheatley, Peter Young, Aaron Simpson, Bryce Stewart, Scott Nickerson, Matt Thorbourne, Todd Duplissie, Chad Parks, Devon Leblanc, and Dustin Matthews.

For immediate help curing your
slice, write the author at
Hancockpt@aol.com.